YOU CAN'T HIDE

MARY MILLS MYSTERY - BOOK 3

WILLOW ROSE

Books by the Author

MYSTERY/THRILLER/HORROR NOVELS

- Sorry Can't Save You
- In One Fell Swoop
- Umbrella Man
- Blackbird Fly
- To Hell in a Handbasket
- Edwina

HARRY HUNTER MYSTERY SERIES

- All The Good Girls
- Run Girl Run
- No Other Way
- Never Walk Alone

MARY MILLS MYSTERY SERIES

- What Hurts the Most
- You Can Run
- You Can't Hide
- Careful Little Eyes

EVA RAE THOMAS MYSTERY SERIES

- Don't Lie to me
- What you did
- Never Ever
- Say You Love me
- Let Me Go
- It's Not Over
- Not Dead yet

EMMA FROST SERIES

- Itsy Bitsy Spider
- Miss Dolly had a Dolly
- Run, Run as Fast as You Can
- Cross Your Heart and Hope to Die
- Peek-a-Boo I See You

- Tweedledum and Tweedledee
- Easy as One, Two, Three
- There's No Place like Home
- Slenderman
- Where the Wild Roses Grow
- Waltzing Mathilda
- Drip Drop Dead
- Black Frost

JACK RYDER SERIES

- Hit the Road Jack
- Slip out the Back Jack
- The House that Jack Built
- Black Jack
- Girl Next Door
- Her Final Word
- Don't Tell

REBEKKA FRANCK SERIES

- One, Two…He is Coming for You
- Three, Four…Better Lock Your Door
- Five, Six…Grab your Crucifix
- Seven, Eight…Gonna Stay up Late
- Nine, Ten…Never Sleep Again
- Eleven, Twelve…Dig and Delve
- Thirteen, Fourteen…Little Boy Unseen
- Better Not Cry
- Ten Little Girls
- It Ends Here

HORROR SHORT-STORIES

- Mommy Dearest
- The Bird
- Better watch out
- Eenie, Meenie
- Rock-a-Bye Baby
- Nibble, Nibble, Crunch
- Humpty Dumpty
- Chain Letter

PARANORMAL SUSPENSE/ROMANCE NOVELS

- In Cold Blood

- THE SURGE
- GIRL DIVIDED

THE VAMPIRES OF SHADOW HILLS SERIES

- FLESH AND BLOOD
- BLOOD AND FIRE
- FIRE AND BEAUTY
- BEAUTY AND BEASTS
- BEASTS AND MAGIC
- MAGIC AND WITCHCRAFT
- WITCHCRAFT AND WAR
- WAR AND ORDER
- ORDER AND CHAOS
- CHAOS AND COURAGE

THE AFTERLIFE SERIES

- BEYOND
- SERENITY
- ENDURANCE
- COURAGEOUS

THE WOLFBOY CHRONICLES

- A GYPSY SONG
- I AM WOLF

DAUGHTERS OF THE JAGUAR

- SAVAGE
- BROKEN

You can try to escape from your real or imagined fears—but they'll catch up with you eventually.

~ Unknown

Prologue
OCTOBER 2015

SHE'S NOT RUNNING, but it is close. Maria Verlinden rushes through the aisles, leaving behind the sections with towels and bathroom accessories. She hopes to be able to get through Target's dreaded toy department without Tara acting up. She doesn't have time to look at toys today. As a single mother with only one income, she can't afford to buy her toys every time they shop. Today is about getting her some new shoes, that's all. Quick in and quick out. Without spending money on anything unnecessary.

"Moom, can I get a toy?"

Maria sighs. She looks at her nine-year-old daughter as they walk past the many teddy bears staring back at them with big cute black eyes, begging Maria to buy them.

"You know Mommy can't afford it today. You need new shoes, remember? The school won't let you wear flip-flops. You have to wear sneakers."

"But, Moom, I really want a Monster High doll. Ally has one."

"Not today, honey. I am sorry…"

"But, Moom!"

Maria pulls Tara's arm a little too hard as she tries to get past the toys and into the clothing department.

"You're hurting me, Mom!"

"I'm sorry, baby. We just need to hurry. Mommy has to go to work."

Maria feels exhausted, thinking about going into the office today. Selling office supplies over the phone has to be the worst job on the planet. But she needs the money. And it sure beats working at Wal-Mart like she used to. Tara will spend the rest of the day with a neighbor who is out of work and who takes care of her when Maria

1

has to work and they're off from school. Today is a teachers' workday so there is no school. Maria hates having to ask her neighbor for help, but what else can she do? She can't wait for Tara to be old enough to stay home alone. Maria has got to work.

"Here it is," she says and stops.

Tara is whining. She is complaining about not being able to have a toy. Maria fights the urge to yell at her. How can she be so ungrateful? She is getting new shoes, after all. Can't she be excited about that at least? Doesn't she know how much Maria has to work and save to be able to afford these shoes?

Maria has promised herself to stop yelling so much at Tara. She wants to be better about it. But the pressure of not having any money and living in a bad neighborhood at the age of almost thirty, with a nine-year-old, is getting to her. She hates her life. Worst of all, she sees no way out of it. It's not like she'll meet someone when she has a kid and as long as she lives in that awful place. She feels so stuck. She loves her daughter, but there are days she wonders how her life would have turned out had she gotten that abortion her parents told her to get, before they cut her off. But how could she? It was a baby, for crying out loud. You don't just kill a baby just because the father doesn't want it.

"This baby will destroy your life, Maria," her mother said the day she also told her to get the abortion or they would disown her. Their daughter being a single mother was apparently too much for them, too much of a disgrace. "The kid will be a bastard," they said.

Maria had no idea beforehand that her parents would react like this. But she decided to keep the child anyway, even though it would never know its father or grandparents. After all, it wasn't Tara's fault.

Maria looks at her daughter as she touches a pair of very sparkly shoes. Maria can't help smiling. Yes, Tara is annoying at times, and yes it has been hard, but she loves her; she is the love of her life. How a beautiful little girl like that could cause so much commotion was beyond her comprehension. Maria would give her the world if she could afford it.

"Can I have these, Mommy?"

Maria looks at the price. It's a little more than what she can afford. "Let's see what else there is," she says.

"Okay, Mommy, but I really like these. Ally has a pair like them."

"Good for Ally. Now, how about these over here?" Maria picks up a pair of shoes and shows them to Tara when she spots a man at the end of the aisle touching a pair of shoes but not picking them up. He spots Tara and makes a face at her. Tara laughs. "That man is funny," she says.

Maria grabs Tara's hand in hers and pulls her closer. "Do you want to try these?"

"They're ugly, Mom."

"All right. How about those over there?" Maria asks, still looking at the man who hasn't taken his eyes off of Tara. Something about him fills Maria with unease. She pulls Tara even closer. Tara looks at him again and he makes another funny face. Tara bursts into laughter. The man smiles. Maria eases up slightly. Maybe she is just being paranoid. Maria picks up another pair of shoes and shows them to Tara.

"How about these?"

"Okay. I'll try them on."

Tara grabs the shoes and sits down on the bench. She takes off her flip-flops. Maria keeps an eye on the man. He seems to be circling them, looking at shoes, but not picking any of them up. She doesn't like the way he is looking at Tara.

"Hurry up, Tara," Maria says. "I have to go to the office. They only allowed me to be an hour late today."

"I don't like these, Mommy. They're too tight on my toes."

"Then try another size," she grumbles, and pulls out a box with the same shoes in another size.

The man is still circling them, making faces at Tara whenever he gets her attention. Maria starts to wonder if there is anyone else nearby, in case he tries to steal her purse. It's very early and she hasn't seen anyone else in the store except for the cashiers at the entrance.

"Do you need help with that?" the man suddenly says to Tara.

Maria turns and sees him kneeling in front of the girl and helping her with the shoe. Maria stops breathing. She doesn't like him being this close to her daughter. But, then again, he is just being nice. Maybe he is just a lonely man. She looks at his basket; he hasn't put anything in it.

That's odd, she thinks, but then shakes the thought again. *Maybe he's just here to buy a pair of shoes just like you. You don't have anything in your basket either.*

Maria laughs at herself. The man smiles at her, then at Tara, as the shoe slides right on.

"There you are. It fits perfect. Just like *Cinderella*."

Tara giggles. She doesn't like *Cinderella*, she is more of a *Frozen*-girl, but she is being polite. The man gets up.

"I think we have a winner, *Mom*," he says, addressed to Maria.

"I want these," Tara says and looks proudly up at Maria.

Maria smiles, relieved. She looks at her watch. Only ten minutes till she needs to be at the office. She can't make it in time, but if they move fast then maybe she won't be too late, not so late they'll fire her. They did that last week to one of the other girls. She didn't show up and the next day they had simply given the job to someone else. They didn't even tell her, so when she finally did show up, she found someone else at her desk and had to leave. There are plenty of other girls out there who want Maria's job. They never hesitate to tell them that.

"Thank you so much," she says to the man.

"No problem, *Mom*," he says, and nods.

She knows it is silly, but for some reason she holds her purse tight to her body as she passes him. She kneels in front of her daughter and takes off the shoes that she puts back in the box.

"All right. Let's get moving," she says to Tara. Tara gets up and they start to walk. Tara turns and waves at the man as they disappear down the aisle. He makes another funny face and Tara burst into a light giggle.

As they reach the check-out and give the shoes to the cashier, Maria spots the man walking towards the exit quickly. She notices that he didn't buy anything.

At least he's gone, she thinks to herself with a light shiver when she hands the cashier the money for the shoes.

October 2015

Tara wants to wear the shoes right after they have paid for them, and Maria lets her put them on before they leave the store. Tara laughs happily and runs circles around Maria as they walk towards the parking lot.

"Look at how fast I can run!" Tara yells.

"You are very fast," Maria says, and looks at her watch again. Just five more minutes. Her office is all the way in Melbourne. There is no way she'll make it in time. She'll be at least half an hour late. Maria sighs. She'll have to stay half an hour longer this afternoon to make up for it. Well, at least Tara is happy. She is jumping and running around giggling.

They approach the car and Maria grabs her keys and unlocks it. Tara jumps inside and Maria hurries to her door and opens it, when someone sneaks around her vehicle. It is him again. The same man that stared at them inside the store.

Maria gasps in shock.

"I'm sorry," the man says. "I didn't mean to startle you."

Maria places a hand on her chest. Her heart is beating fast. "It's okay," she says. "I am just…in a hurry."

"I was just wondering if you could help me," the man says, and moves a step closer.

Maria wonders if she should just jump inside the car and drive off. The man stares at her. Tara is yelling from inside the car.

"Come on, Mommy!"

"I really don't have any time," she says, and is about to get inside of her car.

"It'll only be one second. You see, my wife is in that car over there and she's not well. The car won't start and…"

Maria looks at the man. She feels confused, conflicted. Normally she would always help, but this time…there is something odd about this guy. She turns her head to look at the car he pointed at, but can't see anyone inside of it. Tara is yelling again.

"There's no one in the car," Maria says.

When she turns her head, the man is right in front of her. He pushes her inside the car. Maria screams.

"What are you doing?"

"Mommy?" Tara says.

The man is strong, and even though she fights him, she can't get up. "Help! Someone heeelp!"

She tries to kick him, but can't. She manages to scratch him on his arm with her nails while panic spreads inside of her. She has to get him off her. She has to get away from here, now.

"Lie still, bitch," he yells, and slaps her across the face.

Tara screams when she sees him hitting her mother. "Get out of the car, Tara," Maria yells. "Get out and run for help!"

Tara yells something, but Maria doesn't hear what it is. She just keeps screaming at the child to run for help inside Target. Maria regains more of her strength and manages to punch the attacker in the stomach, when she hears the car door open and Tara scream for help.

That's it, that's my girl.

But the attacker punches Maria in the face and she loses consciousness for a few important minutes. When she opens her eyes, Tara's screams have changed character and sound more panicked and helpless. Maria manages to look outside and sees her daughter in the arms of the man, who is carrying her over his shoulder back towards the car.

"No!"

"Oh, yes," the man says, as he throws Tara in the back of the car and slams the door shut. He approaches Maria and leans over her.

"The deal was for the both of you, *Maria*."

October 2015

Tara?

Maria opens her eyes. She can still taste the fumes from the white cloth that was held against her mouth until she gave up the fight. It makes her want to throw up. She is panicking. She blinks her eyes. Tara is here. Tara is right next to her on the bed. What a relief.

Tara seems to be asleep. Maybe she too is knocked out. Maria has a headache. Probably from the fumes.

We've got to get out of here.

Maria gets up from the bed. She leans over her daughter and can hear her breathing. It fills her with relief again. The girl is alive, sleeping heavily, but alive. Maria walks to the window and realizes she is in a house somewhere. The view is spectacular, but she's got to be at least forty feet up. Beneath her are a tennis court and a lap-pool. She grabs the handle to the sliding door and tries to open it. It is locked and you need a key to open it.

Maria looks around the room. It is sparsely decorated with a queen bed and a dresser. Nothing on the walls. Nothing on the floors. Just white tiles. She looks at the door to the room and walks to it. She grabs the handle but—as suspected—it is locked as well.

Maria sighs and walks back to the bed. She can't see her purse anywhere, so she doesn't have her phone. Tara is breathing heavily. Maria leans over her and kisses her on the lips. She can't begin to say how happy she is that she is still alive and still here with her.

But, now what?

Where the hell are we? Are we at that awful man's place? What does he want with us?

Tara starts to slowly wake up as well. She is smacking her lips, probably thirsty. Maria realizes there is a small bathroom attached to the room and she goes in there to get some water from the tap. She finds a plastic cup and fills it. She wets Tara's lips with water. Soon Tara blinks her eyes and opens them to look at her mother.

"Mom?" she says sleepily.

Maria feels like crying, but she holds it back. "It's okay, baby. I got you some water."

Tara sits up and Maria lets her drink from the cup. When she is done, Maria drinks some as well. It tastes like chlorine, but it's better than nothing. She finishes the cup.

"Where are we, Mommy?"

"I don't know, baby."

"I wanna go home now."

"Me too. But we got to wait till the man lets us out, all right?" Maria can hear her own voice shivering as she speaks. She is terrified by what the man wants from them, but she is also determined to get out of here, alive and with her daughter in her arms. No matter what.

"What do you mean, Mommy? Has the man kidnapped us?"

"I…I don't know."

Tara is about to cry. Maria wants to cry as well, but she doesn't allow herself to. She grabs her daughter in her arms and holds her tight.

"It'll be all right, baby. Mommy will get us home; don't you worry, baby. Don't you worry."

October 2015

There is a sound behind the door. The handle is moving, and a key is put in the lock. Maria gasps and grabs Tara. She pulls her close to her while staring at the door handle.

Who is behind that door? Is it the guy from Target? What does this person want with us? Will he kill us? Will he take Tara from me?

Maria swallows her desire to scream, as the door slowly opens. A face appears. He is big. His hair thick for his age. She has seen him before, she thinks. He reminds Maria of some actor, but she can't remember which one. The way he looks at them makes her very uncomfortable. He is wearing a suit that looks very expensive to Maria. The kind of suit her dad's clients would wear when they came to his office at the law firm.

The man places both hands on his sides and smiles. He walks towards Tara and strokes her cheek gently, with slow yet firm movements. Tara becomes stiff in her arms and Maria tries to pull her away from him.

"Look at you two," the man says. "Even prettier in real life than in the pictures. I have been looking forward to seeing you both."

"Mommy!" Tara says and throws her arms around Maria's neck.

"Where are we?" Maria says, snorting in anger. "Why are we here?"

Maria notices that the door to the room is still left open. She wonders if she can make a run for it.

The man shakes his head. "Tsk, tsk. Now don't you worry your pretty little heads with that. You're finally here, and boy how we are going to have fun together."

"I wanna go home, Mommy!" Tara says, while clinging to her mother's neck.

"Now, don't say that," the man says. "This is your new home. You will stay here with me until I get tired of you. As long as you do what I say, I will keep you alive, huh?" He touches the tip of her nose. He smiles and tilts his head. "Now, let's see what I have here." He puts a hand in his pocket and pulls out a red lollipop. He hands it to Tara. She doesn't want to take it and turns her head away while clinging tightly to her mother.

"Please, sir," Maria says. "Please, just let us go."

The man sighs. "Now, that is the only thing I can't do. See, I paid good money for the two of you and I can't get that money back if I let you go. So...well..." he shrugs and pushes the lollipop at Tara. "Here."

She shakes her head. Maria doesn't like the expression in the man's eyes when she rejects him. Anger is building and it scares her. She has seen it before in one of her earlier boyfriends.

"Take the lollipop, Tara," she says.

"But, Mooom! You always say..."

"I know what I say; just take it. Do as I tell you to."

Tara sniffles and looks at the man. He places his hand on her back and caresses it gently. Maria can't stand the way he is touching her. She feels like screaming at him, but she doesn't dare to.

Finally, Tara reaches out and grabs the lollipop.

The man sighs. "There you go. Now, that wasn't so hard, was it?"

"Say thank you," Maria says.

"Thank you," Tara sniffles.

The man reaches out and touches Tara's hair. Everything is turning inside of Maria. The man stares at Tara's hair. "You're welcome."

"Now can we go home?" Tara asks.

The man burst into a sudden laughter that makes Maria jump. "Ha!" He leans over them and says: "No, you can't. But we can play a game. Now, what would be fun to play? I know it! How about hide and go seek? Yes, that is my favorite game of all time."

"I love hide and go seek," Tara says.

The man clasps his hands. "How wonderful!" He grabs Tara by the chin. "I have a feeling you and I are going to be GREAT friends." He leans over and whispers. "Now, go...hide."

Part I

GENTLEMEN PREFER BLONDES

1

April 2016

"WELCOME TO CHEATER'S."

The half-naked woman greeting Danny Schmidt in the doorway smiles. Danny nods and walks to the back of the place and finds somewhere to sit. Two girls are dancing on the podium, slithering up and down the poles. Another girl approaches him and asks him what he would like to drink. He orders a beer and hands her a tip that she puts in her bra. She winks and leaves him. Danny watches the dancers. One of them is young, barely eighteen, he thinks. Her eyes are blurry. She is very pretty and the men seem to like her. Especially one guy smoking a cigar, he claps at her every move and rains money on her. She barely notices it.

The waitress comes back. She places his beer in front of him. He gives her another tip that disappears into her bra. As she is about to leave, he grabs her wrist.

"Say, don't you have anyone younger than these two?" he asks.

She stares at him for a few seconds, scrutinizing him. "Sure." She rubs her fingertips against one another to tell him it'll cost him.

Danny smiles. "Naturally."

He hands her a hundred-dollar bill. She smiles even wider now, then leans over and whispers.

"How do you prefer them?"

The way she is standing, Danny can look down her cleavage. "Blonde and young."

"How young?"

"Fourteen-fifteen?"

She doesn't react. She is used to this kind of request. "Sure. We can get them even younger if you're willing to pay. But it's very expensive."

Danny nods. "The younger the better. He opens his jacket and shows her a bundle of money."

"All right, cowboy. Come out the back. To the VIP-section."

Danny throws a bill on the table, throws one last glance at the dancing girls, then follows the woman out behind a curtain. She tells him to sit on a couch while someone brings him a bottle of champagne. The girl opening it rubs herself against him. When it has popped she pours him a glass, then sits on his lap and rubs herself against his crotch.

"Enjoy the show, tiger," she whispers in his ear, and bites his lip before she leaves.

Danny sips the champagne while he waits. A few minutes later, the woman returns followed by three young blonde girls all dressed in sexy lingerie. By looking at their faces, he guesses them to be no more than twelve or thirteen. They're all wearing heavy make-up. The woman tells them to stand on the podium in front of Danny. They're posing for him. He rubs his chin while observing them. Music is put on and they are told to dance. They show him what they can do. He is very impressed and smiles. The woman approaches him.

"You like what you see, huh?"

"Yes."

"You want to touch? Touching costs more."

He hands her more money. She signals the girls to come closer. They swarm Danny now and he leans back on the couch. Their hands are on him, everywhere...on his chest, in his crotch. He looks into their eyes. They're all drugged, blurry. One of the girls is younger than the others, he realizes when looking into her eyes. He grabs her by the chin and looks at her face.

"You like her, huh?" the woman asks. "This is August."

"I like her," he says.

"Very good," the woman says. "She is a beauty."

"I'd like to spend the night with her."

Before the woman can say anything, Danny pulls out more money from his jacket and places it on the table. The woman doesn't say anything else.

"The back entrance is over there," she says, and grabs the two other girls and disappears.

2

April 2016

"YOU FORGOT TO PACK HIM A LUNCH?"

I stare at Joey. We're standing in his townhouse. There is a mess everywhere. Clothes on the floor, cereal boxes left out on the kitchen table, dirty dishes in the sink. He looks like crap. Hasn't shaved in a week, or even showered, from what it looks like. I only stopped by to grab Salter's stuff. He's been with his dad for a few days.

I've brought Snowflake so he can say hi to his old friends. Clyde is barking at him while Snowflake sniffs Bonnie's behind. It doesn't seem like the animals have been out much, with the way they're acting up when they see us.

"Well, I didn't forget; I gave him some money to buy something."

"You know I hate it when he has to eat that food they serve in the cafeteria at the school. What is going on, Joe? You never used to be this sloppy."

He shrugs with a sigh. On the floor, I see a bra that, for obvious reasons, isn't mine. I look at it. "Is that…hers?"

Joey chuckles. "Yeah. Probably."

"So, that's it. You're partying with her and not taking anything seriously anymore?" I ask.

"What's it to you?"

"We have a kid, Joe, that's what it is to me. I don't want him to come here if you don't take care of him and if there is underwear lying all over the place." I pick up the bra, holding it between two fingers and hand it to him. "Please, tell your girlfriend to stop throwing her undergarments everywhere. At least keep it where my son won't find it."

"You tell her yourself."

15

"She's here?"

"Yeah. She kind of…lives here now."

My eyes widen. "What? She moved in? Just like that?"

He shrugs again. "It was easier."

I can't believe him. I don't know what to say. I don't want to say any more. I am exhausted with this entire situation. I feel so hurt that he would move in with the woman he cheated on me with. Of course, to him it wasn't cheating, since we were separated at the time. I can't just move on. My son needs his dad and I need Joey to be a good role model for him. He isn't with the way things are right now. Joey is hardly working, he hangs out with Jackie, his girlfriend, who now apparently has moved in; they drink beers and party while I am left picking up the pieces of my son's broken heart. Salter is ten now. He is beginning to figure out what is going on and asking questions I have a hard time answering.

"So, that's it now? She is definitely a part of our lives?" I ask. "Because I sure hope you're planning on staying with her, since you chose to bring her into your son's life."

"Don't be so uptight. It's annoying," he says with a groan.

I want to shake him. I want to yell at him and tell him I need him to snap out of this, whatever it is that's going on with him. I owe the guy so much. I owe him my life. We have known each other since we were in preschool and we were married for what felt like an eternity. But now, as I am standing in front of him, I don't recognize him anymore. All my life I have known and loved this guy, but…now I feel like I don't know him at all. Why would he choose this life?

"Don't you have to work today?" I ask.

"Nope. Nothing out there for me."

"You're telling me no one needs a carpenter today or even later this week?"

He rolls his eyes at me. It makes me angry. I can't believe him. Joey has barely worked in two months. I can't help wondering if he isn't doing enough to get something, to get the jobs. Is he even out there, or does he just stay at home with her? She works at Juice 'N Java downtown, but only a few times a week. She can't be making much. I have no idea how they're getting by, how they're paying the rent.

"You know what, Mary? It really is none of your damn business," Joey growls. Clyde is barking and Snowflake runs after him. Bonnie trots after them, not really engaged in their little fight.

Joey picks up Salter's sports bag, pulls a few clothing items from the floor and throws them in, then hands it to me.

"Here. This is what you came for, right? Now you can go."

April 2016

She is almost bursting with excitement. Paige Stover can't hide it in the car when she sees the rec center. Paige just started taking basketball lessons and loves hanging out with Coach Joe. Once a week, he gives her a private lesson, since she is very new to the game, and then the team meets every Saturday. It's expensive for her mother, Nicky, but since her parents died, Nicky inherited a good sum of money.

It feels good to finally be able to give Paige what she wants in life. After twelve years of being a poor, single mother, Nicky is finally able to give her daughter what she deserves. What all the other kids have. Paige is such a good girl, does well in school, and wants to do a lot of sports, even though she isn't among the most athletic around.

"There she is. There's my Paige-girl," Coach Joe yells when they enter the center.

Paige grabs the ball from between her mother's hands and runs towards him. They hug.

"Have you been practicing flipping your wrist like I told you to?" he asks, and shows her how to do it.

Paige repeats the gesture and he laughs putting his hands on both her arms. He hugs her again. "You sure have."

Nicky sits down and pulls out her phone, while Coach Joe starts instructing Paige. He asks her to run first to warm up, then dribble while running with the ball. Then he asks her to shoot hoops. Twenty-five shots. She misses most of them. Coach Joe laughs heartily and makes her run again, then do push-ups to build up the strength in her arms. Paige is skinny. She hasn't played many sports until recently, since they can now afford to pay for it. But she has barely any muscles.

Nicky looks at the display of her phone and goes through her emails. Her decorating business is doing well and there are several requests from new costumers. She looks at Paige and the Coach, then walks outside to make a few calls.

Nicky is very pleased to finally be able to make a living for herself. It has taken her years to get to this point, where the costumers come to her and not the other way around. It all travels by word of mouth, but it takes years to get people talking. It used to be that she had to work another job on the side. She has held many jobs as a secretary for years, but her dream has always been to have her own business. Like her father always used to say, there are two ways to live your life. Either you are busy making someone else's dream come true or you're busy making your own come true. Nicky has always known she would one day make her own dream come true. But being a single mother, after Mike left when Paige was just a baby, was hard and required that she have a steady income for many years. She couldn't just quit her job and devote herself to her business. Not until she had enough clients.

Nicky makes a couple of new appointments and plots them down in the calendar of her phone. She looks at the clock. The time is almost up. She hurries back inside, but finds the rec center empty.

"Hello?"

Nicky looks around the empty basketball court. Where can they be?

"Paige? Coach Joe?"

Nicky's heart is in her throat as she walks to the office, only to find that empty as well. "Coach Joe? Paige?" she yells again, this time slightly panicking.

They can't have left, can they? I was right outside all the time. I would have seen them. Could they have used the back entrance?

"Mom! We're right here!"

Nicky turns and sees Paige. She is standing in a doorway leading to a room Nicky hadn't noticed before. Behind her is Coach Joe, both his hands placed on Paige's shoulders. He is smiling.

"I just showed Paige a small clip from a game last weekend. We have a TV in here."

Nicky swallows hard while the worry and anxiety are pushed back. She curses her own paranoia. Of course, everything is fine.

Saigon, Vietnam, 1975

DANH NGUYEN LOOKS at his sister. She smiles and unwraps his present. He feels the excitement in every bone of his body. He has been looking forward to giving her this doll. His sister is his everything. His beautiful—three years younger—sister, Long, who makes every room brighter when she enters.

Today, she is turning eight years old. All her siblings, five brothers and four sisters, and her parents and grandparents are gathered in the house on their father's estate. Their father is a wealthy businessman, and they're fortunate enough to belong to the upper class.

"Thank you! Thank you!" Long exclaims when she sees the doll. She throws her arms around his neck. Danh holds her tight and closes his eyes.

"You're welcome," he whispers lovingly. "Only the best for *your majesty*."

Long giggles. She loves it when Danh calls her that, when they pretend she is a princess.

"Let's eat," their mother says and claps her hands.

Her face is growing new wrinkles every day, it seems to Danh. He knows she is concerned by what is happening to their country these days. Everyone is afraid of the Communist Government and what they might do next. Danh understands some of it and sees it on his parents' faces, but he feels certain they are very safe. Their dad is a respected person in the area. He has always kept all of them safe.

Danh looks at the table with all the food and smiles again. Unlike many others, they have money enough to live well, even though they can't get the supplies they usually do, they manage to get by anyway.

"Did you hear what happened to Uong?" his grandmother suddenly says when everyone has started eating.

Danh looks up and sees his parents' reaction. Uong is the man who lives only two houses down the street. Danh hasn't heard what happened to him.

"Not now, *me*," his mother says.

"I would like to hear it, *bà ngoại*," Danh says, adressing his grandmother. He has known Lan Uoung since he was born and likes to hang out around his store. "What happened to him?"

Danh's mother shakes her head. "Not now, Danh. Today we're celebrating."

"But…"

"*Không! No!* I said not today, Danh."

Danh can tell by the look on her face he has to let it go. He sinks into his chair and goes quiet. Still, he can't stop wondering what it is they won't talk about. Sometimes he hates being one of the young ones. His older siblings all know when to stay quiet and when to speak. Danh never does. At least he isn't the youngest anymore.

They eat in silence. Long doesn't look as happy any more and Danh makes a few funny faces at her to cheer her up. It is, after all, her birthday.

Long giggles and clasps her mouth. Danh feels better when he sees her happy. As long as she is happy, there is nothing wrong with the world.

Not until the door is kicked in.

They all hear it, but it goes so fast, Danh hardly realizes it before they have them surrounded. Ten police officers storm inside, guns pointed at them. Danh's mother starts to scream when they throw themselves at Danh's father and hold him down while putting him in handcuffs.

All Danh can think about is Long. He grabs her in his arms and covers her eyes.

"It's all part of a game, your majesty," he whispers in her ear. "They're here to celebrate your birthday and they'll just get upset if we don't play along."

The policemen order all of them to sit on the floor in the living room, while they drag their father away. Danh's mother tries to stop them, but is knocked down and beat up by an officer. The grandparents and siblings scream and cry for them to stop. Finally, they do. Bruised and beaten, their mother crawls back to her family.

Danh closes his eyes too and tries to imagine being in his favorite spot, in a canoe on the river, fishing with Long by his side. While the policemen trash the place and steal all their belongings, Danh whispers stories in Long's ears of the many times they have been fishing together, trying to get her to stop crying.

"Remember the time you fell in the water? Do you?"

"*Vâng. Yes*," she whimpers.

"We couldn't stop laughing, remember?"

"I remember," she whispers, and he feels how she calms down in his arms, while the sound of glass shattering becomes nothing but a distant noise.

Hours later, when the sounds slowly disappear, Danh dares to open his eyes again and look around.

Everything is gone. All their belongings are either gone or destroyed. Nothing is left. A note on the wall tells them the house now belongs to the government, along with the family's other houses.

They have one day to leave.

April 2016

MY DAD's house is so quiet. Salter is still in school, my dad is sleeping, and so is Snowflake. I am sitting in front of the computer wondering if I can shake this morning's fight with Joey. I don't understand why he gets to me the way he does. Well, if I am being perfectly honest, then maybe I can. I am so angry with him for moving on and for acting like a teenager in love all of a sudden, not living up to his responsibilities.

After leaving him with Salter's sports bag in my hand, I had to drive to Subway and buy a sandwich for Salter and take it to the school. Call me controlling...I don't want him eating that food in the cafeteria.

The blank page is staring at me from the computer. I am trying to write an article about a democratic senator that has been travelling to spots around the globe on trips sponsored by private people, people that were known for conservative views. I am sitting on the story, since no one else has discovered this. Chloe is actually the one who gave me the information. Apparently, the guy is also known to be active in the websites and chat rooms she observes for use of child porn. She tracked him down, then broke into his computer and found all the material we needed to take him down publicly.

I, for one, can't wait.

I make myself another cup of coffee, push Joey out of my head, then start writing. Seconds later, the keyboard is glowing, and I can't stop. The material is so good and I can't wait to publish it and see this guy taken down. I know this will be a big story, one that the newspapers will have to quote us on in the morning.

Snowflake wakes up as I press publish, and someone is at the door. I get up and open it. It's Marcia. I smile happily.

"You have time for coffee?" she asks.

"Always. Come on in."

I make a new cup for myself and one for Marcia, then find some cookies in the cabinet that I bring out with it. We sit in the living room overlooking the glittering ocean. The waves aren't very good today. There is too much wind for it to be fun. Suits me well enough. I needed the time to write.

"So, how's it going?" I ask, with a cookie half eaten in my mouth.

Marcia smiles. "I'm getting the kids for the weekend," she says.

"Really? That's amazing!"

She nods. It's been a long time since I have seen that kind of light in her eyes. It makes me happy. She is doing really well on her medicine and with the help from her sister.

"Carl finally agreed to let me have them for three days in a row after my doctor called him and told him I was ready."

"I am so happy to hear that," I say, and put a hand on her shoulder. "And you're sure you can handle it, right? It's not too much? Four kids for three days can be a lot with all you're going through."

"My sister will help me," she says. "I just want to be with my babies again. I have seen them only a few hours here and there since they moved back with their dad. I miss them so much. I miss being a part of their lives, you know? I miss noticing the little differences every day as they grow older."

"I understand. I have to get used to being without Salter for several days in a row. I'm not sure I'm doing so well on that part," I say with a light laugh. "I'm not doing well with any of this, having to give up Joey and see him with that…that girl. Knowing they're together as a family with Salter when it should be me. It ain't easy, I tell you that."

"I hear you met someone?" she asks.

I grab another cookie. "You mean Tom? Yeah. We've been on a few dates. I met him through Tinder. I can't believe I tried that, but Chloe persuaded me to. He seems like a nice guy. Not a local, which is good, since we know all of them from back then. Moved here four years back from South Florida, works at the Space Center. Something with the weather stations, I am not quite sure I get it. He's tried to explain it to me several times, but I just pretend like I understand. Basically, he's the guy who tells them if the weather is good enough for a launch or not. That's how far I am." I laugh again and eat yet another cookie. Marcia follows me, which pleases me immensely, since I hate eating alone.

"Have you heard from Sandra lately?" Marcia asks.

I shake my head. "No. Not in a really long time. I have a feeling she's avoiding me. She's probably fooling around with Alex still."

Marcia stares at me and I clasp my mouth. "Whoops."

"She and Alex are fooling around?"

I make a grimace. "Yeah, well, I wasn't supposed to say anything. Me and my big mouth."

"That totally explains everything," Marcia exclaims. "I've noticed how they look at each other, but always thought it was all about them longing for each other, since they can't be together. But they're both married?"

"You're telling me. I've tried to explain that to them. I even threatened to tell their spouses, but they still continue this charade behind their backs. I can't get myself to meddle in it, though. They're grown-ups; they'll have to deal with it themselves."

"Wow," Marcia says, and leans back on the couch with her coffee between her hands.

"I know, right? To be frank, it's actually nice to have told you, because now I'm not the only one who knows."

"Speaking of betrayal, are we getting any closer to catching that brother of yours?" she asks.

I grunt. I hate talking about my brother, Blake. He is the one who poured acid on Sandra's face, making her lose her modeling career and destroying her marriage. He is a killer on the run, and I want to get him so badly.

"There's nothing new since Naples, where they found the body of Olivia Hartman," I say. "Detective Fisher has tried to work with the local police over there, but so far they haven't found any traces of him. He was long gone when they found the body inside the mattress at the motel. They're looking for him in the area, but there is no way he'd stay there after he killed her. He's not that stupid."

"Where do you think he is now?" Marcia asks.

I shrug. "Chloe is trying to track him, but he is being very clever. Doesn't use any credit cards, not any in his own name. His picture has been shown in the news over there, but they have no idea where he is. He is gone, again."

I grab another cookie, deciding if I make this my lunch, then I am allowed to have a couple more. Talking about Blake always makes me want to eat.

"So, what's the plan?" Marcia asks.

"There is no plan," I say. "We wait. We wait for him to make a mistake. Which he will sooner or later. I know that much about my dear baby brother."

April 2016

THE WIND FEELS WARM. The strong engine of the silver Ducati lifts the bike off the road as it roars into the wind. Blake laughs out loud and speeds up. He zigzags between cars and trucks on the road. The motorcycle rockets forward. Blake yells when feeling the power beneath him.

This is the way to ride!

He stole the bike outside a restaurant in Naples right before he left town. He bought himself a helmet in Fort Meyers, a black one with a black visor. He looks badass when he wears it.

When Blake reaches a busy intersection, all the cars around him slow down. Blake doesn't. He turns the throttle, picks up even more speed, and barely avoids crashing into a stopped car as he zigzags between them across the intersection, speeding through the red light. A car hits the brakes and honks the horn aggressively. Blake doesn't give the driver the time of day. He is doing seventy-five, steering straight towards a building. The wall is approaching rapidly, but Blake doesn't brake. He aims the bike closer and closer, while the adrenalin is pumping through his veins; while imagining the collision, he sees the faces of the girls he has killed. He sees their eyes, the fear as they scream, and he feels it all over again, feels the torment, the intoxicating power.

At the last possible second, he steers the bike and spins it hard to the right. The bike tips to the side and screeches across the asphalt. Panting, he manages to get it to skid to a stop before he turns the throttle again and accelerates back onto the road, heart pounding heavily in his chest. He yells out into the air as he continues to zigzag between driving cars.

Never has he felt this free, this invincible. So many lives he has taken, so many lives destroyed, and still they haven't caught him yet; heck, they're not even close. They have no idea where he is or what will be his next move.

Freaking idiots. They'll never know. I am always gonna be one step ahead of them. Ha!

Blake zooms across the road and hits the bridge where the air shifts to the fresh salty air coming from the ocean. He takes in a deep breath. How he loathes that smell. How he hates this place.

He approaches ninety miles an hour as he crosses the bridge. The traffic is getting heavy now, as he gets closer to the island.

Freaking tourists.

The traffic is soon blocked up and Blake is going so fast he can't stop. He sees the rear end of a Toyota pick-up truck approaching fast. He can't go left or right. There is no way out.

In the last second, Blake yanks the bike across the road and is now driving against the oncoming traffic. He speeds up, the engine roaring loudly as he sees the approaching car, flickering its head-lights, honking its horn. Blake is standing up on the bike now, yelling and screaming as he faces death, prepares himself for not surviving this, until the second before the car hits him…he turns and ends up in between the cars going in each direction. Knocking their side mirrors off one after the other with his fists, he drives straight through the line of cars until he can get in front of them and back onto the road.

Blake is laughing loudly at the blaring horns as he gets ahead of all of them and reaches the end of the bridge. Running another red light, he makes a turn and drives onto the island, speeding up across A1A.

As he reaches the house on the corner of 7th Street, he finally hits the brakes. The tires screech on the asphalt and the bike slips underneath him, making him turn really fast.

He is stopped.

He stares at the new house they have built that looks a lot like the old one, only bigger. In there. Behind that gate, behind those doors and walls, lives his father. His poor and helpless father, the man he has hated for his entire life, along with the sister he has always wanted dead.

April 2016

DANNY DRIVES up to the man standing on the corner of Barton Boulevard and Huntington Lane. He rolls down the window and the guy approaches him.

"I saw your ad on Craigslist," Danny says.

"Yeah? So what?" the man asks with a sniffle.

"Personals."

The man's fingers drum on the car. He has a lit cigarette in his other hand. He smokes it and the smoke enters Danny's car.

"All right," the man says, and nods in the direction of a building. "Apartment number 245. The code is 111 for the gate."

Danny rolls up the window and drives to the gate. The complex is nice. Not among the most expensive ones around, but not cheap either. The type you'd expect retired people to live in when they come down here for the winter. It has a pool with a hot tub, a tennis court, and a small clubhouse.

No one would ever suspect what this place really hides.

Danny punches in the code and the gate opens. He drives inside and parks the car in front of the building. It's been painted in nice bright colors, in the Key West-style that many use in Florida to make it look exotic.

Danny takes in a deep breath, then walks down one of the hall-ways. He finds the elevator and rides to the second floor. When he gets out, his phone rings. He picks it up.

"Hey, Junior," he says, keeping his voice low.

"Dad, we're out of milk."

"I'll grab some when I come home," Danny says.

His teenage son sighs from the other end. "When will you come home? I'm really hungry."

"Maybe grab some toast instead, huh? This might take a while. How was school today?"

"Boring."

"Got any homework?"

"What do you think? I'm graduating in a month. Of course I have tons of homework."

"Then go do that, and I'm sure I'll be home to make some dinner."

"You don't sound sure. Where are you, anyway? I thought this was your day off from the fire station?"

"Yeah, well, I had some paperwork I needed to finish up. I'll be home soon. Do your homework."

Danny hangs up and looks at the display for a few seconds before he puts the phone away. He thinks about his son and the fact that he will graduate high school in just a month. He can't believe his son is growing up so fast. Life has been hard on Junior since his mom died, but at least he has his school. And then what? Junior has shown no interest in college. Will he move out? Will he get a job? Danny might be able to get him something at the fire station. He always wanted for his son to follow in his footsteps, but he has shown no interest in becoming a firefighter. Lately, it's like nothing really interests him anymore.

Danny takes in a deep breath and walks to the door with the number 245 on it. He knocks and the door is opened.

"I'm here about the ad," he says.

The woman at the door nods and he follows her inside. When the door is closed she looks at him. "Money first."

Danny nods, grabs the envelope in his pocket, and hands it to her. The woman's face lights up as she counts the many hundred dollar bills. The apartment smells bad. Like cigarettes and sex.

"She's right in here," the woman says, and walks ahead of him towards a door. She knocks on the door and a big guy opens it. "New client," the woman says.

"We're just finishing up," the big guy says. He looks at Danny. "He can watch if he likes."

Danny walks inside. Just as he enters, another man walks past Danny towards the door. They don't look at each other or exchange glances. They don't want to know who the other one is. They never want to see each other again.

The girl on the bed isn't moving. She is too drugged. Danny looks at her. "I paid extra for privacy," he grunts, and seconds later they're left alone.

April 2016

I DRIVE Marcia to Publix and help her get groceries. It's hard for her to do even little things like shopping because she has no license after her DUI. Usually, she just goes on her bike, but she can't carry much on her bike. So her sister sometimes drives her, and every now and then I take her. Gives me time to talk to her and I enjoy that. Especially now that she is doing so much better. I realize I have missed her and who she used to be before the drinking started.

I decide to make lasagna tonight. Lasagna is Salter's favorite dish. He is supposed to stay at my house for the next week and a half, and I intend to spoil him rotten. I miss him while he is with his father. I'm not used to it yet.

"Will you come and surf with us soon, please?" I ask Marcia, as we carry out our groceries and put them in the back of my car. Marcia hasn't been surfing for a very long time.

"Yes. I was just thinking about it today. I think it would be good for me to get back out there. What does the forecast say?"

"Tomorrow is supposed to be good. Maybe once Salter is back from school around low tide? I have a date tomorrow night, and I would like to get a little exercise in before I pull on a dress again," I say with a laugh. Not because it is funny, but because I am embarrassed by how much weight I have gained lately. I don't know if it is the break-up with Joey or what, but I can't stop eating sweets. I don't even count the amount of cookies I eat in a day anymore. I don't want to know.

"A date, huh? That sounds great," Marcia says. "I should be able to go out with you two for a little while tomorrow."

"Yay," I say, and close the trunk.

I open the door to the car, and then pause. "Is that Danny?"

"Where?"

"Over there getting into his car," I say and point.

"Looks like him, but who's the girl?" Marcia asks, wrinkling her nose. "She looks a little young."

I stare at the young girl in the very short skirt. She doesn't seem to be able to walk on her own without Danny supporting her.

"Could it be one of Junior's friends?" I ask.

"If Junior had friends in a brothel," Marcia says. "That girl is doped. She looks like a junkie and a prostitute. What is he doing with her?"

I shrug. I don't like this feeling. I know Danny has had a hard time since his wife was killed last fall. I know he is lonely, but still. It is hard to tell the girl's age with the clothing and the heavy make-up, but she doesn't look a day over eighteen—if that.

Marcia waves. "Hey, Danny!"

He sees her and nods while helping the girl inside of his car. He doesn't seem to be his usual happy self, and he doesn't come over to talk to us. Instead, he nods again, gets into his seat, and drives off.

So unlike Danny.

"What was that about?" Marcia asks.

I shrug again and get in behind the wheel. "Maybe he was in a hurry."

"Danny is usually so friendly."

"I know. Maybe he didn't like us seeing him with her."

"You think he was embarrassed?"

"Yeah. Something like that. Wouldn't you be?"

I back out of the parking spot.

"Yeah," Marcia says. "I knew he was lonely, but not that he was *that* desperate. You think he likes young girls like that?"

"I don't know what he likes, but I can tell you that it worries me. Last week, I saw him come out of Cheaters in Cape Canaveral with another girl. Much like this one, only I'm pretty sure she was even younger."

"Oh, my."

"I know."

9

April 2016

THE YOUNG GIRL in the picture is smiling. Her front teeth are too big for her face, but she is still pretty. Her eyes are sparkling as she holds her surfboard up for the camera. Boxer clicks the picture and looks at it more closely. He watches her features. She has brown eyes. Long dark hair. Just like what the client is asking for. But is she the one?

He is not sure.

He closes the picture again, and then continues looking through the timeline on the mother's Facebook page. The mom is stunning. He wonders if her breasts are real or not. They look almost too perfect in that light summer dress she is wearing in the next picture. Not that it usually matters to his client.

Boxer closes Facebook and moves on to the mother's Instagram. She has a lot more pictures here, and he can go through everything she has posted over the past year or so. Lots of pictures of her and her daughter. Of them at Disney World, of them at Brevard Zoo, of them eating ice cream. The mother is very into the environment and posts a lot about the dead fish in Banana River and how to save the lagoon. On Facebook, he has seen that she plans on being at the rally next weekend.

Maybe he will be there too.

A message pops up in the chat room and he turns to the needs of his client.

>What do you have for me?<

>I think I have your match. Sending pictures now.<

Boxer downloads the woman's photos to his own computer, and then uploads them in the secure chat room. He sits back in his chair and drinks from his coffee while waiting for the client's answer.

>Are the breasts real?<
>I don't know. Does it matter?<
>Not really. But do you have others?<
>I do. Give me a sec.<

Boxer grumbles as he goes back to Facebook and finds another mother and daughter that he thought of as a match. He really thought his client would like the first ones better. He downloads a few more pictures, then posts them in the chat room. This woman has smaller breasts, but a bigger behind. She is a good match, but she has recently gotten a boyfriend, and Boxer doesn't like that. Usually he only goes after the single mothers, since they're easier. They're alone more often and it takes longer before anyone discovers that they are gone.

Single moms, especially those that struggle financially, are the easiest targets. They're flakier and move around often, either for jobs or because they met someone.

>I like the first one better,< the client finally answers.

Boxer smiles widely as he looks at the pictures again. >Good choice, sir. That's a nice pair. Both of them are truly beautiful. Ready and ripe.<

>Then let's harvest. ASAP.<

Boxer smiles. He closes the chat and stares at the young girl with her surfboard. He touches the bridge of her nose with his pointer and lets it run across her young face. A beauty like her is going to make him a lot of money.

April 2016

"I AM SO sorry for springing this on you at the last minute."

I move aside and let Chloe come in. "It's no problem, Mary," she says, and puts her laptop on the kitchen table.

Salter is on the couch with his iPad. He doesn't even look up. I know he can hear us, but he just doesn't want to. He has been in a bad mood all afternoon since I told him Chloe was going to look after him tonight.

"So your date changed his plans, huh?" Chloe asks.

"Yes," I say with a sigh. "We were supposed to go out tomorrow night, but he had to change it, so I said yes to today; otherwise, we couldn't see each other till next week. I hope it's not a big problem."

Chloe shakes her head. "It's not. Not for me at least." She throws a glance at Salter, who still doesn't pay any attention to us.

"I know. Salter is pissed. He's been at his dad's for a week and we were supposed to hang out together. But what can I do? I really want to see this guy. I think I like him."

"Salter will be fine. You'll have plenty of time together the rest of the week. It smells divine in here," Chloe says.

"I made a lasagna for you three to share."

Chloe's face is lit up. "Yum. I love your lasagna."

"I hope you didn't have other plans for tonight," I say, as I storm around, setting the table for them, wearing my dress that is a little too tight. Well, maybe not just a little.

"Me?" Chloe says. "Only work. I brought the laptop, so I can do it from here when Salter is asleep. And I brought Twister to play with Salter."

"That's awesome," I say, and take out the sizzling lasagna from the oven. "Salter loves Twister, don't you Salter?"

"Nah. Not really," he grumbles from the couch.

"Don't mind him," Chloe says. "We'll have a great night, the three of us. Don't you worry."

"Yeah, that reminds me. My dad is in his room watching TV. He's already in his chair, so if you could just roll him out here. I usually give him a fork to hold; now that he has regained sensitivity in eight of his fingers, he is actually able to hold it, and he can move the lower part of his right arm. He usually misses his mouth, so you'll have to help him out, and he spills a lot…I mean like *a lot*, but it's important for him to do it, in order to get better. I can clean up later when I get back. You don't have to think about it…and…there was something else, but now I can't remember what it was…"

Chloe places her hand on my shoulder. "We'll figure it out, Mary. Don't worry. We're going to be fine."

I sigh. "You're right. I'm obsessing. My dad can tell you what he needs. Guess I am just a little nervous about this date."

I take in another deep breath and straighten my back. "How do I look?"

She stares at me like she needs to find the right words. It's not a good sign.

"That bad, huh?" I ask.

"No. I mean. Yes. I'm sorry, Mary, but that dress is way too tight."

I chuckle. "Thanks for being honest, at least."

"Let's go upstairs and find another one," she says.

I follow her to my bedroom, where she disappears into my walk-in closet. I sit on the bed.

"We saw Danny today," I say.

"So?"

"It was so strange. Marcia and I were at Publix. We saw Danny in the parking lot. We waved, he didn't wave back, only nodded like he didn't want to talk to us. And he was with a young girl."

"So?" Chloe repeats.

"So…it's not the first time. Last week, I saw him coming out of Cheaters with another young girl on his arm."

Chloe pokes her head out of the closet. "Ah, come on."

"I'm serious, Chloe. I worry."

She disappears back inside. "You always worry."

"Well I'm worrying a lot, then," I say.

"You always worry a lot. It'll make you sick someday. I'm sure there's a perfectly good explanation for it."

"Yeah, that he likes young girls."

Chloe comes out. She looks angrily at me and points a finger at me. "No. Not Danny. Not him." She throws a dress at me. "Here, try this."

I pick it up. "Why not? Maybe he's always done this. We knew things were bad with Jean even before she was killed. Maybe this is what he was into. I just don't know what to do about it."

I put on the dress. When I look up, Chloe is right next to me.

"Let it go."

I shake my head. I can't believe her reaction to this. "I'm not going to let it go. It's illegal. And so...so wrong."

She helps me zip up in the back. The dress tightens on my body. I suck in everything I can.

"It's none of our business."

"Of course it is; how can you even say that? I love Danny, but I am not going to stand by and watch if he...if he hurts..."

Chloe turns me around and we're face to face. "Stop! Danny would never hurt anyone. You know that!"

"That's what I thought, but..."

"I don't want to hear any more about it, Mary. You do this all the time. You get this idea in your head and then you obsess about it till it drives all of us nuts. Danny is a sweet guy. He's our friend."

"Sorry. I just..."

"No. Not one single word more about this."

"All right. Geez."

"Now look at yourself and tell me you don't think this is better."

I look at myself in the mirror. The long blue dress looks really nice on me.

"See?" Chloe says. "You better listen to me."

I nod, bend forward, and kiss my friend on the forehead. "All right," I say. "I'll listen to you from now on. I'll let it go."

"Good. Now go have fun on your date."

"Yes, ma'am."

11

April 1975

THE LARGE EXPLOSION makes the windows shake in the small one-room house in Saigon, where Danh and his eight siblings have lived with their mother since their homes were taken by the soldiers and their father sent to prison.

Danh is sitting on the floor with his younger sister when they hear it. Long whimpers and looks up at her big brother. Danh glares at his mother. Her face is worried.

Another explosion sends shocks through the children. They all look to their mother, who looks as scared as they are.

"What is it?" Long asks.

"Probably just thunder," Danh says. "Nothing to worry about."

Danh gets up and walks outside with his brothers. In the distance, they see smoke. Lots of smoke. Then another loud explosion. Screams in the air and lots of people in the streets. A neighbor comes running past them. Danh's older brother, Bao, stops him.

"What's going on?"

"The Vietcong's coming. They're making their way to the capitol building. We're getting out of here while we still can."

Bao looks at Danh, then at their other brothers. "What's going on?" Danh asks, confused and bewildered. He doesn't understand what is going on, but he knows it is bad. Just like on Long's birthday two months ago.

"They're coming," Bao says. "They're taking over."

With his heart in his throat, Danh walks back inside with his brothers, where their mother and sister are waiting.

"What is it, son?" their mother asks, seeing the concern on their faces.

"It is what we feared," Bao says.

Being the oldest, he has been the man of the house ever since they took their father. The responsibility has weighed on him and he looks a lot older than he really is, Danh thinks.

Their mother nods. Danh doesn't like the look on her face. It scares him.

"Get your bikes," she says. "Ride out of town and don't come back till things have calmed down. You hear me?"

"No!" Danh yells. "We're not leaving you here!"

"You must," his mother tells him. "They will make soldiers of you and rape your sister. Take her and get yourself as far away as possible, do you hear me?"

"But…but…"

Danh's mother grabs a crying Long in her arms and hands her to Danh. "You take care of your sister. You protect her, you hear me? You protect her with your life."

Danh is crying heavily now. He sniffles and nods. "Why can't you come with us?"

"I have to stay behind in case your father comes back. Besides, I'll slow you all down."

Danh looks at his mother's leg that is still bad since the beating she received when they arrested their father.

"Come on, Danh," Bao yells, standing in the doorway. "We have to hurry. They're getting closer."

Danh takes one last glance at his mother, and receives a worried look back. "Go," she whispers. "I'll be fine. I'll see you soon."

Crying, he carries his sister out the door, where Bao is waiting impatiently on his moped.

"Hurry up, Danh. Jump on the back."

12

April 2016

TOM MEETS me in front of Heidi's Jazz club. I feel weird meeting someone else here, since it used to be mine and Steven's favorite place to go. But even though things went bad with him, I don't think it is fair to blame it on the Jazz club.

He whistles as he sees me walking towards him. "Wow. Look at you."

It's our third date, and I am glad the dress is classy and long and doesn't signal that I want to get laid. 'Cause I really do. Well, a part of me does. It has been forever. At least that's what it feels like. The other part of me just wants to call Joey. I can't get used to not being with him.

Tom holds the door for me as we walk inside. It is a Monday night, so I don't expect there to be a whole lot of people. That is actually another reason for us coming here. It is spring break in Cocoa Beach, and that means lots of people everywhere. I want to have Tom to myself.

Tom is not the most handsome guy I have met. Not like Steven or even like Joey. As a matter of fact, he is a little chubby, but that suits me well. I am tired of being the only chubby one in my relationships. Tom enjoys good food just as much as I do. That counts for a lot in my book.

"I got your table ready for you, Miss Mills," the lady greeting us says. We follow her to the small table close to the stage and sit down. It is dark inside, the kind of darkness that gives it a big city nightclub atmosphere. I like that about this place. The waiter approaches us and hands us menus and small flashlights to be able to see.

"Sorry that I had to change our plans in a hurry," Tom says and corrects his shirt. He is wearing a suit for our date. I love that. Joey

38

never wore a suit for me. Not even a tie. Doesn't like the way it feels, he would say. He felt like he was being strangled. I have to say, I enjoy that Tom dresses up for me. Makes me feel like I matter to him.

"I would like a glass of Chardonnay to begin with," I say.

"I'll have an Oktoberfest-bier," Tom says, referring to the Austrian beer. The owner of the place, Heidi, is Austrian.

"And we'll have red wine with the dinner, right?" he asks.

"Yes. Red wine with the lamb," I say. That is another reason for me to choose this place. For Easter, they have the greatest lamb for the whole month of April. It is divine.

"So, why did you have to change your plans?" I ask when the waiter is gone. On the stage, the house band is setting up.

"I have a basketball tournament that I completely forgot about."

"You play basketball?" I say in surprise, thinking about his short, out of shape body.

"What? I don't look like I could play basketball?" he asks with a grin.

"I'm just surprised," I say.

"I coach basketball. Never was able to make it big myself, so now I am a coach, all right?"

"That makes more sense," I say, and sip my white wine, trying to look delicate and elegant. "Where?"

"At the rec center."

My face lights up thinking about him coaching little kids. "Aw."

"I knew that would hit a home run," he says, grinning even more. "Always works."

I chuckle as the waiter arrives with our food. The band opens by playing "Fly Me to the Moon." I secretly watch Tom as he sings along, not hitting a single note, and I notice that so far there is nothing I don't like about this guy.

April 2016

NICKY COMES home from visiting a new client just before six o'clock. She pays the neighbor's son ten dollars and thanks him for picking up Paige and looking after her this afternoon while Nicky was in Melbourne looking at fabrics for a woman's couch.

How one woman can take so long making one little decision is beyond Nicky's comprehension. She had her go through all of her books. Nicky now worries about the rest of the house. If one decision takes this long, how will she ever finish that eighteen thousand square foot mansion? There will be other couches and furniture, and don't even get her started on the curtains.

"Hi, sweet pea," she yells up the stairs. "I'm home."

"Hi, mom," Paige answers from her room.

"I'll start dinner."

Paige doesn't answer. Probably busy on that computer again. Nicky shakes her head as she unpacks the groceries and starts dinner. She almost regrets buying it for her, since she spends so much time on that thing, but it just felt so good to finally be able to give her something that big and expensive, so as soon as she got the inheritance from her parents, she went to the Apple store and bought the biggest computer she could find and placed it in Paige's room. The girl hadn't been able to play Minecraft or Roblox like all the other kids, and was constantly left out when they discussed those games at school. It used to torment Nicky to know that her daughter was falling behind in school where computers became more and more important every year.

Nicky turns on the TV and watches the local news as she peels the potatoes. It's all about those dead fish in the lagoon again.

Today, thousands of dead fish have been seen in the Banana River and in people's canals.

Nicky stops peeling and turns up the volume. The condition of the lagoon concerns her greatly. She wants to leave a world for her daughter to grow up in. The reporter talks about the rally, arranged by a local celebrity, that is planned for this Saturday, while showing more dead fish and then interviewing concerned tourists who have come here for spring break to fish.

"It's really disgusting what is going on here," a tourist from Canada says. "I used to come here and there would be fish jumping into my boat and the water would be crystal clear. This is bad. This is really bad."

Nicky feels a pinch of anger in her stomach as she returns to her potatoes. Meanwhile, the experts on TV argue whether the fish deaths are due to fertilizer from people's yards, leaking septic tanks, or overpopulation of manatees.

Nicky hurries up and puts all the potatoes in a pan with carrots and other vegetables before she throws a Mahi Mahi fillet on top and puts it all in the oven, thinking it is going to be terrible to not be able to eat local fish anymore.

She runs upstairs, knocks on the door, and enters her daughter's room. Just as expected — Paige is on the computer.

"Have you been on that thing all day?" Nicky asks.

"No. I had basketball as well."

"That's right," Nicky says. "Did you do well?"

"Yes. Coach says I can play in the tournament. We have a game on Saturday at two."

Nicky smiles. She is so glad that Paige enjoys doing sports. There really is no need to worry about her use of computers, is there?

"I'll have to make sure to be there for that, then," Nicky says. "Maybe we can go together to the rally for the lagoon in the morning, then head over to the game. How does that sound?"

Paige doesn't even look at her. She is all into her game and tapping away on her keyboard.

"Sure, Mom. Whatever."

April 2016

I TAKE Salter out surfing the next day after school. I feel bad for disappointing him the night before. He seems like he is still angry with me as we paddle out. I have texted Marcia to let her know that we're going out, but I secretly hope that she won't come, since I feel like my son needs to be alone with his mother.

"So, how was your day today?" I ask, when we're on the outside and wait on the next set of waves.

Salter has hardly spoken to me at all since he got back from school, and I can't stop thinking that something else is bothering him. I can't believe he can still be this mad about last night.

He shrugs. "Okay, I guess."

"Did you do anything fun?"

"Mom. This is fourth grade. We don't have time for fun."

"Ah. I forgot. Everything is so serious these days. Are there at least any girls you like in your class?"

He rolls his eyes. "Mom. Please."

"What? You used to always tell me these things."

"Well, I won't now."

"I'm not going to stop asking. I want to know everything about you, just so you know."

He rolls his eyes at me and I splash water at him. He smiles slightly. A set of waves is rolling towards us. We both start paddling for the same wave. Salter catches it. I don't. He laughs at me as he rides past me. He does a nice turn on the lip and my heart is filled with pride.

"You know, there was actually room enough for the both of us on that wave," he says, teasing me as he comes back out.

"Very funny," I say.

"I can't believe you couldn't catch that one," he continues.

"Well, I am a little out of shape, all right. Let's leave it at that before someone gets hurt."

"A little?" he says with a grin.

"Hey!"

"Sorry," he says, laughing.

Another set of waves comes towards us. "Watch me catch this one," I say, and start to paddle.

Salter follows me. We give it all we have and share a party wave. I ride it longer than him and come back out, laughing.

"Now who's the cool one around here?"

"Certainly not you when you talk like that," he says.

"What? No street cred for that one?"

"Okay. I'll grant you a little cred. That was pretty cool."

"Thank you."

Salter goes quiet all of a sudden. He looks down in the water and his smile disappears.

"What's going on?" I ask.

He looks up. "What do you mean?"

"Come on. I'm your mother. I can tell when my son is troubled. Spit it out or I won't stop asking about it."

"It's nothing, Mom, really."

"Don't do that to me. That look on your face tells me it is a lot more than nothing. Spit. It. Out."

He looks me in the eyes. My heart starts pounding. This is serious. I know my boy. This is not a little thing.

"Promise you won't get mad," he says.

"All right. Kind of depends on what you've done."

"It's not like that. I just don't want to see you mad or sad."

"Okay. You're starting to scare me a little here, Salter."

He bites his lips while looking into my eyes. A set of waves rolls towards us, but we let it pass.

"I was thinking…that maybe I could go and live with dad for a little while?"

No!

I stare at him. My sweet baby boy. My accomplishment when everything else went wrong, the only one I knew I could trust and would always have by my side. He wants to leave me? He wants to go…live with his dad?

Please tell me you're kidding. Please say it is a joke. A cruel one, but just that. Just you pulling a prank on me.

"I'm serious, Mom. I really want to. I miss him. You had me for all that time in New York, and now I feel like it's his turn. He's my dad."

Joey put him up to this. It must be him. Damn you, Joey.

I swallow hard and don't even notice the next set of waves passing us. I can tell Salter is concerned; he is worried how I will react to this. He is afraid I might be sad or angry. I am angry and sad. Very much indeed. But I can't show him that.

"Well, if that's what you want, then I guess…"

I stop. I know it is what I am supposed to say, but that is not how I feel. I want to tell him what he wants to hear, but at the same time I feel like I need to be honest as well.

"You know what? No, I am not okay with it. It is painful, Salter. You know how much I love you and love being with you."

"Well, it hasn't felt like it recently," he says. "Besides, he's my dad. I want to be with him more. You're not my only parent. And it's not like we won't see each other. I'll be right down the street. Besides, I'll see you every other Wednesday and stay the weekend like I do with Dad now."

"I don't know what to say to that," I say honestly. I am pressing back tears. I sincerely wish I could just say it is okay, that I could be mature and adult enough to accept this, but I really can't. I don't want to. "I don't want you to live with your dad. I want you to live here with me."

Salter's facial expression changes. His eyes are angry now.

"I just knew it! I knew you would be like this. Why can't you ever just let me do what I want and not what you want? It's my life."

Salter turns his board before I can answer and starts to paddle for a wave. I try to stop him.

"Don't you leave me out here like this, Salter," I yell at him, but he has already caught the wave and rides it to the beach.

On his way, he passes Marcia, who is just paddling out to me. She is panting as she stops next to me. I bite my lips and hold back the tears while she smiles.

"What have I missed?"

15

April 2016

THE MEN ARE STANDING shoulder to shoulder. Danny counts as many as eight men, all with the same hungry look in their eyes.

They call it a beauty pageant, as they present the girls one after the other. All the girls are wearing the same red dress. The only thing that separates them is the numbers pinned to their dresses.

Danny looks around in the arrival hall of Orlando Airport. No one who passes the windows seems to care or even wonder what is going on inside the coffee shop. They're busy with their own lives and where they're going.

These girls on the podium have just arrived as well. Taken here from countries like the Philippines, Cambodia or Thailand. Brought in on fake passports. The owner of the coffee house is the one presenting the girls, praising their best features to the men, speaking about them like they were models. But they're not. They're slaves. And they're about to be bought.

The man to Danny's right lifts his hand and points at girl number 3. He is wearing an expensive suit and jewelry. The coffee shop owner applauds him for it and takes the girl to him. She doesn't look at him; she doesn't put up a fight. She knows it is useless. She is broken and probably heavily drugged.

These people know how to break a girl. She was probably brought here thinking she was going to be an actress or a model or marry some rich American guy and be able to send back money to her family.

The man leaves with his purchase. Danny watches her as they walk past him. He guesses she can't be more than fourteen. Her family back home probably thinks she made it big, that she is the one who lucked out.

Danny turns to face the other girls. Another man makes his purchase and disappears with his girl. One buys two. Danny looks for eye contact. He tries to get it from one of the girls, to meet their eyes. But they're not there; they can't focus or look straight at him. Instead, they stare blankly into the air.

Except for one girl.

The girl with the number 2 on her dress. Her eyes are different. This girl's eyes are staring directly at Danny with a piercing gaze. There is something about her that makes Danny unable to stop looking at her. A fight. A feistiness.

This girl hasn't been broken, he thinks to himself. *There is still fight left in her. A great deal of fight.*

Danny is ready to make his bid. He wants this girl. He lifts his hand high in the air.

"I vote for number 2."

The girl is still staring at him with her feisty eyes as the owner grabs her arm and pulls her towards him. She walks reluctantly towards Danny and is handed over to him, just as the coffee shop explodes in an inferno of loud voices.

"POLICE! Everyone get down!"

With his heart in his throat, Danny turns and watches, as what looks like thirty heavily armed police officers storm the coffee shop, pointing their weapons at them. Terrified, the men try to escape, but are soon thrown to the ground and arrested. The owner of the coffee shop pulls his gun and Danny turns fast, then jumps near the girl he has just purchased, and at the second the owner fires his gun, Danny forces the girl to the ground to avoid the bullet.

Next thing Danny knows, three police officers are on top of him, dragging him away from the girl. He manages to look into her brown eyes one last time before he is knocked out.

16

April 2016

I CALL up Joey when I get back inside. Salter is in his room and he doesn't want to speak to me. I am so frustrated I am about to cry.

"Did you put him up to this?" I ask, almost spitting the words out.

"What?" Joey asks.

"You must have. I…I can't believe you would do this to me, Joey. After all we have been through."

"I have no idea what you're talking about," Joey says. "Is something wrong with Salter?"

"He wants to come live with you," I say. "He just told me so."

"He does?"

"Don't sound so surprised. I know you put him up to it. What is it? You want to hurt me so badly?"

"What are you talking about? I didn't put him up to anything. If he wants to come live with his dad, well then he is more than welcome."

"How can you say that? You have no idea how to take care of a kid. You don't even pack the boy a lunch!"

"I hardly think what kind of lunch you provide determines whether you're dad of the year or not. I miss him, Mary. I think it would be good for us."

I moan. I don't know how to argue against it. I just know that I can't let this happen. I simply can't. It breaks my heart.

"Yeah…well, I don't think it's such a great idea." I can hear how childish I sound, but can't stop it.

He scoffs. "Well, there's a big surprise there."

"You can't take him from me, Joey. You simply can't. I don't know what to do without him."

Joey chuckles. "You always exaggerate, Mary. It's not like I'm taking him away from you. He'll come live here for a little while, and then he'll want to come back to Mommy after a few weeks. Don't you worry. He is a momma's boy after all. I'll just have to enjoy whatever little I get of him. Get some time one-on-one. Some mantime. It'll be good for him. I promise. You'll see him every other week for five days, like we always do. It won't be that big of a difference, Mary."

"I worry that he'll never want to come home to me again," I say, grabbing a cookie with the other hand and eating it. I am not seeing Tom for a few days, while the basketball tournament lasts anyway, so there is no need to watch my weight. Especially not when I feel sorry for myself.

"Of course he'll come home. Are you kidding me? You're his mother," Joey says, comforting me.

It works a little. Or maybe it's the cookie.

"All right…I guess there really is no other way," I say. "But you've got to make sure you pack him his lunch. Every day. And don't let that little thing of yours leave out any more lingerie, or I'll take him back, you hear me? One more bra and I'm bringing him home."

"I hear you loud and clear," Joey says. I know he is grinning. I can tell by the tone of his voice.

"I'll bring him over tomorrow after school, then," I say. "At least I get to spend tonight with him."

"And next weekend," Joey says. "Plus, feel free to stop by anytime. Bring Snowflake. Bonnie and Clyde are miserable without him."

I get a warm feeling in my body that Joey is the one missing me, but I don't say anything. It is hard being away from each other after spending most of our lives together like we have. I miss him too. Not all the bad stuff, but the good parts we shared. I barely get to indulge in the memories before I am violently pulled out of them, when I hear her voice in the background.

"Who are you talking to, baby?"

She might as well have punched me in the stomach. I can't stand the fact that she is in that house and that soon she'll be there with my son as well. She'll be there with my family. My family.

Now I feel like crying again.

"I'll be right there," Joey answers her. "Listen," he says to me.

"You gotta go. Yeah. I kind of figured."

"Sorry. We have this thing, this yoga paddle board experience that we're going to on the river."

"On the river? With all those dead fish? Good luck."

"Yeah, well, it's this environmental thing too, to make awareness and take pictures of how bad it really is, then send it to the commissioners in Cocoa Beach, hoping it'll force them to react."

"But paddle boarding, Joey? Come on. You hate paddle boarding. You're a surfer, remember?" I say.

He chuckles. "I know. But Jackie loves paddle boarding, so, you know…"

Yeah, I know that you're changing yourself for her. Why? You never changed yourself for anyone else, let alone me.

"All right then. I guess I'll see you tomorrow. I'll bring Snowflake."

I can't see it, but I know Joey is smiling. "Sounds good, Mary. The animals are going to be very happy."

"I bet."

I hang up feeling a lot better. I grab another cookie and eat it while wondering how long Salter is going to last in that house with Jackie in it and how long Jackie is going to like having Salter there. Suddenly, I worry about him and if he'll feel rejected by her and then maybe by his dad because he will feel like his dad spends more time with her than his son.

He's going to come back here all heartbroken, isn't he? How did we get to this, Joey? We weren't supposed to be the ones that got divorced. We were the ones that were supposed to last, remember?

I empty the package of cookies while obsessing over the thought. When my phone rings again, I pick it up.

It's Chloe.

"Hey there. I was just about to call you about my next article; I know you want to…"

"That's not why I am calling," she interrupts me. Her voice is so serious it feels like a punch to my face.

"What's going on, Chloe? You're scaring me."

"It's Danny," she says. "I didn't know who else to turn to. You're the only one who can afford to bail him out."

I stop breathing. "Bail him out? But what…does that mean?"

"That he has been arrested, yes."

17

April 2016

IT'S BEEN six months since he last did a pick-up. Not that the demand hasn't been there for more, but he has to be careful. Boxer knows it is important to lay low for a long time after he has delivered the goods. He has to make sure the police aren't on to him. In the meantime, Boxer reads the paper every day and watches the news closely. It still amazes him how easy it is.

So far, no one seems to be missing the woman and the girl he picked up in October. What are their names again? Marie and Tara. Yes. Or is it Maria? Boxer doesn't remember anymore. It's all in the past. The girl and her mother have already moved on to their new owner, as have all the others Boxer has provided. He sees himself as a sort of a farmer selling off the cattle.

Never get attached to the cow. Don't give it a name.

"Latest news on the fish kill in Banana River Lagoon, when we get back," the lady from News13 says as they cut to commercial.

Boxer gets up and walks to the kitchen. It's time to start dinner. Boxer loves to cook. Today he's preparing lamb. Thyme-garlic lamb with strata, horseradish gremolata and roasted veggies.

He puts on music while he chops the veggies and sings along. This is the time of day he feels the best, when he gets to create something with his hands. It has taken him years to get this good, but luckily Boxer has a lot of time. Since he was fired two years ago from his job, time has been all he has.

A message ticks in on his iPad. It's from one of the secured chat rooms, so he knows he must answer right away. He wipes his hands on his apron and checks who it is from.

His client's name is Dr. Seuss. Needless to say, it is a cover. Boxer isn't his real name either.

<How's my package coming along?>

<Counting on this Saturday for pick-up.>

Boxer waits for Dr. Seuss's answer, but hears a sound coming from the front of his house. He turns the iPad to face the screen down, and then walks outside.

"Hello?"

On the wooden porch, he spots the body of a man. He is lying on his back, eyes closed. Boxer sighs and approaches the man.

"Get up, you drunk," he says.

The man blinks his eyes, and then looks at Boxer and smiles. "Hey, brother. Nice view you have here."

He nods in the direction of the neighbors across the street, where the woman is bringing in groceries from her mini-van. She glances cautiously towards Boxer's house. His brother waves.

"Hello, Mrs. Dawson," Boxer says.

She waves nervously. Boxer looks at his brother. "Come on. Couldn't you at least have used the back door?" He reaches out his hand and his brother grabs it. He pulls him up, even though he is heavy. Boxer is strong.

"This is a nice neighborhood," he grumbles, as he pushes his drunken brother inside. "People don't pass out drunk on porches in nice neighborhoods."

"I know, man. I'm sorry."

Boxer helps his brother get onto the couch, and then runs to the kitchen to take the lamb off the stove. It is burnt black. Boxer sighs. He was looking forward to it.

He returns to his brother, who is half asleep on the couch. He sits down next to him.

"So, how much this time?" he asks.

The brother doesn't even open his eyes to look at him. "Only three-hundred-thousand."

Boxer sighs and nods while his brother dozes off. "All right," he says, and looks at his brother while stroking his leg gently.

"All right."

18

April 2016

"WHAT ARE THE CHARGES?"

Chloe hasn't even gotten in the car before I ask. It's the morning after she called and gave me the news. I haven't slept all night. Chloe didn't want to tell me over the phone. Said she wanted to wait till she could tell me face to face. I can't stop wondering what is going on. I have a bad feeling about all this and really hope I am not right.

Tell me he was speeding; tell me he stole something from a store because he couldn't afford it; tell me has too many unpaid parking tickets. Tell me something I can accept. Not what I won't, not what I fear this is about.

Chloe sighs and closes the door to the car. Danny will be put in front of a judge and hopefully the judge will allow bail so we can get him home. That's what we're going to hear.

"If I am to pay for his bail, then I at least deserve to know what this is all about," I say, and get back out on A1A.

Chloe nods. She is not looking at me. It makes me feel very uncomfortable.

"Chloe!" I say, frustrated. "Please tell me. Why was he arrested?"

"All right. All right. Take it easy. It's just...really hard to say. I spent last night avoiding Junior's many questions."

"What did you tell him?"

"Danny wanted me to say that he had to go out of town for a few days and would be back soon."

"Wow. So you lied. Well, you're not lying to me, Chloe," I say, as we drive onto the bridge leading us to Merritt Island, the island separating our Barrier Island and Cocoa Beach with the mainland.

"Danny was arrested at the airport yesterday afternoon," Chloe says.

"At the airport?"

"He was…taken in because he was trying to…" Chloe looks at me, then out the window.

"Trying to what? Geez, you're killing me here, Chloe," I say, as we reach the last bridge over the Indian River leading to the mainland. The smell was worst going over Banana River, but I can tell the fish kill is in the Indian River as well. I see many dead fish and, with the warm weather, it smells bad.

"He was trying to buy a girl."

I almost crash the car into the guardrail. "He was what?"

"Trying to purchase a girl from Indonesia. She had just arrived in the country, thinking she was going to work in the hotel business, but it was a trafficking ring that was behind getting her here. They were trying to sell her in an auction. A slave auction. The police raided it. It was a set-up. There you have it."

"And Danny was there?"

"It appears so. Please keep your eyes on the road and please slow down a little, will you?"

"Why? What…how? How old was this girl he was trying to buy?" I ask, ignoring her comments about my driving. I am a great driver and right now I am very upset.

"Fourteen," she says.

"FOURTEEN?"

"Please watch out for the truck," Chloe says with a moan.

"Oh, my God," I groan. "I knew it. I saw him with those girls. I knew something was off, Chloe, didn't I tell you?"

"Mary!!"

I hit the brakes when the truck in front of us suddenly stops. I manage to stop our car before we hit it, but Chloe apparently doesn't think that I will and starts to scream. I stare at her while we wait for a green light.

"So, you're telling me Danny, our Danny, the firefighter, the captain of Cocoa Beach Fire Department, the sweetest guy I have known since we were just children, Danny, that Danny was arrested trying to buy a fourteen year-old Indonesian girl. And now…now, on top of it, you want me to bail him out?"

Chloe looks at me, and then she nods. "Yes. That is exactly what I am saying."

19

April 2016

"I SIMPLY DON'T UNDERSTAND how you talked me into this."

I stare at Chloe, sitting next to me outside the courtroom in Orlando. It is all over. The judge set the bail for one hundred-thousand dollars. I have paid it.

Chloe grabs my hand. "You're a good person. Danny had to get out of there. We couldn't just leave him. You did the right thing. Trust me."

"Well, it doesn't feel like the right thing. It feels like I have just bailed out a pedophile."

Chloe closes her eyes and breathes in deeply. "Danny is a good man, Mary. And you know it."

"What the heck was he buying a young girl for?"

Chloe bites her lip. "I think we should ask him about that when he gets out. There he is. I see him."

I look up and spot Danny walking towards us, flanked by two court officers. Chloe gets up from the bench and walks towards him. I stay seated. I don't know what else to do. All I really want is to kick Danny and yell at him for being such a pig, a disgusting pedophile. I can't get myself to hug him like Chloe is doing right now. I simply can't.

Danny lets go of Chloe and approaches me. I feel my heart pounding in my chest. I want to run away. I want to grab my purse and just start running.

"Mary!"

I can't even smile. I look up, but my eyes are avoiding his.

"Chloe told me you paid my bail. Thank you so much."

I clear my throat and press back my desire to scold him. It can wait till the car, I decide.

Oh, my God. I have to give him a ride back!

Finally, my eyes meet his and I sense my tension ease up. In them, I see the same Danny I have loved for so many years. My Danny. My friend.

My creepy friend who buys kids! What else does he do with them?

I don't want to think about it. I close my eyes and get up.

"Mary…I…"

"Not now," Chloe says, and grabs his hand. "Let's get you out of here. Let's get you as far away from this place as we can."

I stare at her, wondering what the heck she is thinking. Why isn't she about to explode with anger and frustration? She, of all people I know, should be so enraged with Danny she can't bear to look at him. Chloe! Chloe who has devoted her life to fighting child-porn online. Chloe who has created the organization Nochildporn.org. Chloe who…created software that automatically tracks…who gives the information to the authorities…"

Hey, wait a minute!

I clasp my mouth and gasp. Both of them turn to look at me as the last piece finally falls into place.

"You…you…you two have…"

Chloe approaches me, eyes wide open, hands stretched out in front of her. "Wait till the car," she says. "Wait till we get there. Then we'll talk. We'll tell you everything you need to know, but you'll have to wait. We can't do it here. Do you think you can wait that long, Mary? Do you?"

I hold my hand tight over my lips, then nod while storming into the parking lot.

20

April 2016

DANNY TAKES in a deep breath as he steps outside the courtroom again. This time as a free man. All he really wants to is to forget the past twenty-four hours and move on, but that is not going to be so easy.

He's got some explaining to do. Some serious explaining.

"Tell me everything," Mary says, as the three of them are in the car.

Chloe and Mary are in the front seats, Danny in the back. He feels like a child being questioned by his parents. Well, at least Chloe knows the entire story, so basically he just has to tell everything to Mary.

"How, how long, when and why?" Mary continues. "I mean, I can sort of guess the why, but…the rest?"

Chloe and Danny exchange looks before she starts to speak. "It started about a year ago. I ran into these ads on Craigslist where they sold young girls, you know…people pay for having sex with them. Usually, I work cases farther away and hand everything to the FBI, but these small local things…in the beginning, I alerted the sheriff's office, but they don't have the resources to crack down on all of them. They don't have a special department working sex trafficking. It's everywhere. I see it all over, Mary. These girls are being hurt and abused. I can't wait till they get the resources or till the FBI thinks it is big enough for them to deal with. It happens all over. Every day that passes by, someone is raped hundreds of times, or sold into slavery. It's nasty. I can't just sit here…and neither can Danny. We got to talking one day and I let out all my frustration about not being able to do anything…knowing about all this."

Chloe looks at Danny, who nods.

"She showed me some of it," he says. "Some of the addresses were local and I got to thinking…I mean, if I could save just one girl, then it would be worth it, wouldn't it? If just one girl could get out of this slavery. I would gladly go to jail for that."

"Okay, so let me get this straight," Mary says. "How does it work? Chloe, you…"

"I do the research and Danny goes to check it out. He goes to the bars, like the dancing places, you know gentlemen's clubs and he asks to pay a bar fine, that's the code word for wanting to purchase a girl. They take him out back and he tells them what he likes."

"Usually," Danny takes over, "I go for the youngest girl there. Or the one with the most fight left in her eyes. These people break the girls before they're sold, but some of them remain fighters and you can tell by the look in their eyes. They are the ones who won't last long. They'll get killed within a few months, often beaten to death because they refuse to submit."

"And what do you do next?" Mary asks.

It is painful for Danny to talk about this and he closes his eyes as he continues. "I buy them. If I can, I buy them for the night and tell them I want to take the girl with me. It's expensive, but worth it. I take her to a local shelter in Titusville, where she'll get the help she needs."

"How do you even afford it?" Mary asks.

"I got a huge insurance settlement when Jean died. Her life insurance. I don't need that money. I don't want it, to be frank. I use it to get the girls instead."

Mary stares at Danny. It makes him uncomfortable.

"Now you might understand why I was defending him, right?" Chloe asks, looking at Mary.

She holds a hand to her chest. Danny sees tears in her eyes. He doesn't want her to get emotional. He doesn't feel like he deserves her tears.

"I can't believe I thought…" she says, her voice breaking. "Oh, my God, I feel like the worst person on the planet right now."

"It's all right," Chloe says. "How could you have known? We kept it a secret for a very long time and would have preferred it stayed that way."

Mary reaches back and puts her hand on Danny's knee while driving. She looks at him in the rearview mirror.

"I can't tell you how sorry I am," she says. "Can you forgive me? I should have given you the benefit of the doubt at least. I should have known you were a hero."

Danny sighs and puts his hand on top of hers. He doesn't feel like a hero. "The worst part is all the girls I can't save," he says. "I've seen them. I was there. I've looked into their eyes and chosen someone else to save. That's what's keeping me up at night. That's what's torturing me every day, every hour of my life."

April 2016

You're the worst friend ever!

The feeling of guilt is killing me as I drive the three of us back towards the beach. I can't believe I was so quick to conclude this about Danny. Danny, who has always been there for me, well for everyone really. Danny who likes to take care of everyone and every problem. Of course he was just trying to save these girls.

Of course.

"I just can't believe they would hold an auction like that in the middle of the airport, where thousands of people pass by every day," I say.

"It's not the first I've been at," Danny says.

"It happens often," Chloe says. "A lot more than you think. The airports are one of the worst places, because they fly the girls in from all over the world, tell them they're going to be models or get work so they can send money home to their families, and then when they arrive some creepy guy brings them somewhere and they're sold. Lord only knows where they go from there."

"Most of them live many years in slavery," Danny says. "They're often drugged senseless and are transported from place to place, where they are used as prostitutes, or even sold again and again. I talked to a girl who had been locked inside a small apartment for three years where she was raped by different men between twenty and fifty times a day. She kept a diary with recordings of it."

"Wow, that's really brutal," I say.

"And, it's also happening here. It's not just girls being brought in from other countries. Many of them are just ordinary American girls," he continues. "One that I saved was picked up in her own driveway while her mother was still inside the house. The girl's best friend had texted her that she would stop by and say hello, and then when she went outside to talk to her, the girl arrived with two men in a car. They grabbed the girl and dragged her inside the car."

"It happens all over, Mary," Chloe says. "Everywhere. Most people just don't see it. But I do. I face it every day."

I nod pensively while thinking that I suddenly have the deepest respect for Chloe and Danny. I just wish they didn't have to put themselves in danger the way they do. I applaud what they do, I really do, but I fear for them. Especially for Danny. He has a son who needs his father.

"But, Danny kind of got himself in some trouble last time," Chloe says. "Not at the airport, but before then."

"How so?"

"Do we have to tell her?" Danny asks.

"I think we do," Chloe says. "You're going to need a good lawyer when they find out. Mary knows one."

Danny scoffs. "Come on, Chloe, we've been over this before. They're not going to find out. I got rid of the gun. I told you."

"Still. It's registered in your name...ballistics will..."

"Hey! Hey! What's going on here?" I ask. I hate how they talk like I am not even there.

Chloe stops. She looks at me. "Danny killed someone."

"Chloe!" Danny says. "Now she is an accomplice as well."

"What? Who did you kill, Danny?"

Danny sighs. "The other day, I rescued a girl from an apartment on the mainland. I answered an ad on Craigslist. They had her in one of those gated condominiums that are usually for the snowbirds. A really nice one. I went there pretending I wanted to pay to be with her, then when I was alone with her, I told her my plan. To make a long story short, I shot the couple guarding her."

"Oh, no, Danny!" I say.

"I was just trying to stop them; I was supposed to just hurt them. Shoot them in the shoulders or legs. That's how I usually do these things. Then I call the cops anonymously and tell them there has been a shooting and they arrive and arrest them. Meanwhile, the girl and I are long gone. But the woman died from her wounds. And now Chloe fears that the police will match the bullet with my gun."

"I understand her concern," I say. "But explain this to me. Why are the people arrested if the girl isn't there?" I ask.

"Oh, we leave some child-porn on their computers and phones as well," Chloe says. "It's really the easiest task in the world."

"All right," I say. "But why do you take the girl? Why not hand her over to the police?"

Danny sighs again. "Most of these girls trust the police less than anyone. Many of them have had encounters with the police that have led to them being sent back on the streets or even sometimes back to their traffickers. I spoke to one girl who managed to escape after nine months in captivity. When she finally found a police station, they told her she was perfectly safe on the streets. They couldn't help her. They don't trust them, and frankly, I don't always either."

"Those are big words coming from you," I say and take a left turn onto A1A. Suddenly, it feels better than ever to enter my quiet little town. Still, I can't stop thinking about what Chloe just told me.

It's everywhere. Even here in this sleepy little town?

22

April 2016

I MAKE us all a strong cup of coffee and make them Irish by adding a little whiskey to them. We sit in my dad's new living room and look out at the waves. My dad is awake, but wants to stay in his room and watch TV, he tells me. I don't tell him what has happened. I have promised it will stay among the three of us. I don't know what Danny will tell his son, but that is none of my business.

The ocean is raging, the strong winds blowing on-shore making it a very bad day to surf.

"Thanks," Chloe says, as I hand her the cup. Danny doesn't speak. He hardly looks at me. I can tell he is troubled.

"I can't believe you two," I say and sip my coffee. "I mean, I knew Chloe was crazy, but you, Danny? Why? Why did you agree to do this?"

Danny sips his coffee. He doesn't answer, but stares out of the big windows. I sense there is more to the story than what he has already revealed. I get the feeling he wants to keep this part to himself. I wonder if Chloe knows. I look at her to see if I can read it on her face, but I never can. She has such a poker face.

"There is something, isn't there?" I ask. "There is something else you two are not telling me."

"You know she's not going to leave it alone," Chloe says, addressed to Danny. "Once she gets an idea into her head, there is no letting go."

Danny doesn't look at her or me. He still stares at the ocean. "That's our Mary," he says.

I chuckle uncomfortably.

"That's our Mary," Chloe repeats and sips her coffee.

Danny draws in a deep sigh. I look from one to the other. It's killing me.

Why is no one saying anything? What aren't they telling me?

I do my best to behave. I sit still on the couch and sip my coffee, while waiting for them to start talking. It lasts about half a minute.

"All right," I say, and put down my cup a little too hard on the coffee table. "Don't tell me, then. See if I care."

Chloe chuckles. "I told you she wouldn't let it go."

Danny sighs again. He turns and looks at me. "All right," he says. "Well. I guess you can say I have been trying to make up for something, making amends of sorts."

"Making up for what?" I ask.

"For me not being there."

"Being there? Where?"

He draws in a deep breath while his eyes catch those of Chloe.

"Being there for Junior?" I say, looking at them. "I don't understand…you have always been there for Junior. You're like dad of the decade for that boy…wait a minute…you have another child?"

Danny nods. "I have a daughter. I never told anyone except for Chloe."

"I've only known for about a year."

I stare at him. "But…but who…how?"

"I cheated on Jean ten years ago. With a woman I met at work. She worked at the front desk for a little while." He shakes his head. "Things were awful with me and Jean. Always have been. You know that. It doesn't matter. It was wrong and I ended it. The girl was fired because of the affair. I had her removed, which I am not proud of, I admit that. Then a year later she showed up at the station carrying a baby telling me the girl was mine. I have paid for her upbringing, sent them a check every month, but I was never there for the girl. I don't know her at all. It tortures me every day."

"So you believe saving these other girls will somehow bring you redemption?" I say.

"I know…ridiculous, right? But somehow it provides peace of mind for me. At least I can do this right, you know? Everything else I have messed up, but not this."

"Well, not until now," I say. "Now you risk losing everything."

23

April 1975

BAO HONKS the horn on the moped, trying desperately to get the crowds of people blocking the road to move. Danh watches the people as they pass them, while holding onto his sister, who is still in his arms. The road is bumpy and she is crying helplessly, wanting to go back to her mother.

Danh wants to go back too, but can't forget his mother's words or the look in her eyes when she told them to get out of the town.

Now they have been driving for at least an hour and the crowds of people are only getting bigger and bigger. On their way, he sees people breaking into buildings, stealing everything that others left behind. He sees women carrying everything from children to chairs, and even some people with washing machines on the back of their motorcycles. Bao is trying to follow their two other brothers on their bikes, but soon they lose track of them. Only now and then Danh manages to spot one of their brother's bags of clothes that he has strapped to the back of his bike, but soon that disappears as well.

When it is about to get dark, they arrive at a small fishing village and finally make a stop. Bao pulls out a little money that their mother handed them as they left and buys a bag of rice and something to drink. They eat and drink without uttering a word. Long is still crying, but not as much as in the beginning. Danh tries to encourage her by making fun of the peoples' faces. The harbor is packed with people trying to get on boats and their faces are all serious and angry.

"Look at that man over there," Danh says with a chuckle. "He looks like he had lemons for breakfast, doesn't he?"

Long chuckles and wipes her nose with her hand. There is no sign of their five other brothers who left with them, but someone in the crowd has a radio. Danh listens in as the broadcaster tells them news.

"What are they saying?" Long asks.

Danh hushes her while Bao walks closer. Danh listens carefully while holding his sister's hand. It's hard to hear everything over her sobbing, but he hears enough to understand that Saigon has fallen into the hands of the Vietcong. The communists have taken over the capital.

"What are they saying, Danh?"

Bao comes closer. "Saigon has fallen," he says with a cold voice, as if he doesn't know he is talking to a child. He looks at Danh and speaks with a lower voice. "We have to get out of here. Fast. They'll come here too. Look, they're already changing the flags on those buildings over there."

"What do you mean it has fallen?" Long asks, directed at Danh. "What about mother?"

Danh presses the tears back and kneels in front of her. "Mother is fine. Don't you worry about her, your majesty," he says.

"But...but, how do you know?"

Danh smiles and touches her cheek gently. "Because they just said so. On the radio. They told us everyone in Saigon was fine. That the communists are giving them all ice cream."

Long's face lights up. "Then we should go back!"

Danh chuckles. "We will. Soon. But not yet."

"When will we go back then?" she asks, disappointed.

"Soon, Long."

"Why not now? I miss my mom. And I want to have ice cream too," she says determinedly. Long starts to pull Danh's shirt.

"We all do," Danh says, "but the thing is, Mommy told us to meet her somewhere, so I think we'd better obey, don't you?"

"She did?"

Danh sniffles. Panic is starting to erupt around them as people realize there aren't many boats left in the small harbor.

Bao grabs Danh's arm. "We have to hurry," he says.

Danh looks into Long's eyes. If only he could make them smile again. "She did. She wanted us to go on a real adventure. Are you up for a real adventure?"

"I love adventures. Will there be ice cream?" she asks.

"Once we get there, I bet there will be," he says.

"And Mommy will be there too?"

Danh bites his lip. "Who else would bring all the ice cream, huh?"

24

April 2016

"I KNOW you don't like the feel of the fabric. I told you I'd have them pick the couches up again, and I have already ordered the new ones."

Nicky sighs and wipes her forehead. It is hot sitting by the community pool wearing her work clothes. Her Melbourne client is yapping on the other end about her couches, while Paige is in the water with her swim trainer, Coach Burnett. He shows her something, a new technique to help her backstroke, and she repeats it. He holds her by supporting her back to have her body float more on the surface.

"Yes, Paige. That's it," he yells, his hand still resting underneath her back. "Now, try it again."

"Yes, tomorrow. I'll make sure it's all taken care of," Nicky repeats. She sighs while the woman continues on the phone.

Why can't she let it go already?

Now she is asking her why it can't be fixed right now. Why Nicky can't just come down and take care of it.

"I don't want these couches in my house."

"Because right now I am at my daughter's swimming lessons. I have just spoken to the company and there is nothing they can do until tomorrow. They will get the right couches with the right fabric," she says. "But it will take a few days to have them shipped from up north."

Paige looks up at her from the water and waves. Nicky smiles and waves back. She wonders for a second if it is all worth it. Her dream of having her own company doesn't really seem to be as glamorous as it used to be. Dealing with these rich ladies is harder than she had expected. It is taking all of her time. And now it's going to cost her as well. She'll have to pay for the transport and shipping of those couches herself that she wrongfully ordered, the company told her. Not that she was the one who made the mistake. The lady asked for these couches, but now she's saying she didn't, that the fabric is wrong, even though they went over what type of fabric she wanted a million times. The lady says she is not going to pay for the shipping, since she wasn't the one who made the mistake, so now Nicky has to.

At least Paige is happy. Isn't she?

Nicky can't help but wonder if everything wasn't better before they got the inheritance, when they had nothing and she worked as a secretary with a low but steady income. Not to mention steady work hours. It seems like she works every waking hour of the day now. She likes it, she likes the part where she gets to be creative and come up with great ways of decorating people's beautiful houses, houses she could only dream of ever living in. That part she really enjoys, that's her dream. It's the people that bother her. The women. Spoiled women who never had to struggle for anything, who never had a dream, who don't understand that Nicky also wants to be with her kid as much as possible, even though she is building her business.

Maybe she simply started too early. Maybe if she had waited till Paige was older and maybe moved away. Of course, that would have been smarter. It's easy to be wise in hindsight, isn't it? It's not like she can stop now. She put down the money, she started it all up, and now she is actually successful, so much that she might even soon be able to move out of the crappy neighborhood she lives in. It is all clearing up for her. She just needs to be patient.

Paige has started to complain about her mother not being home as much as she used to, but that's the way things are right now. She will just have to learn to live with it. And Nicky will have to learn to live with the constant nagging feeling of guilt. *It will clear up, it'll get better.* One day, Paige will understand, and then she'll be proud of her mother, who made it on her own, who beat the odds.

You're setting a good example for your daughter. You're showing her that anything is possible, that women can do things too. It might not feel like it, but you're being a good mother.

"Did you see me, Mommy?" Paige yells, as she runs towards Nicky. "I beat my latest record in the hundred meter backstroke!"

"Careful, sweetie. Don't run on the wet floors," Nicky says, and gets up from the chair. She grabs Paige's towel from the bag and hands it to her. Nicky is sweating heavily in her skirt and shirt.

"Did you see it, Mom? Did you?"

Nicky smiles awkwardly. "Sure. I was right here."

Paige's smile freezes. "You didn't, did you? You were on the phone again, weren't you?"

"Listen, Paige," Nicky says. "I am so sorry. But I had an important client. I had to take care of it."

Paige gives her the look, that awful look of disappointment and…yup…the feeling is back. The nagging feeling of guilt.

"Okay."

Coach Burnett comes up and gives Paige a hug. "That was awesome today, kiddo," he says. "I am so proud of you."

Paige's smile lights up again. She looks at him in a way she never looks at Nicky anymore.

"I couldn't believe how fast I went. I just kept going and going."

"It was really great, Paige," he says, and high-fives her with a laugh. "You keep that up and you're going to beat my old record soon."

She grabs him around the waist and holds him tight again. "Thank you. Thank you. You're the best coach in the world. I love you, Coach Burnett."

"Well, I love you too, Paige," he says and puts his hands on her shoulders. "Next time we'll go for a new record in front crawl all right?"

"You betcha'."

She smiles from ear to ear as Nicky's phone rings again. "I am sorry," she says and steps aside. "I have to take this call."

"No worries," Coach Burnett says, while Paige looks like she finds it to be a bigger problem.

"It'll only take a sec, honey," Nicky says to her.

Nicky walks away for a few seconds while speaking to the woman once again. Meanwhile, she observes Paige and Coach Burnett as they chat and laugh together. Nicky is so pleased that Paige gets along so well with her coach. They have known each other since she was in Kindergarten and started swimming. He practically watched her grow up, as she joined the local swim team when she was only five years old. Since Paige doesn't have a father, her swim coach is one of the few male role models she has in her life, and it makes Nicky feel good that Coach Burnett is one of them. Nicky has made many bad choices in her life, but raising her child in the safe and protected environment of Cocoa Beach is not one of them.

25

April 2016

WHEN CHLOE and Danny finally leave, I cook for me and my dad. My famous salmon dish. I put it in the oven, and then walk Snowflake on the beach, even though it is illegal.

I am thinking about the things Chloe and Danny revealed to me earlier in the day. It's a lot to take in at once, and even knowing the two of them as well as I do, I have to say, I am surprised. I knew Chloe did a lot, but I thought it was just from behind the computer. Danny, I understand better. He has always been a fixer, one who wanted to find a solution to problems and do something, instead of just talking about it. But, still. Risking his career, his beloved job as captain of the fire station like this? I would never have thought he would go that far.

And then he tells me he has a daughter? A daughter he has never met, never been a part of her life. That part surprises me most of all, I think. Danny has always been such a devoted and loving father to Junior, and it was all for him that he stayed with that wife of his.

Snowflake and I stay on the beach till the sun has set over the mainland and then we walk back up to the house. I think about Salter and wonder if he has done his homework. It is so strange to not have him to take care of at the house anymore. Now it's just my dad and me.

I grab the dish out of the oven and put plates on the table, then go and get my dad. I roll him into the kitchen and hand him the fork. He smiles when he sees what is on his plate. Dinner is his favorite part of the day. He has changed a lot since he was hurt in the fire. It used to be all about his work and career or about him and his new wife Laura. Now it's all about the little things in life. Eating, being with family, or the joy of simply being able to hold a fork between his fingers.

"You made my favorite," he says.

"Food is your favorite," I say, and help him get some fish on the fork. He can now lift it and reach his mouth on his own. I feel like I am seeing improvement every day now. It's truly amazing. I am very grateful to Jack, his physical therapist, who seems to do wonders with him.

The fork hits his mouth, and a little salmon falls off and lands on his chest, but most of it ends up in his mouth, and he chews with his eyes closed. "Ah. This is heavenly, Mary."

I chuckle lightly and eat some myself. I glance at Salter's empty chair while chewing. I wonder what he is eating, if he took a shower, and if he has enough clean underwear.

I feel something on my arm and realize my dad is poking his fork at me.

"He's fine," he says. "He'll be back before you know it."

"I'm not so sure," I say, and stuff my mouth with salmon and potatoes, trying hard to make the feeling go away. "I'm scared he'll like it more at his dad's than here. I don't want to be alone, Dad."

"Bah. You won't be alone," he says.

I reach out and touch his hand. "I know. I have you and Snowflake, but he's my son, Dad. I love him. I want to be with him every day. I want to talk to him when he comes home from school; I want to know every little thing that is going on with him. I don't want to just see him every other week from Wednesday till Sunday. I want to be a part of his life. A big part. He's going to grow up without me. I'll be nothing but a vague memory. I'm losing him, Dad."

"No! You listen to me, Mary. You won't lose him. Never. It's just a phase. A boy needs his mother too. But he needs both of you. And right now you have to accept that he needs his dad. A boy needs his father."

I sniffle and hold my dad's hand. I know he is right, but I don't feel like admitting it. Instead, I wipe my eyes and look at my father. I can't believe how many years I lost out on of having him in my life. It took almost losing him to understand how important he was to me.

"Just like a girl needs her dad as well," I say.

"Yes. Just like a girl needs her father."

26

April 2016

MY FATHER'S words linger with me all night as I toss and turn, wondering if Salter got to bed on time, if he will get up in the morning and not miss the bus, if he will be all right without his mother. I gave him a call after dinner to say goodnight, but he didn't have time to talk for very long. He, Joey, and Jackie were watching a movie. *Inside Out.* My favorite movie to watch with Salter. Apparently, Jackie had never seen it.

The next morning, I try to sleep in, but can't. I get up, walk Snowflake, and then make breakfast for my dad and me. I can't stop thinking about what my dad said, and I call Chloe to help me with a plan that has started to shape in my mind. Early in the afternoon, I drive to Danny's house and ring the doorbell.

"Mary?"

"A girl needs her dad too," I say.

"What?"

"A girl needs her dad just as much as a boy does."

"Eh…okay…are you all right, Mary?"

"Not really. I miss Salter like crazy since he moved to his dad's place, and that got me to thinking. It's never too late, Danny."

He sighs. I can tell he is confused. "I don't know what you're talking about, Mary. And, frankly, I'm not feeling so good. I'm afraid I might get suspended from the station when they find out about my arrest."

I throw out my arms. "What better time to make amends?"

"What?"

I grab his hand in mine. He looks at me, perplexed.

"Come with me."

He follows me to the car. "Where are we going?"

"You tell me," I say, and jump in the car.

He gets in the passenger seat. "What do you mean?"

I start the engine. "You're the one who knows the address, even though you've never been there."

"What?"

"Yes, Danny. You told me you sent her a check every month. You must know the address."

Now he is getting it. "No, Mary. I can't go."

"Why not? School is out in half an hour and then she'll be home. We can go there, ring the doorbell, and see her."

Danny sighs. "I can't do that!"

"Why not? It's killing you that you haven't been there for her; now I'm telling you that you can be there. At least show her you care."

"Don't you understand? I can't just show up out of the blue. I haven't been there before. I can't just come barging into their lives like that. It's not fair to her mother. Besides, I don't think they even want me in their lives. It's too late, Mary. Now, let it go, will you, please?"

"How can you say that? It's never too late. This girl needs a father in her life just as much as anyone else. And you can give her that. It's never too late. It might be hard; it might be really hard for the both of you, but it is never too late. Ever. The girl deserves a father."

I fall back in my seat with a sigh. Exhausted from speaking. I feel so frustrated and I want to shake Danny.

"All right," he says.

My eyes grow big. "Really?"

He nods. "I mean, what's the worst that can happen? She can tell me she never wants to see me, but at least I will have tried, right?"

"That's more like it. That's the Danny I know."

Danny scoffs, then laughs.

"What?" I ask.

"It's sweet."

"What is?"

"You. How you always think you can save the world."

"Guess I'm not very good at it, huh?"

He puts a hand on my shoulder. "I think you're doing an excellent job. But it's an impossible mission, you do realize that, right? To save everyone?"

I look at him and smile. I turn the wheel. "That may be, but that never stopped me before."

27

April 2016

<So what did you do today?>

Boxer looks over at his brother sleeping on the couch. He was drunk again when Boxer came home last night, even though he had promised to stay off the booze. Boxer sighs. He doesn't know what to do about him, how to help him. For years, it has been like this... nothing changes despite all the promises.

But he can't turn his back on him. He simply can't. It's not an option. His brother can't help himself. He's sick.

His brother stretches and opens his eyes. He looks at Boxer.

"Hey there," he says.

At the same time, the girl answers in the chat in Minecraft. Boxer pretends that he is a thirteen year-old boy in the game. Finding them is the easy part. It's getting them to talk to you that is hard. Actually, it's not that difficult. It's all about knowing what young girls like, how they talk, what they want. That and then listening to them, to what they have to say. Unlike their parents, Boxer takes the time to really listen. He keeps a list of their usernames and if they have given him their real names and the different aliases they use on the different social media. Lately, they're all on this new app called Musical.ly, where they make videos of themselves. Boxer loves this new thing, since he can really get a good look at the girls when they pretend to be singers and dancers in the videos, acting like grown women. If he thinks a girl might be interesting, he sends the videos to his client.

<I had school,> she answers.

<Me too. Most boring day ever,> he writes back.

<Same here.>

<So what are you doing now?>

"Hey, brother, can I grab one of these?"

Boxer looks up from the screen and spots his brother standing with a bottle of whiskey in his hand. It is fifty years old. Boxer is a collector of fine spirits and has them displayed in the living room. The bottle in his brother's hand cost him a thousand dollars.

"I'm heading over to a friend's house for dinner and I don't want to come empty-handed," the brother says.

Boxer feels the tension in his entire body as he stares at his brother and the bottle in his hand. He knows his brother isn't going to any dinner at a friend's house. He is more likely going to one of those illegal casinos in the back of some club, where he'll lose more money because he is so drunk from drinking the whiskey on his way there. Boxer knows this will happen; he knows his brother will come to him again and again asking for more money, and Boxer will give it to him. He will welcome him inside and sober him up before it starts all over again.

He knows this will happen because it has been going on for years.

You should just say no. Tell him he can't take that bottle…that he needs to clean himself up, to get a job and stay off the booze and gambling. By giving in, you're enabling him. It's not what is best for him.

"So, can I?"

Boxer sighs as his gaze meets his brother's and he is reminded of how they looked at him back then. Back when everything changed.

"Sure. Have fun."

His brother smiles. "Thanks bro. Cheers."

Boxer doesn't say anything. He feels like screaming, but is holding it back. His eyes return to the screen.

<Homework,> the girl has answered. <But I am looking forward to this weekend.>

<Because of the basketball tournament?>

<Yes. We're playing a game Saturday. I have to go to this stupid rally first with my mom, to protest against the fish-kill, but after that I am going to play with my team>

<Maybe I'll come and watch,> he writes.

<Really? But I thought you were all the way in Daytona?>

<Maybe I'll come down to see you.>

<That would be awesome. I would really like to see you IRL.>

<Me too.>

28

April 2016

"I'VE CHANGED MY MIND."

Danny turns and looks at me. I ignore him. We're sitting in the car and I have just parked it in front of a very small house on Barlow Avenue. We're still in Cocoa Beach, but on the border to Cape Canaveral. The kids around here go to Capeview Elementary and I don't know many here. I do know it is an area my parents always told me to stay away from, where lots of surf bums and drug addicts live because it is cheap. It seems that nothing much has changed.

The houses are more like small beach-shacks. This one is one of the nicer ones, though. With a small porch out front and a rocking chair. A child's bike is leaning against the porch. Everything looks neat compared to the neighboring houses.

I open my door and get out. I walk to Danny's side and open his. "Come on."

He gets out with a deep sigh. "All right. Let's do this."

I am right behind Danny when he rings the doorbell. My heart is throbbing in my chest, I am hoping and praying that this will go well. If Danny doesn't somehow connect with his daughter now, then he might regret it for the rest of his life. But I also know he is right to be nervous, because there is no telling how she will react to seeing him, or how her mother will react to him showing up like this.

Right now, I just hope they're home.

There's a sound behind the door and it opens. A woman appears behind the screen door.

"Yes?"

"Maria?" Danny asks. He sounds surprised.

"Who wants to know?" the woman asks.

"It's me," Danny says. His voice is shaking. It sounds strange as he speaks his name. "Danny."

"What do you want, Danny?"

He shakes his head. "You're not Maria," he says.

She coughs. "No, I'm her mother, what's it to you?"

"I'm sorry," Danny says. "You just look so much alike."

"Well I was young when I had her; what do you want?"

"Is Maria around?" he asks.

"Nope. She moved about six months ago."

"Moved? But…" Danny looks at me for answers, then back at the woman behind the screen door.

"Listen. I don't have all day," the woman says.

"Wait. This is important," he says. "You have to listen to me. I have to talk to her. I am…I am Tara's dad."

The expression on the woman's face changes drastically. "Well then, we certainly have nothing to talk about."

She is about to close the door, but Danny is fast. He opens the screen door and puts a foot in before she can close it.

"I've got to know where they moved to," he says.

"I've got a gun in here," she says angrily.

"I'm not going to hurt you. I just need you to give me her new address," Danny says.

"I don't have it," the woman says.

"What do you mean you don't have it?" Danny is getting angry now. He pushes the door open and walks inside. The woman backs up into her living room. I follow, and soon we're all in her house.

"You tell me where she and my daughter are right now," Danny says, pointing a finger at her.

"I told you. I don't know," the woman whimpers. "I came here because…well, her father died last Christmas. I hadn't seen her in ten years, not since…the pregnancy. Her father…he was so mad that he never wanted to see her or let me see her again. So when he died, I decided I would go see her, see my granddaughter. I had the address from all the letters she sent me, the ones with pictures of Tara in them, but all I found was this empty house. None of the neighbors knew where she was. I decided to wait for her here, but she never came back."

"Wait. You have been living here since December and she hasn't come back in all that time?" I ask.

The woman nods. "I have no idea where she can be. The neighbor gave me her cell number, but it doesn't seem to work. I don't know where she is. That is the honest truth."

"Did you file a missing persons report?" I ask.

She shakes her head.

"Why not?" asks Danny.

The woman shrugs. "For all I know, she might have run off with some man. Maria is flaky that way."

"Yet you stayed in the house. Why?" I ask.

"In case she comes back," she says.

"I don't believe you," Danny says. "Wait. I have been paying child support all this time. Six months, you say? She's been gone for six months? Yet my checks have been cashed. You cashed them, didn't you? You're living here on my money, on the money that was meant to support my child?"

"I couldn't just leave it there in the mailbox, now could I?"

"And because you look like your daughter, you could cash the checks, am I right? Danny asks. "I bet you even used some of her ID."

The mother looks away.

"Didn't you?" Danny asks angrily.

The mother jumps. She's scared of Danny. "I used her passport. I found it in the drawer in her bedroom."

"Wait a minute. Something is wrong here," I say. "Why would she leave without her passport? Didn't you ever stop to wonder about that?"

The woman shrugs. The place smells heavily of smoke and old wet cigarettes. Danny is mad now. He walks to the woman and grabs her by the collar. He is shaking her back and forth.

"Stop, Danny," I yell.

"How the hell can anyone be this stupid!" he yells to her face. "How can anyone act this selfish!"

I feel like things are getting a little out of control now. I don't know how far Danny will go. He did, after all, just kill someone recently. Trying to save someone else, a young girl, yes, but still. I am scared that he has snapped, that he might hurt this woman and I can't do anything about it.

"Danny!" I say.

He finally looks at me.

"Put her down."

Realizing what he is up to, he finally lets go of her. She sinks into the couch.

"I am sorry about that," I say. I look into her eyes. She is visibly scared of Danny, which could work to our advantage. "Now, do you mind if we take a look around the house?"

The woman opens her mouth as if to speak, but then realizes that we could report her to the police for fraud, and stops herself.

"Go ahead," she says.

29

April 1975

THEY PAY their last money to a man who claims he can get them onboard one of the fishing boats. Hundreds of others, maybe even thousands have the same idea, so they have to act fast.

Bao is running across the harbor towards the ships, Danh and Long try to keep up with him. Bao has the note that shows they have paid. If they lose sight of him, they might not make it on the boat.

Danh keeps an eye on Bao's red shirt in the crowd, while carrying Long on his shoulders and holding the one pack of rice they have left. He fastens his eyes on the red shirt, but soon loses it, before it reappears. This happens a few times before the red shirt and Bao are suddenly completely gone.

"Where did he go?" Danh asks and slows down. There are so many people, so many shirts, and soon he spots a red one and starts to follow it, but seconds later he realizes it doesn't belong to Bao.

Danh is close to panicking now. He tries his best to not let his sister see his panic and keeps going towards the boats, in the direction he thinks and expects Bao might have gone. Meanwhile, his eyes are searching frantically for Bao's red shirt in the crowd.

"I can't wait to see Mommy," Long exclaims from his shoulders. "I bet she missed us."

"I can't wait either," Danh says to comfort her.

He refuses to think about what it will be like once they get to wherever the boats will take them. Or how he will explain to Long why their mother isn't there. He doesn't want to think about when they will see her again, if they ever will.

There is no time to think about those things. Right now, it's all about getting out of there, fast. The explosions and sounds of gunfire are coming closer by the minute, and it won't be long before the entire area is surrounded and there will be no way out for them anymore.

But where are we going? Will there be anything for us there?

Danh has no idea. All he knows is, he promised his mother he would take Long away and he promised his brother he would follow him to the boats. Where the rest of their brothers are, there is no time to worry about either.

"Bao!" he hears Long exclaim. He looks up and sees that she is pointing. "Bao!" she repeats.

"Where?" Danh stands on his tippy toes to better see, and there, in the middle of a big crowd, fighting to get onboard an old fishing boat, he spots him; he sees the red shirt and soon recognizes his face.

"Bao!" he yells, but the sound of his voice is drowned by another explosion, this time closer to them.

He sets off to run towards Bao, when he suddenly feels hands on his body and he and Long are both lifted into the air.

"Long!" he yells, and tries desperately to see where she has been taken, but seconds later, he loses her as well, as he is shoved towards the bottom of a small boat, underneath a grating used to hold luggage and cargo. He lands on top of another body and there are arms and legs everywhere, kicking and hitting him before he can finally fight his way up and breathe again. He is fighting his growing panic and can't stop looking for his family members when another child is shoved next to him. It is dark in the boat, but her laughter gives her away.

"Danh!" she says happily.

"Your majesty!" He grabs her and holds her tight in his arms. He takes in a deep breath as he feels the boat rock. His heart starts to race as he calls out Bao's name, but receives no answer. With all the noise from the many people shoved together at the bottom of the boat, Danh realizes it is no use to yell. He'll have to wait till they arrive at their destination to start looking for his brother.

Wherever that might be.

30

April 2016

THE WAVES ARE CRASHING LOUDLY on the beach when we return. I have called Chloe and asked her to come over. I make coffee for all of us and we sit on the porch while telling Chloe what has happened.

"So, you're telling me this mother never reported her daughter and grandchild missing, even though she's been gone for six months?" she asks.

I roll my dad out to sit with us and serve him some coffee and cookies. He enjoys sitting on the porch so much it makes me feel like I should be out here more, enjoy it more. All I can think about right now is Salter and whether he had a good day at school or not. I look at my phone, but he hasn't called. I guess he isn't missing me as much as I am him.

"I know. I am so angry right now," Danny says.

"And you're telling me she left everything behind?"

"Well, her car is gone, we didn't find her phone or credit cards or a wallet, but other than that, it seemed like everything was there. Her passport, lots of clothes, and even her daughter's iPad."

"She would definitely take that if she was planning on going somewhere with her kid in the back seat, right?" Chloe asks.

"Sure thing," I say. "The mother said she believes they left town either on the night of October 22nd or during the day on Friday, October 23rd. The 22nd at night was the last time one of the neighbors saw her. She was supposed to take care of Tara the next day. Maria came to her house on the 22nd and asked her if she could look after Tara the next day, on the 23rd, when Maria had to go to work. Apparently, it was a day off from school, a teacher's workday, so she had nowhere for Tara to go and the neighbor was out of work, and she had watched her before. She told the neighbor that she was going to Target with Tara in the morning to get her new shoes, and then she would drop Tara off at the neighbor's afterwards, but Maria never showed up. The neighbor waited till noon, then took off. When she came home in the evening, Maria's car still wasn't there. She hasn't seen her since."

"She didn't go to the police?" Chloe asks.

"Not the type that would," Danny says.

"I see," Chloe says and sips her coffee.

"I called her office on our way back," I say, "and she never showed up for work that day either and she never has since."

"Could the mother be right?" Chloe asks. "Could she have run away with some guy?"

Danny shrugs. "I don't know her very well, but I do know the mother is right, Maria is flaky. I mean, if he had enough money and promised to take her away from here, I bet she would."

"But leave her passport behind? And all her belongings, along with her daughter's iPad?" I say. "Kids today are very attached to their iPads; let there be no doubt about that."

"So, what are we looking at here?" Chloe asks. "Do we think something bad happened to her? To them?"

I sigh and look at Danny. He looks worried, conflicted even. I can sense how the guilt is tearing at him. I can understand why.

"All I know is, I want to find my daughter," he says. "I need to know what happened to her. If it hadn't been for Maria's mother cashing my checks, I would have noticed something was wrong a long time ago. Now six months have passed and I have no idea where to start looking for her."

I reach into my bag and pull out Tara's iPad that Maria's mother agreed to let us take when we went through their stuff. Reluctantly, of course, and only after a few threats to report her to the police.

I place it on the table in front of Chloe. "How about we start here?"

Part II

READY OR NOT

31

April 2016

NICKY RUSHES THROUGH CVS, throwing remedies for lice treatment into her basket. There are so many to choose from, she doesn't have time to read the labels. She simply grabs everything and walks to the counter. There's a woman in line before her who seems to have a thousand things she needs to buy. The woman asks the cashier for something and the cashier disappears.

Nicky grumbles and looks at her phone. Five unanswered calls from her Melbourne-based client with the couch issues. Now she is calling again. Nicky can't pick it up. Not here. She can't tell her when she can make it back to the house to look at the fabric. Right now she has to go get her daughter from school, where she is waiting in the clinic because they found lice in her hair during a random check.

Why today of all days!

Today was supposed to be the day she devoted completely to her Melbourne client and her fabric issue. She really wants to get this couch issue out of the way. Getting the old ones removed cost her two hundred dollars that she can't afford to lose. She wants to move on to the carpets upstairs, since she knows she can make a lot of money on that once they get to it.

But now she has to spend the day washing and combing through Paige's hair, while washing every sheet, cover, and pillowcase in the house.

Argh!

When it is finally her turn, Nicky throws all her remedies on the counter and the woman picks them up. She moves very slowly and it annoys Nicky. After every item, she stops and checks her phone.

Come on. I'm in a hurry here.

"That'll be one hundred twenty-six dollars and forty-five cents," she says, and looks lazily at Nicky. Nicky doesn't have time to complain about the price. She swipes her card through, picks up her things, and rushes groaning out of the store.

She drives to the school and finds Paige with the nurse.

"Mom, I have lice," she says, her voice breaking.

Nicky tries to smile, while her heart is pounding with stress and adrenaline. "I know, sweetie. I got the treatment at CVS, so we'll get rid of those little bastards. Don't you worry."

They drive to the house and Nicky starts treating Paige's hair. She goes through it with the comb while Paige screams and squeals. She finds four live lice and hundreds of nits. It doesn't matter how much she combs it, new ones just keep showing up again and again.

Meanwhile, her phone is on the counter next to them, lighting up every time the woman from Melbourne calls. She puts in the shampoo that has to stay for ten minutes, and finally Nicky calls the lady back, while Paige is allowed to go on the computer until she has to wash the shampoo out. Nicky knows she'll have to comb her hair again afterwards to get the last—hopefully—dead ones out.

"Hello, Mrs. Robbins, yes I am aware I promised you I'd be there today, but you see...No, no, I know. I had another engagement, an emergency this morning, so I had to...I know...yes, yes of course, I'll be there later this afternoon. Yes. No. This time I will be there. Of course. I understand you're upset. I will be there. You have my word on this. Okay. Goodbye."

Nicky draws in a deep sigh and sits down to close her eyes just for a second. That was a close one. She almost lost her client. She's got to get better at this, as soon as she gets past this little thing.

"All right, Paige. Let's wash that hair," she yells up the stairs towards her daughter's room.

Paige doesn't answer.

With an annoyed moan, Nicky walks up the stairs while calling her name. She enters her room to find it empty. The computer is still on, Minecraft is on the screen, but there's no sign of Paige.

"Paige? Sweetie?"

She sees light coming out from her closet and opens the door. In there on the floor sits Paige, her hair still wet from the shampoo, her iPad in her lap. She has taken her shirt off and is wearing only her training bra.

"What are you doing?" Nicky asks.

Paige looks at her and blushes. She turns her iPad to face downwards. "Nothing, Mommy. Just playing."

"Why did you take your shirt off?"

"I was hot. Can't we wash that stuff out of my hair now? It feels really gross."

Nicky grabs the iPad and looks at the screen where Skype is open, but no one is there. Nicky shakes her head. She doesn't have time for this.

"Well, come on then. We need to get you showered and then Mr. Lee will be here to look after you till I get back from my client."

"Oh, no, Mommy. You know I hate math."

"I do and that's why you need a tutor, now come on, I'm in a hurry here."

32

April 2016

He got her to take off her shirt for him. Boxer can't believe his luck. Calling her on Skype and telling her his camera didn't work was genius. He has never tried doing this before, but it won't be the last time.

Brilliant. Absolutely brilliant, he thinks to himself, as he goes through the pictures he took of her while talking to her, asking her gently and nicely if he could see her without a shirt. He didn't think the girl would go for it, but she did. Especially after he told her how beautiful she was and that he really liked her.

The pictures don't do anything for him. Boxer isn't into that stuff, but his client is. He hopes Dr. Seuss will be especially excited to see these.

Boxer downloads the pictures to his computer, and then sends them. He gets up from his chair, feeling triumphant. If all goes well, he'll be able to make a load of money on this beauty. And her mother. Cause that's what his client likes, the girl and her mother. What Dr. Seuss does with them after he delivers them to him is none of Boxer's business. As long as he gets his money.

Does he sometimes feel bad? Does he have nightmares about the girls he takes? Yes, of course he does. He would be a monster if he didn't.

Boxer walks to the hallway and puts on his shoes and jacket. He is wearing a tie today. She loves it when he wears a tie.

While thinking about his brother, he walks to his car and drives out of town. His brother never came home last night, and Boxer is worried what kind of trouble he has gotten himself into this time.

Boxer parks the car in front of the hospice in Titusville and greets the lady behind the front desk. She recognizes him and waves.

"She's in her room," she yells after him.

"Got it," he yells back and storms to the door. He corrects his tie and hopes he doesn't have too many sweat marks on his white shirt, before he knocks.

"Come in," the thin small voice behind the door says.

Boxer pokes his head in. "It's me."

She gesticulates with her arms. "Oh, my sweet boy. Come closer so I can take a good look at you."

Boxer walks up to her wheelchair and grabs her hand. "How are you, Mom?" he asks.

"You know how I am," she says.

"I do. But is there any news? How's your blood pressure?"

"Son. I am dying from cancer and you worry about my blood pressure?"

"No. I mean…yes, I do. Last time I was here the doctor said it was too high, remember?"

"You know what I like, son? I like to sit here and watch those cars drive by. At a certain point, you get to recognize some of them. Every day they go in the morning and then come back in the afternoon. Every day. Back and forth. Always in a rush."

"That's nice, Mom. That's very nice."

"How's the job coming? They make you manager yet?" she asks.

"The job's great, Mom. It's really great."

"Good, my boy. You make me proud."

They sit quietly and look out the window for a few minutes, when the door is opened and the manager of the hospice pokes his head in.

"Could I have a little chat with you?"

They walk outside. The manager clears his throat. "Sir, I hate to bother you with this, but we haven't received your payment for the last two months."

Boxer pretends to be surprised. "Really? Well, my bank was supposed to have sent the checks automatically," he lies. "I'll have to check with them. I'll have the money for you shortly. Don't worry."

The manager eases up. He smiles and rubs his hands. "Oh, good. It's always a delicate matter when someone…I mean we wouldn't like to have to…"

"Oh, I understand. Of course you need your payment. I'll have it to you as soon as possible."

33

April 2016

I CALL Salter when the two others have left. I have been waiting for him to call me, but since he hasn't done it, I finally break down and call him. I can't believe how long he can go without talking to me. As I wait for him to pick up, I debate with myself whether to tell him how angry or maybe disappointed I am or to pretend I haven't noticed that he didn't call me.

Oh, my God! When did it become this complicated?

"Hi, Mom," he says when he finally picks up.

"Well, hello there. Good to know that you're still alive," I say, trying to sound like I am joking.

"You sound mad. Are you mad?"

Kids. They see straight through you.

"No. No. Not at all. Just been missing you, that's all. How was school today?" I ask, trying hard to sound casual, as if I haven't been obsessing about him every second of this entire day.

"Oh, I didn't go to school today," he says.

"What?" Okay, now I am sounding angry. But rightfully so. I try to calm myself down. Maybe there is an explanation. "Are you sick?"

"No. No. But Dad and Jackie took me standup paddling instead."

Stand up paddling?

"What?"

"Calm down, Mom. It was just one day. It's not that big of a deal."

"Wasn't it today you had the FSA test?" I ask.

"Crap. You're right. I forgot about that."

"You forgot?"

"Yes, I forgot, all right? Sometimes people forget. They can't all be perfect and remember everything like you."

"That is the lamest argument I have ever heard," I say. "Pass me to your dad, please."

"No."

"What do you mean no?"

"No. You're just going to yell at him and blame it on Jackie, and then he's going to be all sad afterwards. He's trying his best here. He's never taken me out paddle boarding before, and I really enjoyed it."

I want to scream, but I can't. I am in too much shock. When did my son become this teenager?

"I need to speak to your dad, please. Put him on," I say.

"No. You can call his own phone," Salter says.

"Salter!"

"I'm leaving now. Goodbye," he says, then hangs up.

I stare at my phone. *What the heck was that?*

"Pick your battles, my dear."

I turn my head and look at my dad, who is sitting in his wheel-chair watching TV in the living room.

"What?"

He looks at me. "You've got to pick your battles," he repeats. "Is it really worth getting so upset about? Is it worth starting a fight with Joey about?"

I gnarl. "Why are you always on Joey's side, not mine?" I ask.

"Just trying to give you a piece of advice I wish someone would have given me before I had children. You can fight and argue over the smallest of things if you want, but that's just going to make your life miserable. Think about it. This thing you're arguing about, will it matter a year from now?"

I put the phone down and get up from my chair. I don't want to hear anymore and I have to start dinner.

"It will if he doesn't pass the FSA," I say. "Then he won't get into fifth grade next year, so yes, it does matter. I'd say it matters a lot."

34

April 2016

TOM CALLS me Friday morning and we chat for an hour on the phone. I feel like a teenager, lying on my bed talking to him, flirting over the phone, but it is nice. He is nice. "So, when will I see you again?" I ask.

"We have one last game tomorrow afternoon, with the junior girls team, then it's all over," he says. "Maybe we should go out to dinner tomorrow night?"

"Yes," I say, feeling my heart throb. I am already looking forward to seeing him again.

"So, what are you up to this weekend?" he asks.

"I'll go to the rally tomorrow morning. Got to support our locals when they fight for the environment, right?"

"I know. It's terrible with all those dead fish. I can't believe they can't even figure out why this is happening."

"That's what gets me infuriated as well," I say. "I'm thinking about writing a piece about it for my blog. Maybe take some pictures at the rally."

"Sounds like a great idea," he says. "You are very powerful with that blog of yours. Maybe if the outside world hears about it, the politicians will finally step up and do something. This is sure to kill the tourism."

It is time for Tom to go and we hang up. I catch myself smiling as I get out of bed. I look at the clock. It is almost ten. I can't remember the last time I stayed in bed this long. I realize my dad hasn't gotten his breakfast yet and get dressed real quick.

"I am so sorry, Dad," I say, as I enter his room. He is not mad; he is smiling, as always.

"That's okay, sweetie. I watched the most beautiful sunrise from my window and now I am watching TV," he says, and lifts the remote with his fingers. It won't be long before he'll regain all the strength and mobility in his hands again, his physical therapist told me the day before, just before he left. I am thrilled to see the progress he is making.

"Tell you what? How about I make you some pancakes?" I say, to make up for my guilt. Plus, I am starving myself and really in the mood for pancakes.

"Sounds great, honey," he says.

I whip together some batter and start to make the pancakes. My heart is hurting when my train of thoughts stops at Salter. I can't believe he is being so defiant towards me. Am I losing him?

I don't like the thought and replace it with something else. I try to imagine being Danny right now and feel bad for him. He still doesn't know if he'll be charged with anything, and if he is, he'll lose his job. On top of it all, his daughter and her mother are missing. Where could they be? I wonder how people can just disappear like that. Being gone for six months and no one does anything? What about her friends?

I think about myself and know in my heart that people would start wondering after a few days if they hadn't heard from me. That's how tight our little crew and community are. Then I think about Sandra and the fact that I haven't spoken to her in almost a week. It is strange, since I had just gotten used to having her in my life again, but it seems like she is avoiding me. Or maybe I am avoiding her. I really don't feel like having to deal with her and Alex and their affair and betrayal of their spouses. I can't take it. Not after all I am going through with Joey.

I finish making a stack of pancakes when someone knocks at the door.

"Come in," I yell, while Snowflake is all over me because he can smell the pancakes. I let him out in the yard to do his business, while Chloe walks through the front door.

"Good morning," she says. "Do I smell pancakes?"

35

April 2016

I SET an extra plate on the patio table on the porch, get my dad out of bed and into his chair, then roll him outside. It's one of those gorgeous spring mornings with no wind and the ocean is glassy. It's already eighty-three degrees and the sun is shining directly at us, so I put up the umbrella.

"So, I took a look at the girl's iPad," Chloe says after her first pancake.

"And?" I ask, not getting my hopes up. It was a long shot; I know that very well. I really don't know what I expected to find on her iPad. Maybe a new address or a message to one of her friends telling them she'd be moving, or just anything to indicate they didn't just vanish, that it was somehow planned.

Chloe grabs another pancake, pours syrup on it, and takes a bite. She chews and swallows before she answers. "And I didn't find anything about them moving or her talking about having to move or anything like that."

I sigh and chew my pancake with Nutella. "I had a feeling you wouldn't."

"But I did find something else," she says. "I went through all of her history and Tara was quite active both on Twitter and Instagram. And she played Minecraft a lot."

I shrug. "So do most kids her age."

"Sure. But there's something else. She chatted with this guy, he calls himself Boxer, and he seems to be talking to her on all the platforms. He would comment on her pictures on Instagram, they were Skype friends and chatted in there, and in Minecraft and Twitter as well. She had a Facebook account, but never used it much. But it is strange how this guy seemed to appear everywhere, so I went to check on her chat history in Minecraft. The two of them started chatting two months ago, and after that it was every day."

I shrug again. "So what? They were friends. Salter has a bunch of friends he only knows from social media or Minecraft. They play together and call each other on Skype or they use the chat to communicate and find each other in the different worlds."

"I know, I know," she says and takes another bite.

I watch my dad as he is struggling to reach his mouth with the fork. His hand is shaking, his fingers white with effort. I fight my urge to help him, since he has told me he wants to do it himself. It's the only way he'll get better at it. I know he is right. But it is so very painful to watch every time he misses; the disappointment on his face is crushing me.

"Have they been talking about anything creepy?" I ask. "Like is he a pedophile, is that why you wonder about him?"

"Not that I know of," she says. "I mean, he does tell her he likes her, but it all seems very innocent. But what strikes me is the fact that he is the last person she wrote to. On October 23rd, in the early morning he wrote to her: *We don't have school today. Do you want to meet me in Roblox?*" Chloe looks at me. "Roblox is another game very similar to Minecraft..."

"I know what Roblox is," I say. "I have a ten-year-old, remember?"

"Right. Well, he asks her this, and then she writes: *I can't. Going to Target with my mom to buy new shoes. Maybe later?*"

Chloe looks at me from above the iPad again.

"Is that it?" I ask.

She puts the iPad down on the table. "Yes."

"That's really not telling us much, is it?" I say.

Chloe sighs and leans back in her chair. I realize how much my dad's new patio furniture has already rusted. Especially the legs. Good thing Chloe isn't very big, or I would fear it might break. It's amazing how fast things rust when you live on the ocean. All that salt in the air just eats right through it.

"I don't know," she says, resigned. "I just had an odd feeling about this guy, that's all. It might be nothing. I guess I was just reaching for something. I feel so bad for Danny."

"Yeah, me too," I say, and reach for my third pancake. "I wish there was more we could do."

36

April 2016

THE SUN HITS him in the face and he blinks his eyes. Blake looks at his watch. The sun is right outside of his window at the Hilton where he rented a room. The hotel is right on the beach and Blake asked specifically for a room with a view, yet there is no balcony even though it overlooks the beach. Blake finds that to be very odd. He wants to sit out there at night looking over the ocean, a beer in his hand like he used to when he still lived with his father.

There is a knock on the door and Blake gets up to open it. Room service brings in his breakfast, and he digs in while thinking about his next move. He has been in Cocoa Beach for almost a week now and kept a close eye on his father's house and especially on his sister. It still amazes him how close he can get to her without her knowing it. Twice he has been right behind her when she goes into Publix to buy her groceries and he walked just a few steps behind her all through the store. Of course, she probably wouldn't recognize him even if she stared directly at him, now that he has shaved off his hair and grown a beard. But still it strikes him how very inattentive she is to her surroundings, how easy she makes it for him to get really close…and how easy it is going to be to hurt her.

Finishing his croissants and fresh fruit, Blake wipes his hands on the napkin, grabs his coffee cup, and walks to his new laptop that he just bought at the Apple store, using Olivia's debit card, of course… the secret one that she created in her aunt's name while she was still alive.

Blake touches his face and his beard. It feels strange. He hasn't quite gotten used to the feel yet. The same goes for his reflection. He can hardly recognize himself anymore.

The computer starts up and Blake starts working the keyboard.

He has been planning this for quite some time and working on perfecting it. He knows Mary is completely clueless when it comes to computers, but she has Chloe. Oh, yes. Chloe, who fell for Blake once.

It has taken him all these days to create the perfect weapon against his dear sister, but now he is ready to fire it. The only regret he has is that he won't be there to see her face when it explodes.

You won't know what hit you, dear sissy. But it ain't over yet. This is just the beginning.

Blake sips his coffee while focusing intently on the computer screen. The coffee is too bitter. He walks to the remains of the breakfast table and grabs the sugar bowl, then pours a couple of teaspoons of sugar in his coffee, while watching his program unfold on the screen. Nothing but numbers to most people, but to Blake it is more beautiful than the sunrise. He drinks more coffee. It tastes better now. The numbers run over the screen and Blake feels a chill of joy in his stomach.

Almost there. Almost there.

He presses a few keys, writes some numbers and a code. The computer thinks for a few seconds, then more numbers appear before the final stage arrives. Blake looks at the screen, and then down at the return key, knowing all he now needs to do is press it and all hell will break loose.

Blake takes in the moment; he closes his eyes and pictures his sister's face. He looks at the screen again. It's a thing of beauty, isn't it?

Then he leans over the keyboard, places his finger on the return key, and presses it.

37

April 2016

PAIGE HAS to stay home from school because of the lice, and Nicky has no idea what to do with her while she attends to Mrs. Robbins in Melbourne. She can't really bring her. It would be torture for everyone, and if Mrs. Robbins were to ask why Paige wasn't in school today, Nicky would have to tell her the reason, and then she would definitely be fired for bringing lice into her house. Even though they had gone through all the treatment and there were no lice in Paige's or Nicky's hair this morning when she combed through them both. There is still the risk of re-infestation.

If you miss just one of those little bastards, you'll have to do it all over again.

Nicky has thought of another solution for Paige today. One she won't be too happy about. She has called Mr. Lee and asked him to come and teach Paige some math for a few hours.

She knows she'll be very unpopular, so she hasn't told Paige. Paige is in her room, playing on her computer when Mr. Lee arrives.

Nicky opens the door and Mr. Lee bows politely. "Good morning, Mrs. Stover," he says with that cute accent. "How are you today?"

"I'm great. Thank you so much for coming on such short notice," she says, and lets him inside of her house.

Nicky likes Mr. Lee a lot. He is probably the first man she has felt attracted to since she became a mother. It is strange, since she never used to like Asian people, but Mr. Lee is different. He is tall and muscular underneath the tight white shirt. And he has that handsome smile. He has told her he works as a math teacher at a private school in Viera.

"So you had no classes today?" she asks as they walk into the kitchen.

"No. Not today."

"Guess I was really lucky then, huh?"

"Yes," he says with a wide smile. "Very lucky."

His smile warms her and she blushes. Nicky looks away, feeling silly. "There is coffee in the pot; I have made some snacks for later, some fruit and crackers, and there is lunch in the refrigerator. I hope to be back by one," she says. "Will that be okay?"

He smiles and nods. "Yes. It's just fine." Mr. Lee then grabs her arm. She feels a warmth go through her body at his touch. "Don't worry. Don't stress," he says. "It's no problem at all."

Nicky sighs happily. "You have no idea how glad I am to hear that."

"Now, go. Do your job, make your clients happy. Paige is in good hands."

"I know she is," Nicky says and grabs her purse in her hand. She picks up her phone from the charger, then yells up the stairs:

"Paige. I'm leaving. Mr. Lee is here to do math with you."

"Aw!" Paige groans from her room. She appears at the top of the stairs. "Do I have to?"

"Yes," Nicky says and throws her a kiss.

"But I was doing something on the computer," she continues.

"Don't start arguing," Nicky says. "I don't have time for this."

"You never have time. For anything anymore!" Paige yells.

"Don't give me that," Nicky says, feeling the pinch of guilt in her stomach. "You do what Mr. Lee tells you to, do you hear me?"

But Paige has already stormed into her bedroom and shut the door.

"I'll take care of her," he says. "Just go. We'll be fine."

Nicky draws in a deep breath. She looks into the eyes of Mr. Lee. He makes her feel safe. She knows Paige will be fine with him, even though she has to do math. He is good with her and makes her laugh.

"Thank you," she says as the phone starts to ring in her purse. She picks it up. "I'm sorry," she says. "It's my client. I have to go. Call me if there is anything." Nicky runs with the phone to her car.

"Yes, Mrs. Robbins, no, I am on my way. Just caught in heavy traffic, that's all. Be there in a few minutes…"

Nicky runs to the door. The last thing she sees before she closes it is Mr. Lee walking up the stairs towards Paige's bedroom.

38

April 2016

"So, I was planning on writing a piece about the fish-kill in the lagoon," I say.

We're done eating breakfast and Chloe is helping me clean up the kitchen. I have a tendency to make quite a mess when I cook.

"For the blog," I continue.

She nods while putting a cup in the dishwasher. "That sounds like a good idea. And an important case. Very local, though. You need to really have a good angle on it to make it interesting for your readers."

"I know. I think I'll go to the rally tomorrow, take some pictures for the post, and talk to some people. Get some info from the locals. I want to figure out who is to blame for all this."

Chloe scoffs. "Don't we all?"

"I know. I feel like something is off here, you know what I mean? There are so many theories out about it being because of people using too much fertilizer in their yards or pesticides, and then others believe it's caused by the septic tanks leaking, some even blame it on the manatees. But, I'm asking, why now? These things have always happened around here; why are the fish being killed now? The other day I saw a picture from one of the canals where you couldn't see the water for all the dead fish on the surface. It looked so creepy. We've never had this kind of fish-kill before. There must be something that has changed within the past few months."

"I heard people say it might be pollution from that power plant up north. Take a look at that and you might find some answers," Chloe says. "But I do agree. It does feel like someone is covering something up in this case. Something is off. If you can find out who, where, and what, then you have your story."

I throw out the remains of my fifth pancake and feel sick to my stomach. I ate way too much again. I decide I just won't have lunch today. That should even things out.

"I'll try that," I say.

"By the way, I've made some design changes to your blog," Chloe says and walks to my computer. She taps on the keyboard while I continue to clean up. I wipe off the stove and put the last dish in the dishwasher.

"Our blog, Chloe. You're as much a part of it as I am, if not more. I don't think I pay you enough," I say. "I mean, without you there would be no blog and no income from all those advertisers."

I turn and look at Chloe when she doesn't try and argue with me, which she always does when I try to give her money for her work. She is staring at the screen, eyes wide open, and her face pale.

"What's going on?" I ask and throw my dishtowel on the counter. The look on her face is scaring me.

"Chloe?"

"Something is very wrong," she says and taps on the keyboard again.

I walk up behind her and look over her shoulder. Then I gasp. "What on earth is this?"

She shakes her head. "I don't know. I think we've been hacked. Someone has placed a bomb in here sending out all kinds of messages to your followers. Completely spamming them. This is bad, Mary. People are going to be so pissed. We've already lost five thousand fans. If this goes on, we'll end up losing every one of them."

"What kind of messages?"

"Like this one," she says and points at the screen.

"What the heck? I never said that! And that picture of me? Where did that come from?"

Chloe shrugs. "I don't know. What are you doing in this picture anyway?"

"I was stuck in the toilet. Hey, don't judge me; I was like ten years old. How did this get on here?"

"Who has access to these photos?" Chloe asks. "Do you have them on Facebook? Instagram?"

"No. I don't have any of my childhood pictures online. Most of them were lost in the fire. I don't think my dad has any left…wait a minute," I say. "There is someone who could have had access to them before the house burnt down."

Chloe nods. "Blake."

"Yes, Blake."

"Looks like he wants a war," Chloe says, while tapping on her computer.

"How has he done this?" I ask. "I didn't know he could do anything remotely like this on a computer."

"Well…I taught him," she says. "Now, if I could only…I need to stop this before…"

"You did what?"

"I taught him everything, all right? Remember I had a thing for your brother a while back? Well, it is very clear to me now that he used me. I taught him how to hack and how to destroy webpages like this. I was using it to destroy child-porn sites. He wanted to know more; he was interested in what I did. I thought he was interested in me…but now he is using what I taught him to get to you."

"But that means you can also stop it, right?" I ask hopefully, while Chloe's fingers dance crazily across the keyboard.

"I don't know yet," she says. "This bug he has created is pretty advanced. I can't seem to get back into the page."

"But you can stop it, right?"

Chloe doesn't answer. I stare at the screen while she works her magic. I have never seen her like this, so frantic. Meanwhile, the number of followers drops drastically by the minute. I feel so helpless. It frustrates me that I know so little about computers and the world of hacking.

"Oh, no!" Chloe exclaims.

"What? What's happening?"

"He knew I would try this, so when I did, I activated another bug."

"What bug? I don't understand anything that is going on, Chloe."

"Neither do I," she says and looks up at me.

Meanwhile, my blog is crashing on the screen, in an inferno of old pictures of me flashing on the screen one after the other, numbers and letters flying around until the screen suddenly goes black and one message remains, blinking:

READY OR NOT, HERE I COME!

39

April 1975

PEOPLE on the boat are cheering as it pulls away from the shore. On the outside, some people are still trying to jump on the boat, most of them without success.

Danh holds his sister tightly in his arms. He doesn't know whether to cry or join the cheering crowd, so he chooses to do neither. He can only hope one of his brothers is on the boat with them or will be waiting for them wherever they are going to end up.

Soon after, the cheering subsides and everything in the bottom of the boat goes quiet. They have entered the big ocean.

Now what?

In the ocean, the small fishing boat hits rough seas. It feels like the boat is being thrown high into the air only to slam back onto the waves. Soon people are screaming instead of cheering. And some of them start to get sick. One after another starts to puke. Being on the bottom, a lot of it comes down on Danh. He lies on top of Long, covering her so it won't hit her as well. She is scared and whining, so he starts to sing for her, the songs their mother used to sing. It calms her down and soon she falls asleep.

By some miracle, or pure exhaustion, Danh manages to fall asleep as well. When he wakes up, it is light outside. The seas have calmed down. Many people are still asleep. That's when he sees it. Up on the deck. The red shirt.

"Bao!" he yells.

The red shirt turns around and looks towards him. Danh waves. "Bao!"

Bao walks closer, then reaches down his hand and grabs Danh's. He pulls him up and they both help grab Long. They carry her up, away from the crowd of sleeping or sick people. Danh's heart is beating so fast. He is so happy to see his older brother he is almost about to cry.

"We're actually allowed up here on the deck," Bao says. "We're among the few who have paid for this ride."

Danh looks down at the many people at the bottom of the boat. There has got to be at least a hundred and fifty people. It seems like a lot of people for such a small boat.

"They disguised it as a cargo ship," Bao said. "Clever, huh? They hope no one will stop and check for refugees. They're carrying colas." Bao points at the many bottles.

Danh doesn't look at them. He keeps staring at his brother, wondering about the word, refugees. Was that what they were now?

He struggles with this term and wonders if that means they'll never go back again. But what about their parents? What about their many brothers? Will they ever see them again?

Long moans in her sleep and Danh hopes she won't wake up yet. He doesn't have the answers she will be seeking and he doesn't know how long he can keep lying to her, pretending everything will be all right, when he doesn't know. When he is terrified they won't.

Bao grabs a cola and throws it at Danh. "Here. The captain says we can drink these to stay hydrated. He has rice too."

Bao puts his arm around Danh's shoulder and pulls him closer. "We'll be all right, brother," he says. "Don't you worry."

Danh eases up and smiles. For a few seconds, he believes his brother is right. Until he looks down at the crowd of people on the bottom and then back at the sodas, and realizes there is far from enough for everyone.

40

April 2016

"I DID IT. I'm back in!"

I literally have no nails left when the words I have been longing to hear for hours finally fall.

I get up and walk to Chloe. The table is filled with empty chocolate wrappings from me binging in anxiety. "Really? Are you sure?"

"Yes. I have taken control back of our site. It's over."

I take in a deep breath of relief, pull up a chair, and sit right next to her. "How bad is it? What's the damage?"

"We've lost a million followers so far. There might be more along the way. We still have almost four million, so it's a sustainable loss."

"Phew."

"Now all we have to do is clean up. I think I might have to make an entire new design. It may take a few days to get it completely up and running, but I think I can manage," she says.

"I have no idea what I would do without you," I say, and pour the both of us some more coffee. It is late in the afternoon and I am exhausted from this emotional rollercoaster.

Chloe sips the coffee, before she looks at me. "Maybe we should spice it up a little?" she asks.

I walk to the cabinet and grab the whiskey. I pour some in both of our cups.

"Just what the doctor ordered," she says.

I close my eyes and take a big sip. The alcohol soon makes me calmer. I am so angry with my brother I can hardly contain it. I push my anger back by eating another candy bar, just as I hear a knock, and seconds later the front door is opened. Danny walks in. He looks tired. Like he hasn't slept at all.

"She's not the only one," he says, his bloodshot eyes staring at us, looking almost manic.

"What do you mean?" Chloe looks up. Danny slams the door behind him. I just hope he doesn't wake my dad, who had to take a nap.

Snowflake attacks him, wagging his tail and whining for him to pet him. Danny greets him with a short pat on the head, then walks to us.

"I mean she is not the only one," he continues. He lifts a stack of papers in his hand. "Look at all this. I have been up all night searching the news, scanning the local newspapers for other missing persons, and look at what I found."

He throws the stack on the desk next to Chloe. "Four cases within the last two years. Four cases of missing single mothers and their child. And there seems to be a pattern to it. If you look at the dates, there are exactly six months between the disappearances. Exactly."

Danny spreads out the papers and shows us the dates. "These two, Kim and Casey Taylor, a mother and a daughter, just like the rest of them, disappeared exactly a year ago. Last seen at the mall on a surveillance camera. Kim's mother filed a missing persons report a week later, when her daughter and granddaughter still hadn't shown up, and these pictures appeared. According to the newspapers, it is believed Kim Taylor ran away with this man that she is talking to in the surveillance video, the one you can only see the back of. They closed the case, stating she had met a man and left town with him. But Kim's mother didn't believe any of that, so she has started a Facebook group to help find her daughter and grand-child. I spoke to her earlier and she told me it is odd that Kim would leave everything behind in her apartment and not even take her clothes if she had left, or made sure the cat was taken care of. She has told this to the police, but they say they believe Kim is on drugs and this is typical addict behavior. If someone comes along, offering them drugs or a better life, they leave. Next, there is this case, exactly six months earlier, to the date, Jenny and Stacey Brown disappeared. They are last seen by a neighbor in Publix, where she greeted them on their way out. Since then, no one knows what happened to them. Again, they live in a bad neighborhood; the police believe drugs were involved. The mother owed a lot of money and was known by the police for petty theft, shoplifting and so on. They believe she left town to start over somewhere else. Jenny's sister, who filed the missing persons report, accepted that explanation and stopped looking for her. Exactly six months earlier, in April 2014, two years ago, Joan and Nicola Williams disappeared. The newspapers haven't written much about it, but they did send out an Amber Alert for the daughter when the father asked the police for help, but they were never found. The story reports nothing about their home or whether they took everything or not. But it fits with the pattern. The same with Maria and Tara Verlinden. Their disappearance came exactly six months after Kim and Casey Taylor's. No one seems to care because that stupid mother of hers doesn't care. There you have it. All four cases are from Brevard County."

I grab the printed out articles that he has found and look at them one after the other. There are a lot of similarities in the cases, I can give him that, but there are still a lot of unanswered questions. It could all be coincidence. But the fact about the dates being so accurate intrigues me. I can't just ignore it.

"Six months, you say?" I look at my phone to check the date. "If you're right in your theory, then that would mean that a mother and a daughter will disappear again tomorrow?"

41

April 2016

A THUNDERSTORM HITS Cocoa Beach that afternoon, just as I park the car behind the building housing city hall and the police department. I don't have an umbrella or a jacket to cover me, so I decide to make a run for it. When I go through the glass doors to the police department, I am soaking wet, and water is dripping from my hair and clothes onto the tiles. I leave a puddle as I walk across them to the front desk.

"I'm here to see Detective Chris Fisher," I say to the woman behind the counter. She seems to be pretending I don't exist and stares into her computer screen, her glasses on the tip of her nose, her red hair in a ponytail.

"Is he expecting you?" she asks, still without looking at me. I try not to let it irritate me.

"No. But it's important. He knows who I am," I say. "Just tell him Mary Mills is here and that I have some very important information for him. It's a matter of life and death." I try to sound dramatic to provoke any reaction from this lady who doesn't seem to care about anything. It doesn't work.

"Have a seat," she says, finally looking at me above her glasses.

I sit down in an uncomfortable chair. I can't sit still. This morning has been an emotional rollercoaster to put it mildly, and I can't calm down. I check my phone excessively to see if Salter has called, but he still hasn't. I worry about him. He ought to be back from school now. I hope he at least went to school today and not paddle boarding again.

I grumble and curse Joey when the door opens and Chris Fisher pokes his very round head out.

"Ah, Mary," he says, sounding like he is everything but happy to see me. He steps out and walks towards me with his usual smirk. I can never tell if he is hitting on me or being a jerk.

"To what do I owe the honor?"

I have known Chris Fisher since he was just a kid. He hasn't changed much since he was that annoying teenager who was always peeking at us older girls. He is still annoying. He is also the guy that is handling my brother's case, and so far he hasn't done much of a job finding him.

"I have several things I need to talk to you about," I say. "We should go somewhere where we can sit down, somewhere more private."

"Want to be alone with the Fisher-man, do we?" he teases me.

I don't react to his comment. Instead, I get up from my chair. He senses his joke fell flat and looks disappointed.

"I was going to Juice 'N Java for a coffee and a muffin anyway," he continues, and points towards the café across the street.

I sigh. Not very private, but if that is all I can get, I'll take it. "All right. I could go for some coffee myself."

He holds the door for me with a grin and I walk out. "So, what's up?" he says when we're in the street.

"Two things," I say. "First of all, there's my brother."

"Go on, I'm listening."

"He orchestrated an attack on my blog. He hacked in and planted something, I have no idea what it was, you'll have to ask Chloe about that, but it destroyed everything and sent out all these fake messages to my followers. He left me a creepy message stating *Ready or not, here I come.*"

Chris nods along as we walk towards the café across the street. We stop at the intersection at Minutemen Causeway.

"All right, so he is now harassing you. That's new. Seems to me like he is being reckless. He probably thinks there is no way we can catch him. That he is invincible. That's actually a good sign. Makes it easier for him to make a mistake, and then we'll find him. I want to say that I'll have my IT department take a look at it, but I don't think they can do anything that Chloe can't do. Plus, they're swamped most of the time, so it might take months before they have the time to take a look at it, and my guess is that doesn't help us much in catching Blake."

"So what you're pretty much saying is you won't do anything," I say. "That's about what I expected."

"Hey, don't be sassy. I am working on finding him. Don't you worry," Chris says while the light turns green and we cross the street. "It's just...well, I have other cases too. And as far as we know, Blake is out of the county now so..."

"I know," I say. "He's under someone else's jurisdiction."

"Until he shows up here, there really isn't much I can do."

We walk past Heidi's and enter the Juice 'N Java. Again, Chris holds the door for me and I walk in first. The place is packed as always. Lots of soldiers from the Air Force base come here for lunch or afternoon coffee, along with mostly locals. I especially like it because you don't see many tourists here. This is our place.

I order a Mint Madness iced coffee and a big chocolate muffin. We sit on the couches by the window. The place always reminds me of the coffee shop in Friends. The old-fashioned furniture, couches and soft chairs, the art on the walls is beachy, made by local artists, and under the ceiling hangs old beautiful surfboards. Sometimes they have live music playing, small bands or local performers. I have been here once for open mic night as well and enjoyed it a lot. The place has a good vibe to it. It's a great place for me to go when I once in a while miss New York, which, to my surprise, actually isn't very often. I don't miss the life I had back then.

"So, what was the other thing?" Chris asks when we're sitting down. I'm on the couch while he grabs an armchair.

I remove the magazines from the coffee table and place the articles Danny printed out in front of Chris. "I know you won't have time to read through them, but I can give you a quick summary."

"Please do," he says and stares at the stack of printed articles like he doesn't want to even touch it.

"Single mothers disappearing," I say. "And their children."

Chris looks at me, tired. "What?"

"Four cases the past two years. There might be more in the years before, I don't know, but this is what we've found so far. And, get this. There are exactly six months between every disappearance. Look here, I wrote down the dates. April 23rd 2014, October 23rd 2014, April 23rd 2015, October 23rd 2015. Look at them," I say, and point my finger aggressively at the piece of paper where I wrote down the dates. I take in a deep breath and bite into my muffin. It's nice and mushy. I realize I haven't had a real meal all day since breakfast. It's all been candy bars and cookies.

Chris just stares at the papers, then up at me. I can tell he really doesn't want to have to read it. He sighs and drinks his Loco Cocoa Latte. He even looks at his watch, as if to tell me he doesn't have time for this.

"It fits, Chris," I say. "The dates do."

He finally grabs the articles and flips through them so fast there is no way he could read anything.

"So, what you're saying is, these mothers…"

"They're all single mothers," I interrupt. "That's a pattern."

"All right, these *single* mothers. You're telling me they have all disappeared with their children? Where is the crime? They could all have left town or something." He picks out an article and reads a few lines. "Like this one, for instance, it says here in the article that she was a drug addict and moved often."

"That's exactly how I reacted in the first place as well, but the dates are very strange, and some of them left all their belongings behind. Even passports and children's iPads. You don't leave your kid's iPad behind willingly," I say, matter-of-factly.

"But it says here they did take their phones and wallets," he says.

"Sure, but why leave your passport?" I argue.

"Where is the last one? You said there were four?"

"Well, the last one was never reported to the police," I say, hoping to avoid too many questions. I want him to know that Maria and Tara are missing, but I also made a promise to Danny to not tell anyone that she was his daughter. At least not until he has told Junior about her himself, which I know he is building up the courage to do, but knowing Danny it might take a while. There is nothing worse for him than to have to disappoint someone he loves.

"So, how do you know they're missing?" he asks, puzzled.

"Well, I just know. Because I know them. I wrote all the details in this document here," I say, and point at a Word document. "Their names are Maria and Tara Verlinden. I spoke to Maria's mother yesterday and she has no idea where they are. They left everything behind. I don't think they disappeared willingly."

"But she never filed a missing persons report? That sounds a little odd to me," Fisher says, drinking his coffee.

"I know it sounds odd, but she didn't because she has no relationship with her daughter, and well…she took the money that Maria received for child support, because she…you're not even listening anymore, are you?"

Chris shakes his head and leans back in his armchair. "Come on, Mary. This is far out. Besides, I can't go into this if there isn't proof of a crime being committed. You know that. I have other stuff on my plate. Lots of stuff. We have to take care of the dog problem too."

I look up at him. "What dog problem? You don't mean people walking on the beach with dogs, do you? Please tell me that is not what keeps you busy?"

He rubs his forehead, squirming in his seat. This is embarrassing for him. "It's just that…well tourists are complaining…"

"You've got to be kidding me!" I say a little too loud.

Some of the other guests in the café turn their heads and look at me. I smile and pretend everything is fine.

"It's political, Mary. There isn't much I can do about it."

"Argh!" I exclaim. "How can that be more important than missing women and their children?"

"It's not," he says, annoyed. "But again, where is the evidence that a crime has been committed?"

"How about the missing persons reports? Some of their families have filed missing persons reports."

"And the cases have been closed. It says so here, in the article about the woman who went missing in April 2014. They closed it, concluding she had left town. I have to say it all looks like coincidence here, Mary. I can't see how they are related." He throws out his arms. "I'm really sorry."

"But the dates," I say, tapping my pointer finger at the page with the dates. "Look at the dates. If this is a pattern, then another mother and her child will disappear tomorrow. How can you close your eyes to that? We have to do something at least. How else will you be able to sleep tonight?"

He sighs and rubs his hair. "Mary. You're blowing this way out of proportion. People leave town all the time. Especially single mothers. They run away from their families, they leave because they meet a guy, or they leave because of drugs. Maybe they owe money, maybe they know someone in another state who can give them a job. Drug addicts leave their belongings behind because they don't think. They just go to for their next fix; maybe they didn't plan on staying, maybe they just stay there for a longer period of time than expected because someone is providing them with the drug they need. It's not that strange. Besides, if I were to believe that someone would disappear tomorrow, a mother and a child, how would I prevent that from happening? These women come from all over the county. Do you want us to tell all single mothers to stay home tomorrow?"

I sigh. I know he is right. We have no way of knowing who or where this will happen again or if it even will. There really isn't much anyone can do. I just feel bad for Danny that we can't get the police to help him find his daughter. But he told me so. Danny said they wouldn't take this seriously. And he was right.

I collect the papers and make them a pile again. Chris grabs my hand. I look into his eyes.

"You know what?" he says. "You have been right about these kinds of things before. You have a hunch, I'll give you that. Let me take a look at these cases and see what I can come up with, all right?"

I smile and let go of the copies. "You're a good guy, Chris," I say. "Even though you hide it well."

42

April 2016

It's pick-up day.

Saturday morning Boxer is looking at his own reflection in the mirror. He is calm. In the beginning, when he did his first pick-up, he was nervous, afraid something might go wrong. He's not anymore. So far, all of them have gone well. And he is getting better at it.

He splashes water in his face while remembering the other times. He doesn't like it much. He doesn't like the way they scream, the way they plead and beg for him to let them go. He can still hear each and every one of them when he thinks about it. So he tries not to. But when a new pick-up date arrives, it is hard to keep those memories away. He has been dreaming about it all night, especially about the girls.

Boxer walks downstairs where his brother is still sleeping on the couch. He came back the night before, drunk and with a new debt. Boxer just paid the three hundred thousand from last week and now he has to help him out with another five hundred thousand. It stresses him out, since he doesn't have that kind of money on hand, not when he has to pay for their mother's hospice as well. Hopefully he will...after today.

"Get up, bro," he says, and grabs his brother's shoulder. He shakes it. Nothing happens. His brother smells of liquor. Boxer hates that smell. He never touches alcohol. He has seen what it has done to his brother.

"Get up. I need your help today," he says.

His brother finally blinks. Boxer doesn't understand why he insists on sleeping on the couch when he has a perfectly good guest bedroom upstairs that he could crash in.

"Help? With what?"

"I have an order for a pick-up."

His brother sits up and wipes his eyes with a yawn. "All right. Give me a few minutes to get ready."

"I'll make some coffee," Boxer says, and walks into the kitchen.

"How about some of your famous pancakes?" his brother asks.

Boxer smiles. "Sure. Why not?"

He starts to whip together some batter while suppressing the growing anxiety inside that he senses when thinking about today's task. He doesn't want to feel it. He doesn't want to feel anything, but it is hard not to.

His brother puts on his pants and comes into the kitchen. He smells and Boxer makes a grimace.

"Go get a shower," he says. "There's still time."

His brother does as he is told and comes down ten minutes later, his hair wet, and smelling a lot better. He grabs the coffee pot and pours himself a cup.

"So, where are we doing this pick-up today?" he asks, while Boxer finishes making the pancakes. He serves them for his brother while grabbing some yogurt with granola and fruit for himself. Boxer doesn't like to eat unhealthy. He wants to take care of his body.

"There's a rally today," he says while they eat. "People are protesting the fish-kill in the lagoon."

"And that's where we pick them up?"

"Yes. They will be there."

"Lots of people, though. Kind of risky, don't you think?" his brother asks. His brother has helped him do most of the pick-ups and knows how it works. There was only that one time when he was on a bender that Boxer had to do it alone. Most of the money goes to pay for his gambling anyway, so it's only fair that he helps out, Boxer thinks.

"They won't even notice," Boxer says. "Trust me. I know what I'm doing."

43

April 2016

"WE'RE GOING to be late, Mom!"

Paige yells at Nicky as they rush out the door with signs in their hands. Nicky's says *Save our water. There's no Planet B!* while Paige's simply says, *It's my future you're messing with.*

Nicky really likes the slogans they have come up with and feels confident that they'll be able to shake the politicians up a little today. She has been looking forward to this day all week. Mrs. Robbins is in Miami all weekend, so now she has time to spend with her daughter. Going to this rally is a great way to bond a little over something important.

They drive to downtown and park behind city hall. They're early, but the space is already almost filled up. The Intracoastal waters and a bunch of dead fish are something that can get people to rise up from their couches.

Nicky is happy to see that so many people care. They grab their signs and walk to the front of city hall, where a sizable group has gathered. Nicky sees a handful of women she knows from Paige's school and walks to them. Paige is falling a little behind. She doesn't seem too interested in this rally and it aggravates Nicky, since she wants her daughter to know the importance of taking good care of the environment. It is, after all, her future they're rallying for.

"Hi ladies," she chirps and waves at her friends.

"Hello there, stranger," her friend Belinda says and kisses her on her cheeks. "Long time no see."

"Well, you know. Been kind of busy with the company and all."

"How's it going with that?"

"It's been good. Yeah. It's been busy, real busy."

"I want you to meet someone," Belinda says and pulls Nicky's arm.

She drags her towards a chunky woman standing with a camera between her hands. "This here is Mary Mills. You know…the famous blogger. Mary, this is Nicky. Her daughter Paige is in sixth grade."

Mary reaches out her hand and shakes Nicky's. "Nice to meet you," she says, and smiles warmly.

"Mary is writing about the rally for her blog. Isn't it exciting? She has like five million followers on that thing."

"Well, I'm technically writing about the fish-kill and what caused it, but I will be writing stuff about the rally as well, and I'll post some of the pictures I take today," Mary says. She has a nice smile.

"Good, good," Belinda says. "Oh, that's excellent. Soon the entire world will know what's going on down here. That'll get them out of their chairs, don't ya' think?" she says and pokes her elbow at Nicky.

Nicky nods. "That is awesome."

"Would it be alright if I took your picture?" Mary says. "You've got an awesome sign. Is that your daughter standing behind you?"

Nicky turns to look at Paige, who stares angrily back at her. "You said there would be other kids."

"They're coming, sweetie," Nicky says. "Now come here and smile for the camera. Hold up your sign so Mary can see it. There you go."

They pose and smile and Mary Mills takes a bunch of photos, then smiles and thanks them. "If you follow me on Facebook, I'll post all the pictures there during the day today," she says. "Are you on Facebook?"

Nicky nods. "Yes. Both Paige and I are. We would love to see them."

"Is your husband here as well?" Mary asks and looks around. "I'd love to get a picture of the entire family rallying together for the future of our children."

Nicky feels heavy. She hates when people ask about Paige's father. "No. It's just the two of us," she says.

"Okay. Say no more. I'm a single mom myself. One last thing. What's your last name?"

"Stover."

Mary writes the name down on a small pad, then looks up at Nicky with a smile. "Great. Then I'll tag you so you can see them once they're up."

"Great. Thanks."

Nicky feels a tug at her shirt. "Mom, I saw some of my friends from school. Can I walk with them?"

Finally, Paige seems to be onboard. "Well, of course, honey, Nicky says. "Remember to yell as loud as you can while you walk and put your sign up in the air. Make yourself be heard!"

44

April 2016

I DON'T FEEL GOOD. I try to suppress the feeling of dread that is constantly nagging at me while I take pictures and talk to people at the rally. It's not the fish-kill that's bothering me. It's not the many stories people are feeding me of how the local politicians are trying to cover up the real cause of the fish-kill, no that's not why I feel sick to my stomach.

It's the hunch.

The feeling that something bad is going to happen. The knowledge that someone might disappear today, that a single mother somewhere might vanish along with her child, and no one knows where to.

I keep looking around at the crowd, staring at the faces of all these people. Most of them are women. Some have brought their children. As a single mother myself, I am terrified. A few minutes ago, I talked to a single mother with a little girl a few years older than Salter. Could it be her? Is she next? Am I? Was it planned, what happened to them, or was it random?

I comfort myself by telling myself that it doesn't have to be right here in Cocoa Beach that the next disappearance is happening. It could be anywhere in the surrounding towns. Rockledge, Titusville, Merritt Island, Viera. Maria and Tara lived almost in Cape Canaveral.

Am I overreacting? Am I blowing this out of proportion like Chris Fisher said? I don't know. But the feeling won't go away. It is sitting in my stomach and eating at me, slowly devouring me, making me anxious for every face in this crowd, including myself.

I am just happy that Salter is with his dad. I spoke to him before

I went to bed last night and he had been to school and was doing fine, he told me. I hope he wasn't lying to me.

You've got to let it go, Mary. Let it go. You can't control everything for the rest of his life.

"Any news?" Chloe asks, as she comes up next to me.

"Good morning," I say cheerfully.

I can't believe she is here. I am amazed that I managed to talk her into coming with me for this. I didn't expect her to show up. She hates crowds and she hates being outside and usually sleeps at this hour of the day. Judging from the look on her face, she isn't exactly enjoying it. In the bright sunlight she looks paler than usual. I can't see her eyes behind those dark sunglasses, but I know they're not happy.

"I got a few leads that I want to follow up on," I say. "You were right that there are a lot of rumors about the power plant."

"I'm not talking about the fish-kill," she says with a deep sigh that makes me want to spring for coffee for her. "What did Chris Fisher say? When you spoke to him yesterday?"

"He'll look into it," I say.

She turns her head and I think she is looking at me, but I can't tell because of those sunglasses.

"He said that?"

"Believe it or not, he did. It took some convincing on my part, but that's what he finally said before he left me."

"I don't see many cops here today, though," she says and looks around us. We're standing in the middle of the crowd, as it is slowly growing bigger when more people join in.

"They're probably watching us from behind the windows while drinking coffee and eating cake," I say, and look at the building behind us. "It is awfully convenient that the rally is right outside their door. But I did see one down in front of the fire station when I got here. I also heard they have blocked off the streets."

"So what's supposed to happen next?" Chloe asks, sounding highly uninterested.

"We're supposed to walk down Minutemen yelling all the slogans," I say. "I think they're waiting for one of the organizers to step up and kind of start the whole thing. You know, take the lead. I heard that Theodor G is going to be here."

"Oh, no. I can't stand that guy. So pompous."

"Well, everyone else loves him," I say, getting a little annoyed with Chloe's attitude. She's ruining my mood. It's enough that I have this anxious feeling inside of me, I don't want to feel depressed as well.

"I loathe rallies," Chloe says. "Too many people in one place. Everyone is so close together it's yucky."

"Yeah, but at least it's for a good cause," I say, trying to lift her spirits a little. Meanwhile, I grab the camera and take some more photos. My new subject is a dad with his young son helping him hold his sign.

"Cute."

"As if this will ever help anything," Chloe says with a scoff. "These people walking around with their signs singing hymns or yelling slogans won't save the fish, if you ask me."

"Don't be so cynical. We gotta do what we can do, right?" I say. "This is all we as a community can do right now. Show the politicians that we are angry about this and that they should do something. Ah, look, News13 is here. That's good. We need all the publicity we can get."

"Where is Danny? Why is he not here?"

"He needed some time with Junior. I think he's trying to find the courage to tell him he has a sister."

"Ouch. That's gotta hurt," Chloe says. "Got any food?"

I reach into my purse and pull something out. "Candy bar?"

"Sure. I'll take it."

"Looks like someone is stepping up," I say, as a woman walks out of the crowd with a megaphone in her hand.

"Welcome, everyone," she yells. "First of all, I want to thank everyone who has come out to support this important cause today."

A vague bit of applause spreads through the crowd, then dies.

"Oh, my," Chloe complains.

"Shh," I say, while the woman with the megaphone tells us what is going to happen.

"Did she just say that we'll be walking all the way to the country club?" Chloe says. "You've got to be kidding me! In this heat?"

"I gotta say, the idea doesn't appeal to me either," I say, as the woman is replaced by a big broad-shouldered guy that I recognize as Theodor G, the football player who started a fast food chain called Pull 'N Pork, when he retired. Like Kelly Slater, he is one of the local heroes around here. We need them today.

Theodor grabs the megaphone and the crowd finally manages to applaud loudly. He talks about the river and how it has never been this bad and how he used to play in the water as a teenager and fish. When he is done, the crowd starts to walk, Theodor in the lead, chanting and singing.

I see many mothers with their children and feel a pinch in my heart, thinking about Maria and Tara. Where are they now? What has happened to them? Why doesn't anyone care?

"I'm not walking that far," Chloe says.

"Ah, come on," I say. "You know...when in Rome and all that."

"Kill me," Chloe says, before she finally trots along behind me.

45

April 2016

BOXER PARKS his car and gets out. His brother is right behind him. Minutemen is blocked off; no cars can go through while the rally is going on. The crowd is starting to leave city hall now and is walking towards the main street. Boxer and his brother grab the signs Boxer has made for them and join in. Boxer nods and greets some of his neighbors.

"Hi. How are you?" he says again and again.

His brother doesn't know anyone and he stays behind Boxer. He is not very good with people. Not like Boxer is. Boxer knows how to talk to them, how to make them feel like he is one of them, that he is part of the community. Just like when he speaks to the girls online, he has a way of making them feel like they can talk to him.

Like he's a nice guy.

"How do we find them? There are hundreds of people here," his brother finally whispers in his ear.

"I showed you their Facebook pictures. Just look for them," Boxer hisses angrily, trying to stop his brother from talking about why they are really there.

"But how? There are so many people?"

"I know," Boxer says, and holds onto the gun in his pocket. "We gotta just wait for the right moment."

"As you wish," his brother says and trots along.

"Save our lagoon. Save our river home!" Boxer yells, along with the rest of the crowd. He is holding his sign up high in the air. "This is the future for our children. Save our water!"

They walk like this for about ten minutes when his brother starts to get impatient. "Where are they?" he asks.

"I don't know," Boxer hisses.

"Well, you should know. It's all your plan."

"I didn't know there would be this many people, all right?"

"So, what do we do? All these women look alike. Many of them have children. Why don't we just grab one or the other?"

"We can't. I have a particular order for this one. I've been working on it for months. We can't take any chances here. It'll ruin everything. They have to be single moms and they have to be the ones I've picked out and the client has approved of," he whispers, hoping his brother can hear him over the crowd's loud singing and yelling. "Just trust me."

"All right. All right. I just figured it would be easier if we…"

"No! Just walk."

"All right. You're in charge."

Boxer's brother finally goes silent when Boxer's phone vibrates in his pocket. He pulls it out and sees a notification from Facebook.

"What is it?" his brother asks.

Boxer is smiling. "Someone tagged Paige in a photo. I've set it up so I get all notifications about her. If she posts anything or if someone tags her in something." He touches his screen and a picture shows up of Paige and her mother standing by city hall holding their signs.

"It looks like it was taken before they started walking," Boxer says. "But at least now we know that they're here and what their signs say."

Seconds later, the phone vibrates again. Another notification from Paige. It's the same lady who posted the first picture, but this time it shows Paige with three other girls walking on their own.

"This one is newer," he says. "Look, they're right ahead of us. That building there is the school. Roosevelt Elementary. It's no more than fifty feet ahead of us."

46

April 2016

I AM KEEPING myself very busy during this rally and completely forgetting how far we are walking. I take pictures of everyone and post them on Facebook right away, trying to tag everyone, but it's getting more and more difficult.

The latest picture I took was of four young girls between eleven and twelve years of age, walking with their signs and singing along. I thought it was the cutest thing, so I had to take their picture. I love it when young kids get involved.

I tag all four girls, then move on. I photograph an elderly lady who is walking steadfastly, keeping up with everyone else, and I interview her while we walk. She tells me she is ninety-six years old.

"The river has never been in this bad a shape," she says, determined. "We've had fish-kills before, but not in this amount. It's outrageous. I am here today to support my community and show my anger towards what is going on. Those politicians are sitting on their hands and doing nothing. It's outrageous."

I write her comments down. I want to use them both on Facebook and in the article I am writing for the blog.

Chloe is trying to keep up with me, but is snarling more and more the further we go.

"Are we there yet?" she keeps asking me.

I, on the other hand, am trying to make the best of it. I find that I am actually enjoying myself. And doing something like this makes me forget that nagging dread I have been feeling since last night. I am beginning to hope that I am actually wrong about this...that Chloe, Danny, and I are only seeing ghosts.

"If I'd known this was going to happen, then I would never have..."

"Chloe," I interrupt her. "You've got to stop complaining. I am grateful that you are here, but if all you're going to do is complain, then maybe it would be better if you went back home."

"I thought you needed me here."

"I thought so too, but as it turns out, I don't. I am doing it all by myself. I love you. I am all for you. I love to hang out with you, but if you don't want to be here, just go home and I'll see you later."

Chloe looks disappointed. I still can't see her eyes, but I know how they look. I know her all too well. "So you're saying you don't need me here?"

I grab her and hug her, even though I know she hates people touching her. "See you later, Chloe."

"All right. I guess I'm going back then."

I wave and follow the crowd as it passes Chloe, who is now standing still. Some guy elbowing his way through the crowd accidentally pushes her aside.

"Hey!" she yells.

"Sorry," he says and hurries on.

I chuckle. That is so typically Chloe. Never was very good with people. And people were never very good with Chloe.

I turn around and start shooting pictures of the crowd. The guy who pushed Chloe is right in front of me and I take a few pictures, but mostly of his neck. I wonder why he is in such a hurry to get up front.

I am very pleased to see that the police have blocked off Minutemen completely for cars and they are all present by the blockade. I remind myself to put that in my article. How the local enforcement is backing up our protest. Should give them some goodwill. I need to stay good friends with them.

I take a few extra photos when something happens behind me. It starts with the unmistakable sound of tires screeching. It is followed by someone screaming. The scream makes me turn to look. I face hundreds of people who have started to run towards me. It's like a stampede.

What the hell is going on?

Between the screaming and running people, I manage to spot a car. It seems to have driven through the police blockade and into the crowd.

There is blood on the front of the car.

47

April 2016

BOXER DOESN'T LOOK BACK. The people surrounding him all do. They turn to see what the screams are about while he continues ahead. In front of him, not very far away, he can see the girls. Four young girls walking in a line. They too hear the screams and the commotion coming from the back of the line and turn to look. Panic erupts as the stampeding crowd from behind surpasses Boxer and chaos is everywhere. The girls are pulled apart, some of them start to run, others are crying helplessly, calling their mother's names.

Boxer's eyes remain fixated on the girl, on Paige. She is standing still, frozen, while everything and everyone around her moves frantically like recently beheaded chickens. As he approaches her, their eyes lock.

She smiles, but not for long. The seriousness on Boxer's face causes her to stop. He approaches her and grabs her by the shoulders.

"Something happened. You've got to come with me," he yells through the screams. "Something terrible happened to your mother."

Fear spreads in her eyes. "What? What happened?"

"Something terrible. She was taken away in an ambulance. Come with me. I'll take you to the hospital," he lies.

Boxer grabs Paige's hand in his and pulls her out of the crowd. "I have my car over here, it's parked behind city hall," he says. "But we must hurry."

Screams and panic continue behind them as they leave the main road and cross the parking lot. The girl is whimpering.

"Is it bad?" she asks. "Is she hurt?"

"I don't know. But I gotta tell you, kiddo, it doesn't look too good. She was in pretty bad shape when they took her away."

"Oh. How did it happen?"

"A car drove through the blockade and hit some people."

Boxer looks around to make sure no one is watching him. Not a single person sees them. They're too busy screaming and running around. The officers present are all running towards the car that apparently did hit someone. Boxer has no idea who or how it happened or who drove the car, but he is very grateful to whoever it was. It was perfect timing. It was just the type of panic he was going for.

Boxer's own plan had been to use the gun to fire a few shots outside the crowd and create chaos that way. But since the car did all the work for him, he didn't have to.

"My car is right over here," he says, and points at the white van. He looks around to see if he can see his brother anywhere, but he doesn't seem to be there. Boxer opens the back door.

"You need to ride in the back. Jump in."

Paige hesitates and looks at him, slightly skeptical.

"Come on," Boxer says. "We've got to get out of here before everyone else gets into their cars and starts driving, then we'll get stuck in traffic. You hear those sirens? Well, that's your mother being taken to the hospital. You want to be there, right?"

Paige nods while looking at him with big brown moist eyes. He can't believe how great a liar he is, how convincing his little act is.

"Well, get in then."

Paige finally jumps in and Boxer slams the door shut behind her. *One down, one to go. Now where is that no-good brother of mine?*

Finally, he spots him as he comes running towards the car. Boxer growls when he realizes he's alone.

"What the hell are you doing?" he yells. "Where is the mother? You were supposed to bring her here. You were supposed to tell her that her daughter had been hurt and that she needed to come with you, where is she?"

His brother pants heavily and leans forward to catch his breath. "I'm sorry, Boxer. I really am. She…" he pauses to breathe. "She…I couldn't find her."

48

April 1975

THE DAYS ARE long and the food sparse on the boat. They have no water, only sodas, so they cook their rice in it and it tastes terrible. Danh is losing weight fast and so is his brother and especially his sister. But at least they're being fed.

Far from everyone onboard is getting anything to eat or drink for days. Most of the people on the bottom of the boat haven't paid the fare and therefore don't get to get up on deck and don't get anything. They're getting sick down there and it is spreading fast. Danh sees it every day. More and more people are getting sick and they look like they're all dying.

Danh feels awful for being one to get food, but Bao tells him to just ignore them, to be happy there is food and drink for him and his family. Long soon notices it too. That people are suffering. She doesn't understand why they can't just give those people some food.

"There are children down there," she says, crying. "They're hungry. They're thirsty."

"So are we," Bao says harshly. "It's them or us. We won't survive if they drink everything we have. Don't you understand anything?"

He has never been very good at talking to Long. He wants her to toughen up, he wants her to grow up, while Danh tries to keep her a child. He loves her innocence, her naivety, and would prefer she stayed that way all of her life. He simply loves it about her. So he tries to play games with her. As always, when he wants her to think about something else, he tells her it's all part of a game. Using empty cola bottles, he plays music for her and hopes that will make her forget everything. Most of the days, they pretend to be royalty on a ship and they have to look for pirates. That forces her to look away from the sick people. They talk about dreams and about how they are going to bathe in water when they arrive at the coast.

"There will be so much food we'll all get fat," he says.

"Also ice cream?"

"Especially ice cream, your majesty. We won't eat anything else for weeks. We'll get so fat we'll have to roll everywhere," he says, putting air in his cheeks to look fat, then trying to roll around on the deck.

Long giggles.

"No one will even be able to carry us, so fat will we be," she says, laughing her light childish laughter. The sound is like medicine for Danh's tormented soul. He has lost count of the days, but knows it has been more than two weeks so far since they left the harbor. He is sick of the ocean and longs to see land again, to feel steadfast land under his feet. But, most of all, he wants to be able to drink as much water as he can. Drinking only sodas makes him want to throw up. Once he sets his feet on solid ground again, he'll never touch a soda again. Especially not a cola.

But no matter how much Danh tries to make Long forget about the starving people at the bottom of the boat, it is no use. Every day, the smell coming from down there gets worse; the sick get worse and they all wonder how many are already dead.

Without anyone noticing it, Long rations her own portion of rice for days in a row and saves up, hiding it in the pocket of her dress. After a week, when Danh isn't looking, when he is dozing off for one unforgettable second, Long grabs the rice and walks down the ladder to the bottom, where she feeds a boy and his mother.

Danh doesn't realize what is going on until someone from the deck starts to yell at her. He opens his eyes just in time to watch Bao go after her and pull her crying and screaming up on the deck.

"Don't ever go down there again! You hear me?" He has placed his face close to hers and Danh can tell he is hurting her arm. "Never again! These people are sick. The captain won't hesitate to throw you overboard if you get sick too!"

49

April 2016

I can't believe what is happening around me. Such a peaceful rally, suddenly turned into an inferno of screaming people running like a mad shooter was after them. To be fair, I think most of them think that is what happened, but still. The panic is overwhelming. Kids are crying and mothers rushing them away to their cars.

Meanwhile, I am running to the scene to see what happened. I approach the area that is heavily surrounded by police and paramedics.

I can see someone lying on the ground. I see blood on the car and lots of people kneeling beside the woman who was hit by the car that accidentally ran through the police blockade.

I manage to get a step closer when I realize I know who it is.

It's that woman that I photographed earlier. What was her name again? Nicky! Nicky Stover! Oh, my God!

I spot detective Fisher among the officers and elbow my way forward. He nods and approaches me.

"You can't get through, Mary," he says and stops me.

"Where is her daughter?" I ask.

"You know this woman?"

"Not very well. But I do know her name is Nicky and that she has a daughter, Paige. Who is taking care of her?"

"Right now, we're just trying to keep her alive," he says. "The car crashed straight into her."

"Oh, my God. Do you have the driver in custody?"

"Yes. She says she didn't see anything. I mean, how hard could it be to see a police blockade and three officers guarding it?"

"Drunk driver?" I ask, while my heart pounds in my chest.

Where is Paige while her mother is fighting for her life? I sure hope someone is taking care of her.

"We don't know yet. She's been taken to the station. Says she mistook the gas pedal for the brake. Tourist in a rental car."

"Oh, my."

One of the paramedics yells something and Chris disappears. He comes back towards me just as I am about to leave.

"You said you knew the daughter, right?"

"Yes," I say. "Well I don't know her. I know who she is."

"The mother is asking for her. She doesn't know where she is. Could you make sure she gets to the hospital?"

I nod. "Sure thing."

Chris nods, blinks, and points his finger at me and pretends it's a gun.

He's such a cliché.

"What's going on?" The sound of the voice coming from behind me makes me turn around with a gasp.

"Tom? What are you doing here?" I ask and hug him.

"I was down at the rec center when I heard something was going on downtown. Someone said people had been killed. What happened? What's going on? Is that Nicky Stover?"

"Yes," I say. "Someone ran into her. A tourist ran their car through the police blockade. You know her?"

"I know her daughter. She plays on my team."

I grab his collar. "Then you have to help me find her."

50

April 2016

I HAVE no idea where to start. With Tom next to me, I walk back onto Minutemen Causeway, which is now slowly getting emptied of people. I see many mothers dragging their kids away, but no Paige, no little girl all alone. We search the parking lot behind city hall where most people are getting inside their cars. We ask a few people if they have seen her, and one of them tells us she believes she saw Paige down by the high school, but she is not sure. We decide to walk in that direction.

"Who was she with?" Tom asks.

"She was walking with three other girls, also sixth graders from Roosevelt last time I saw her. They were all up front. Her mother was walking further in the back with other moms. I can't believe it… I am in shock."

I feel his hand on my shoulder to calm me down. "First, we find Paige. Then we freak out, all right?"

"Gosh, I am glad you're here with me," I say. "I would have completely freaked out by now. Thanks."

He smiles. He is not the handsomest of men, but he is slowly growing on me. I am beginning to see a beauty in his eyes that I hadn't seen before.

"Do you think she might have gone with those girls when all the panic started? Or maybe with some of their parents?" he asks. "Maybe one of the other moms took her home when they heard what happened?"

"Would you do that?" I ask, knowing he has adult children.

"No. Of course not," he says. "I would take her to the hospital so she could be with her mother."

"So, what if you don't know what happened?" I ask, my eyes

steadily searching, scrutinizing the area for any young girls. The few I spot are not Paige. We keep walking down Minutemen to see if maybe some are waiting down by the school or maybe they continued all the way to the country club, maybe a group of people up front didn't hear what happened and just continued the walk?

"I would still try and get a hold of the girl's mother somehow. Call her or look for her."

"Did they have cell phones when your kids were young?" I ask with a grin.

"Very funny. I'm old, ha, ha," he says.

"Sorry. It was just too tempting," I say.

We meet some people walking the opposite way and I stop a man. "Do you know if there are any more people down that way?" I ask him. "We're looking for a young girl around eleven-twelve years old."

He shrugs. "There might be. We made it almost all the way down there before we heard what happened and decided to walk back. Terrible thing."

"All right," I say. "We'll keep walking. Thank you."

"You're welcome."

We pass the elementary school, then the high school, and meet a few people walking back, dragging their signs behind them. Somehow, the fish-kill doesn't seem all that important anymore.

I think about Nicky Stover and wonder if she'll survive being hit by that car. I get a chill, wondering how Paige will react to being told what happened, when her world will crumble. I realize I might have to be the one to tell her and I am not looking forward to that.

"It's going to be fine," he says, and puts an arm around me. I like how much he is paying attention to how I feel. Being in a new relationship is great.

"I know," I say. "I just wish we would find her, you know? She needs to know what happened to her mom."

51

April 2016

It's NOT until we reach the country club at the end of Minutemen Causeway that I realize something is very wrong. There is hardly anyone there, a few women are packing picnic tables back into a van and removing signs. When we ask them if they have seen four young girls and show them a picture of Paige, they shake their heads.

Now I am seriously worried.

"She's not here either. What do we do?" I ask, my voice shaking.

Tom is biting his lip. "Could she have gone to the rec center? She is, after all, supposed to play in the game in a couple of hours."

"But certainly she has heard about her mother by now?" I ask, while we walk back towards city hall. "Someone must have told her."

"Maybe she went with some of her friends," Tom says. "Let's not panic here. They probably walked to the rec center…all of them together."

I grab my cell phone and look at the display. My son is in fourth grade. I wonder who I know that might know the number of some of the sixth graders or their parents. I think of Marcia. Her daughter Rose is twelve. She's in sixth grade. I call her up.

"Hi Mary. What's up?" she says on the other end.

"Do you know Paige Stover?" I ask.

"Sure. She's in Rose's class, why?"

"Do you know if Paige has a cell phone? It's important."

"I'll ask Rose. What's going on, Mary? Your voice sounds so shaky it's scaring me."

"Sorry. There was an accident at the rally. Paige's mom was hit by a car. I promised her that I would find Paige and help her get to the hospital."

"Oh, my. I'll ask Rose. One sec."

Marcia disappears for a few seconds, then returns. "She just got a cell phone, according to Rose. I have the number. I'll text it to you so you don't have to write it down. Okay?"

"Perfect," I say, and hang up.

Tom looks me in the eyes and plants both his hands on my shoulders. "I'm sure Paige is fine. I'm sure she already knows what happened and is at the hospital with her mother. You're probably getting yourself all worked up over nothing."

I nod as the phone in my hand vibrates and the number appears on my screen. I press it and wait for the tone.

"Hi…this is Paige Stover…"

"It goes directly to voicemail," I say. "I'll leave a message, just in case…Hi, this is Mary Mills. If you already know this, then you don't have to listen to it, but I just want to make sure that you know that your mother has been taken to the hospital, after a car hit her at the rally. I have been looking for you and can't find you anywhere, so if you hear this message, please be kind and shoot me a text or call me back so I know that you've gotten it. Okay. Thank you."

I hang up. We walk in silence back past the high school, the elementary school, and past the place of the accident, where the police are still working the scene. The paramedics are all gone and so is the ambulance. I feel terrible when we walk past it. Detective Fisher catches up to us.

"Mary! Did you find the daughter?" he asks.

I shake my head. "I checked the parking lot behind city hall. We walked all the way to the end. No one there had seen her. I left a message on her cell phone. I take it you haven't seen her either then? I was hoping…"

"No! She isn't at the hospital either. Her mother has been asking for her excessively."

My heart drops. I can't believe this. "She's not at the hospital either? But…but where is she then? Could she have gone home with someone?" I ask.

"Or maybe she's at the rec center," Tom repeats. "She does have a game there later today."

"I think I'll send a patrol out to look for her."

"Check the rec center," I say. "Or her friends. She was walking with three other girls from her school last time she was seen."

Fisher nods and puts a phone to his ear. "Got it," he says. "We'll find her. Don't worry. She can't have gone far."

52

April 2016

"How COULD you have messed this up?"

Boxer is yelling at his brother. They're back at the house; Paige is sedated and they put her in the dog crate in the back. She won't wake up for hours.

"I am sorry," his brother says. "I looked everywhere like you told me. I saw them, and followed them. I found the women she was walking with, and then I saw her, but then the car went through that blockade and I lost sight of her. Everything was so chaotic. Everyone was screaming and running around. I searched and searched, but then all the police came running towards us and I had to get out of there. You told me to wait for the gunshot, but there wasn't any. Only the car and then the panic. I did my best, Boxer, I really did. You must believe me."

"The order specifically was for both mother and child. Not just the girl. Her mother as well. I can't deliver her now. I can't deliver half a package. If I can't deliver, we won't get paid. I can't pay for mom's treatment or pay off your debt. Do you understand what I'm saying? This was a big deal. This was supposed to bring in a lot of money."

"I am sorry," he repeats, but it's not enough for Boxer. He doesn't tolerate failure. It's simply not acceptable.

Boxer sits down and runs a hand through his hair. He closes his eyes and thinks of something calming. It usually helps him. But he can't seem to calm his thoughts down. Behind closed eyelids all he can see are images of war. People running for their lives. Him as just a young kid in his twenties, armed with a machine gun, pointing it at a child wearing a vest packed with explosives and a detonator in her hand.

"What do I do?" he hears himself yelling to his commander in charge.

"Shoot! Damn it! Shoot her before she detonates the thing and blows us all to pieces!"

"But she's just a kid!"

"Don't trust her. Don't even trust a kid. It's her or us, soldier. They train them for this shit. Shoot her. It's an order."

And then it happens. Boxer hesitates just long enough for the kid to lift her grip on the detonator and explode herself to pieces, taking Boxer's best friend who was standing closer than Boxer, to the grave with her.

Don't even trust a kid.

Boxer is pulled out from this memory by his brother speaking. "I can't believe I messed up so bad. I am so sorry. So, what do you want to do next?"

Boxer opens his eyes and looks at his brother. His beloved brother who has saved his life more than once, before he became a wreck, before the drinking, before the gambling.

"It's okay," he says, when he suddenly notices Paige's cell phone that he has taken from her vibrating in the basket on the table, where he places all their phones when he takes them.

He walks up and sees she has a voicemail. He presses the button and listens to the message. As he hears the words meant for her, he feels the rage once again expanding inside of him so fast it feels like he is going to burst.

When the message is over, Boxer throws the phone against the wall. The screen cracks and the phone falls to the ground. He grabs all the phones in the basket and throws them in the trash can.

"What?" his brother asks. "What is it?"

"Her mother is in the hospital. That's why you couldn't find her," he says. "It turns out she was actually the one who was hit by the car. If she's in the hospital, it'll be hard for us to get to her."

"Uh-oh, so what do we do now?"

Boxer sits down heavily on the couch. "I don't know," he says. "I have to think. I have to come up with something. And quick."

53

April 1975

A FEW DAYS LATER, Long loses her appetite. She simply stops eating, and no matter how hard Danh tries to stuff rice and cola into her, she refuses. Soon, she grows weak and small and is burning up.

Danh sits with her in his arms all day and all night, trying to hide her from people, and especially from the captain. Every now and then he tries to wake her up; tears rolling across his face, he asks her if she wants to play princesses and pirates again.

"If you don't wake up, the monster will take you, the sea monster will come for you and drag you away to the cave under-water where it keeps all its princesses, you know that, Long. You must wake up, your majesty. Please, wake up," Danh pleads, tears rolling rapidly from his eyes.

After two days, Bao starts to notice something is wrong. He stares at Danh, holding Long.

"Put her down," he says.

Danh shakes his head defiantly. "No."

"Yes, Danh. Put her down. People are starting to talk."

Danh looks at Long's small and fragile face. Her skin is so pale, her eyes are closed, and small droplets of sweat make her forehead shiny.

"No. I can't. She's sleeping," he says. His heart is hurting. He keeps hoping, telling himself repeatedly that she's not sick, she's just tired, so very tired and feeble from the long trip.

If only she would eat or drink something. If just I could get her to drink some cola.

Bao approaches them, he reaches down and touches her head. The look in his eyes terrifies Danh to the core.

"She's burning up," he says with a loud whisper. "She's sick,

Danh. She's very sick."

He shakes his head. He doesn't want to believe it, he refuses to. Not his Long. He has seen what happens to those down in the bottom of the boat. They wither and then when they start to smell, they're thrown overboard. They have even thrown some overboard that weren't even dead yet. To stop this disease from spreading, they have to do it as prevention. No one has been sick on the deck yet. Not until now. There is no telling how they'll react.

"No. No. She's just resting," Danh says, and pulls her away from Bao.

He covers her face with part of his jacket that he wrapped her in when she first said she was freezing. At first, he couldn't stand how she was trembling, but now he misses it. The feeling of holding a lifeless body in his arms fills him with despair.

"What's going on over here?"

"Look what you did," Danh hisses. "You woke their suspicion."

A man who has been staring at them for days finally leaves and walks to the captain. Seconds later, the captain stands in front of them flanked by two men, his gold chain necklace dangling in front of Danh's face as he bends down.

"She sick?" he asks. "They tell me she has the disease."

Danh shakes his head rapidly. "No. No. She's just tired, that's all. Weak from not getting enough food and water. She can't eat the rice, she says, tastes terrible when cooked in cola."

"Let me look at her," the captain says. "Move the jacket so I can see her face."

Danh is sweating. He is shaking in fear as he pulls back the jacket and her face is visible. The captain pulls back with a startled look. He doesn't speak; he walks backwards a few more steps, turns around, and walks away.

Still shaking, Danh pulls the jacket back to cover her face. Long is still so pretty, so delicate. Bao sinks down next to him on the deck, simply whimpering in fear till the captain returns.

"You have to go," he says. "She's too great of a risk."

"NO!" Bao says and jumps up. "You can't do that. You can't do that to us."

The captain shakes his head. "People are getting scared. She'll infect us all and then we'll be dead too. You have to go. All of you. You have all been exposed to it now. We have a small boat. It has oars. You can row."

"But...but...we'll die!"

"This is a good offer," the captain says. "Everyone else around here wanted to just throw you all overboard, but I give you this boat. You take it. It's a good offer. Boat or no boat, you're going in the water."

54

April 2016

I SAY GOODBYE TO TOM, who needs to be back at the basketball tournament. I go home, and feed my dad some very late lunch, still with a worried and heavy heart. I had been right in my hunch that something bad was going to happen, I just didn't know that it would be this.

After lunch, I call up Salter. I miss hearing his voice.

"Hi, Mom, what up?"

What up? Is that how we speak now?

I decide to ignore it. "I just wanted to hear your voice. How are you?"

"I'm good."

"Did you hear about what happened at the rally today?"

"Yeah, Cayden texted me. He was there with his dad. Some tourist ran into the crowd?"

"Yes. Crazy thing. A woman was hit and is in the hospital now. She has a daughter, Paige Stover, you know her?"

"I know who she is. She's in sixth grade at my school. Plays basketball."

"Yes, that's her. I feel so bad for her."

"Me too."

I hear softness in Salter's voice again. It makes me happy. He's usually such a sweet boy. I don't like when his heart hardens into a rock like it's started doing recently, especially when talking to me.

I think about Danny and the daughter he never got to know and now maybe never will, since we can't find her. I can't stop thinking about all the single moms and their daughters that have gone missing over the past few years. Where did they go? Have they simply moved?

"Was there anything else you wanted, Mom?" Salter asks. "'Cause Dad, Jackie, and I are going fishing today."

"Not in the lagoon, are you?"

He scoffs. "No, of course not. It's filled with dead fish. Dad has borrowed a boat and we're going out on the ocean. We're leaving from Cape Canaveral."

"Wow. That sounds really great, buddy. Say, you do know not to ever go with anyone you don't know, right?"

He sighs provocatively. "Mom."

"I'm just a little worried, that's all. You do know not to trust anyone you don't know, right? You know Stranger Danger and all that, right?"

"Mom. I am not a moron."

"I'm not saying you are; I just want to make sure you realize that there are people out there who steal kids."

Okay, now you're just terrifying the kid!

"I mean, there are bad guys in this world who might…"

"Mom!" Salter says harshly. "I know these things."

I can hear Joey's voice in the background, and soon Salter disappears and Joey is there.

"Stop babying him," he says. "You gotta stop it. You are so freaking controlling. Geez."

"I am not trying to baby him. I just want to make sure everything is alright," I say. "I have the right to worry about my son."

"Why wouldn't everything be all right? Huh? Because you don't trust me, that's why. Because you don't trust anyone with your child. No one can do as good a job as you, right? Well, guess what? We're doing pretty good around here without you."

Ouch!

An awkward pause follows, where I try to gather myself. "I'll stop by with some clean clothes later today," I finally say, holding back tears.

"No need to," he says. "Jackie bought him lots of new clothes; they went to the mall this morning."

"The mall? But Salter hates the mall."

"Well, not any more. He loved it with Jackie," Joey says.

He loved it with Jackie? What's going on here?

"So, what you're basically telling me is you don't need me at all, is that it?"

"Don't start that," he says. "They're bonding. Salter and Jackie are. It's a good thing. Don't make this about you."

"But it is about me. It's all about you replacing me, leaving me out of my own damn family!" I yell.

I hear a click when Joey hangs up. I groan and throw the phone down, then I pick up a pillow, place it in front of my face, and scream into it.

55

April 2016

I SPEND the rest of the afternoon working on my article, but I can't really focus on it properly. I keep writing things, then deleting them. I drink loads of coffee and stuff myself with chocolate bars, and as the day passes, I even dive into the ice cream. Ben and Jerry's, Brownie Batter. That's when you know you're in trouble, that things are really bad.

I try hard not to feel sorry for myself as I get into the story, researching online all the many theories about the fish-kill, and try to find an angle that all the newspapers haven't already covered. I know my audience is different from theirs; they're spread all over the world, so they might not have heard about the fish-kill, but I still need to add something to the story that no one has heard before, and so far I don't have anything.

Just before six, the doorbell rings, and I walk over to open it. Outside is Detective Fisher. He isn't wearing his usual smirk. It frightens me.

"Chris?"

He runs a hand through his hair several times in a row. I can tell he has been doing that a lot today, since his hair is slightly greasy.

"We haven't found her," he says.

My heart drops. "You're kidding me, right?"

He looks surprised. "Why would I kid about something like that?"

I shake my head. That was a stupid thing to say. "No. Of course not. It's no joke. She wasn't at the rec center?"

"Never showed up for the game. I had a man there all afternoon to wait and see if she did show up, while we contacted everyone that knows the family. I've spoken to all the parents from the sixth grade;

142

no one has seen her since the rally this morning, since before the accident."

"You're scaring me," I say.

"Well, you should be. We all should be. I mean…what if something happened? I can't bear to think about if…"

"Let's not get ahead of ourselves, Detective," I say. "How's the mother, how's Nicky Stover?"

He draws in a deep breath and calms down. "Better. Lots of broken bones and temporary memory loss, doctor says. Many months of recovery in front of her, but she'll live."

"That's a relief," I say.

"Yeah. But imagine if her daughter doesn't show up after this. It's almost too cruel to bear, you know what I mean?"

"I know. I'm sure you'll find her," I say, but I know I don't sound very convincing.

"We have to find her before it gets dark, so we're walking door to door now through the entire community, asking if anyone has seen her, and we're having a big search of the entire Minutemen area. We only have one dog to help us, but it's better than nothing. We're starting here at six o'clock. We're asking the public for help, asking all who can to join us look for her. So, if you can?"

"Of course," I say. "I'll be right there. Just let me feed my dad first."

"Sure. Bring flashlights and maybe that dog of yours. We need all the help we can get."

I look at Snowflake behind me. He is wagging his tail trying to get out to the detective and talk to him. But I am holding him back. He has a tendency to jump people when he gets excited.

"Of course. No problem."

"See you down there."

56

April 2016

BOXER IS out of his mind with anger and frustration. He tries not to think about it as he joins a group of people outside of city hall. They have all showed up to search for Paige Stover. A policeman came to his door earlier and asked for his help. Of course, Boxer will take part in the search. They need all the eyes and hands they can get.

An officer holds a picture up of Paige and others are showing copies to people and asking them to look at them closely.

"Paige Stover was last seen at the rally this morning. She was seen here, in front of city hall, where this picture was taken with her mother, then later way down Minutemen just before the school, where she was walking with three of her girlfriends. No one has seen her since the chaos erupted. Her mother was hit by a car and we suspect she might have seen or known about it, then run off in shock. We need people to look everywhere. In all the bushes, in the dunes at the beach, under and inside boats, in the canals, anywhere she could be hiding in case she got scared or something. She might not even know about her mother being hit by the car; maybe she was just scared by the panic, who knows? We're asking you to be careful in approaching her. If she is in shock, she might be really afraid. Should you find her, get ahold of a police officer or call 911. We'll get someone out there to help you. I want to thank everyone for coming out to help us. Now, let's find Paige!"

Boxer is handed a picture of Paige and he starts to walk along with the group. He follows them towards Minutemen where the group is split. Some walk towards the beach area while others walk towards Minutemen Causeway and the schools. He greets a couple he knows from his street.

"This is awful," the woman says.

"I know. Poor girl," Boxer says. "I just hope she's all right."

"Yes. So do we. And her poor mother too. Being hit by a car and now this? Now her daughter is missing? Can you imagine?"

Boxer shakes his head in sympathy. "I really can't."

"Well, I'm just glad so many people showed up to help with the search," the woman continues. "I remember last year when Olson's little boy ran away from home. He was found hiding under a boat, apparently too frightened to bring home his report card to his dad. Poor thing. His dad is a police officer. Nice man, but a little harsh on the kid, I can imagine. What do you say, Clark?" she says, addressed to her husband, but he doesn't answer.

As they reach Minutemen, a group of them grab each other's hands and they shape a long line. Boxer looks at the lady next to him. She is holding a dog as well, a white Goldendoodle that seems to be very excited.

Boxer looks at her hand as she reaches it out to him. He has seen her on Facebook. This is the lady that took the pictures of Paige during the rally, the ones that led him straight to her when he couldn't find her.

"It's okay. I can hold both you and the dog," she says. "This is Snowflake, by the way."

Boxer smiles. "Well, hello there, Snowflake," he says. Enjoying the attention, the dog jumps him.

"Snowflake!" The woman says and pulls the dog down. "I'm sorry. He's just very excited about people. If he spots Paige Stover in the bushes, he'll run straight to her, is my theory."

"That's nice," Boxer says.

"Shall we?" the woman says and reaches out her hand again. Boxer grabs it in his. They walk through the street and comb through all of the parking lots. Some look in the bushes along the street, others under cars and in yards in front of the houses. Walking hand in hand, they comb through the entire area until they reach the school. Some are calling her name, others worrying more quietly.

"It's nice when the community comes together like this, don't you think?" the woman asks. "It's good to know that they have your back, right? I mean, you never know when you'll need other people's help, right? It feels good to know that you're not alone around here."

Boxer nods, his eyes avoiding hers. "It sure does. It sure does."

57

April 2016

THIS IS AWFUL. This is so painful I can barely stand it!

I imagine the most terrible things happening to poor Paige Stover. I try not to think about it while walking with the search group around the area of the school, but it is hard not to. I can't stop thinking about Paige's mother and how terrible she must feel.

Luckily, I know Salter is with his dad on that fishing boat. They're probably coming in by now, driving home for dinner or grabbing a burger on the way back, I imagine.

I'll have to call him again to make sure he is all right when all this is over. They can get mad all they want at me; I am a mother, and I have the right to worry.

I am walking with the group, holding hands with Danny on one side, and a man I don't know on the other. I remember seeing him before, but I don't think I have ever spoken to him. He seems very shy. Shy people make me insecure, and I have a tendency to blabber like a crazy woman when I get insecure and when I am with people that don't say much. They scare me a little because you never know where you stand with them, you never know what they think or feel about anything.

By the time we have circled the entire school area, I think I have told him my entire life story. I have even made a few jokes that were completely inappropriate for this situation. I feel embarrassed by myself and bite my tongue to shut up.

But when I do, there is one thought that I can't escape, one thought that keeps popping into my mind, and I don't want to think it.

What if Paige has been kidnapped? What if her disappearance is somehow related to all the other disappearances?

It was, after all, supposed to happen today, according to the pattern.

You can't think like that.

I shake my head and focus on the task at hand. In the distance, the sun is starting to set, and for once, I wish I could stop it or slow it down a little, just for a few hours so we have more time. It is heart-breaking to know that somewhere out there Paige might be sitting, all afraid and scared and out of it. What if she has to spend the night without being found? What if she is stuck somewhere and can't get up? What if she is hurt so badly she can't move?

What if she has been kidnapped?

Danny, on my left side, is very quiet as we walk towards the high school to go through the area behind it. I have a feeling I know what he is thinking about, but of course—nosy as I am—I have to ask.

"You thinking about Tara?" I ask.

I keep my voice low so no one else can hear us, except maybe the guy to my right, but I am guessing he doesn't know Danny or me and has no idea what I am talking about.

Danny nods. He doesn't seem bothered by the question. At least not visibly. "How can I not?"

"I know. I can't stop thinking about it too. All those women and children disappearing. I can't just ignore it. It can't be just a coincidence. I don't think I believe that anymore."

"I never believed that. Not since I found out about them. Something happened to Tara and Maria. Something bad. I just know it."

"Let me ask you something," I say, still keeping my voice low. "Were you in love with Maria?"

Danny looks at me shortly, then turns his head away.

"I think you were," I say, "That's why you could never visit. You couldn't bear the fact that the woman you loved and your child, the family you couldn't be with, was right there. And you couldn't be with them no matter how badly you wanted to. Why the heck didn't you just divorce Jean?"

"In retrospect, that's what I should have done," Danny says. "I see that now. I thought about it every day. But I guess I was too much of a chicken. This was the easy way out. Maria and Tara never expected anything from me. Junior and Jean did. They were the ones who would have been most heartbroken and disappointed with me if I told them."

"So, you chose your own heartbreak over your son's and wife's? Wow. Quite the sacrifice, I think."

"Or maybe I was just a chicken," he says.

"Did you tell Junior yet?"

Danny nods.

"How did he react?" I ask. I notice there is a commotion by the canals on the other side of the road where another group is searching. I look in their direction, but can't seem to figure out what is going on. People seem upset and focused on the area over there. Some are running towards them.

"Well, he's not here with us today," Danny says, "even though I asked him politely to be, and he hasn't wanted to have anything to do with me since I told him. He refuses to even talk to me, so how do you think he took it?"

"That bad, huh?"

"Worse," Danny says with a sigh. "Seems like I am just losing everyone these days. Say. What's going on over there?"

"We found something!" a voice yells.

I look at Danny. "They found something in the canal!"

Hearts pumping, we start to run towards the group that has gathered in a place where the bushes are low and the canal very visible.

Please let her be alive. Please let her be alive.

A man crawls down; everyone waits with tension and worry until he pokes his head up. He looks terrified.

"It's a body," he says. "Help me pull it out of the water."

The men all step up. I watch while the body of a young girl is pulled out of the water and put on the grass. I walk closer and look at her pale face. Danny feels her neck for a pulse, then looks up at all of us and shakes his head.

"She's dead."

A gasp runs through the crowd.

"Is it her?" someone asks. "Is it Paige?"

I turn and look at them, then shake my head. "No. That's not Paige Stover."

"This one has been in the water for a long time," Danny says, examining her arms and neck.

"There are more," the man who spotted the body suddenly says, terror in his voice. "I see an arm sticking out between the dead fish over there! Oh, my God, the river is filled with dead bodies!"

Part III

HERE I COME

58

April 2016

He takes off his shoes as he walks across the tiles to not make a sound. He knew his sister would forget to lock at least one of the sliding doors to the beach. She never was very careful.

Blake walks across the tiles in the living room. It's the middle of the night. He walks by the light of his flashlight. He waited outside the house till it grew dark; it felt like it took forever for Mary to get to bed. It was way past midnight before she turned her light out, the last one in the house. He then waited an hour to make sure she was completely away in dreamland.

He stops and looks at the pictures hung by the stairs. Lots of them of Salter and Mary, the stupid dog, and even of dear old daddy, taken both before and after he was paralyzed.

But none of Blake.

He walks closer to one of Mary with her surfboard. It is from back when she was a lot younger. Blake remembers the picture. He doesn't remember the day she got that board. It was shortly after their mother had been shot. He was no more than a baby. But the picture has been staring at him from his father's desk for all of his childhood. Now, looking at it again, makes the rage come right back up in him. All the times he was called to his father's office only to be yelled at or told he was useless, meanwhile resting his eyes on that exact picture of his sister who could do nothing wrong.

"Why can't you just be a little more like your sister?" He can still hear his father going at him. On and on and on again. All through his childhood. It came to a point where Blake would know the exact words that would come out of his father's mouth. He would mimic them as they flew across his lips.

"Your sister would never have done that!" or his favorite: "You could learn a lot from your sister, young man."

Blake scoffs and walks up the stairs. He stands still by the door to Mary's room and listens, then opens it slowly and walks inside. Snowflake jumps down from her bed and runs to him wagging his tail, the crazy animal. He pets it gently and hushes it when it whimpers because it is so excited to see him.

Stupid dog.

Blake feels the knife in his pocket with his hand as he walks closer to his sister. She has not gotten smaller. Her plump body is lying heavily on the bed, half covered by her sheet. It's hot tonight and their dad has always been cheap with the AC, especially at night. Blake is guessing nothing has changed on that front.

Mary is snoring lightly, lying on her back, facing him as he leans in over her. She grunts something in her sleep. Blake looks at her fat neck and wonders how much strength he'll need to strangle her.

Mary's sleep is restless and she starts to toss and turn. By her whines and grunts, he senses she is tormented, dreaming heavily.

"What are you dreaming about, dear sister?" He whispers close to her face. "Did I bother you with my little trick destroying your blog? Are you having a nightmare? Well, you ain't seen nothing yet. I'm just getting started. I'm going to make your life as miserable as you did mine."

Blake is overwhelmed by the feeling of great power he possesses in this exact moment. He fights the urge to kill her right here and now. It's been awhile since his last kill. The sensation, the longing, the desire is back. Big time. But he can't. No, not yet.

Blake walks backwards and pets Snowflake on the top of the head before he leaves the room, a chill still running down his spine.

He hurries down the stairs and finds his dad's room, then enters. The old man is heavily asleep as well. Furor wells up in him as he approaches him. All the anger, all the frustration of never being good enough, engulfs him, and he clenches one of his hands into a fist, then holds on tight to the knife with the other.

Blake's body is trembling with anger; he bites his lips as he leans over his father's lifeless body, then whispers.

"I'm coming for you, Daddy dear. I'm coming for all of you. I'll take care of you last."

59

April 1975

It's dark in the water. The small boat is being thrown around between the waves. It feels like the waves are playing with them, Danh thinks.

Like a lion plays with its prey before devouring it. Toying with them to wear them out, before the fatal strike is set in.

Danh holds on to his sister, who seems to grow even smaller by the hour now. She doesn't make a sound and barely breathes. Bao sits by the oars and rows, using up all his strength. Danh has no idea how long it has been since they were left there and they watched the fishing boat sail away. Six-seven hours? Maybe. It is nighttime now and they have no idea what direction they're going in, where land is. So far, they have just tried to keep in the same direction as they saw the fishing boat go, but they have been tossed and turned so much by the waves, they could have been going in circles without even noticing it.

"It's no use," Bao says, and puts the oars down.

Danh wonders if he is angry with them for putting him in this situation. Danh is shivering in fear and wants badly to cry, but has no more tears. He is terrified for Long and worries that she'll die. Her fragile body seems so lifeless in his arms.

"Please, don't leave me, your majesty," he whispers in the darkness, while Bao lays down to rest. The ocean seems to calm down a little, even though they're still being thrown around and water keeps coming into the small rowboat.

Danh wonders how long they will be able to keep the water out and how long they will be able to survive without anything to drink. They haven't had much for weeks as it is, and now they're completely without anything. Danh sobs tearless cries while smoothing his hand over her head.

"Please. I promised Mother I would take care of you. I made a promise! I can't go on without you, princess. Don't leave me."

Somehow, Danh manages to doze off way into the night, and when he wakes up, his mouth is dry and nasty, and the sun is right in his face. His skin is burning. The ocean is calm now. The first thing he sees is Bao. He is still sleeping. Half of his body is sunken into water in the bottom of the boat. Danh blinks a few times, then remembers where they are, and looks down.

"Long," he says.

She is in his lap, still wrapped in his jacket. There is no color in her face, her lips are cracked, her eyes still closed. Terrified, he leans over her small body and listens. He can't hear anything. Is she dead?

Please, don't be dead!

"Your majesty?"

Finally, she draws in a small breath. Danh leans back with a sigh of relief. Long is still alive. Bao wakes up, but barely has the strength to lift his head, let alone his body. He blinks a few times and licks his lips, but it doesn't help. Danh knows how it feels.

"We're going to die out here, aren't we?" Bao asks.

Danh shakes his head, but it barely moves. "No," he whispers. "I promised Long she would get ice cream."

Bao tries to laugh, but only a strange wheezing sound comes out of his throat. He leans his head down and closes his eyes again. Danh wants to sleep as well. He is so tired, and as hope oozes out of him, so does his will to survive.

You gotta stay awake. For Long. You gotta take care of Long!

Danh forces himself to open his eyes. They soon become heavy again and close. He has no idea for how long, but when he opens them again, he sees something. At first he believes it is a part of his dream, or an illusion of some sort. It can't be real. It simply can't.

Yet, it is still there even after he blinks.

He parts his dry lips and tries to point. "Boat," he whispers, but no one can hear it. He tries to speak again, but no sound leaves his lips, and soon he can't hold his eyelids open anymore. Seconds later, the darkness swallows him completely.

60

April 2016

I HAVE the worst nightmare and wake up screaming. It's still dark outside. I sit up in my bed. I feel thirsty and walk out of my room, Snowflake running right behind me, wagging his tail because he thinks it's time to get up.

On the way down the stairs, I think about Paige and how she still hasn't been found. I wonder where she is and if she is scared. I also think about the two bodies they ended up pulling out of the canal.

Who were they?

The police had quickly arrived and blocked the area off so we couldn't see much, and soon I went home, tired and depressed because we hadn't found Paige, and slightly scared because of the bodies. It took me many hours to calm down and be able to sleep, and when I finally did, I had the strangest dream about my brother Blake.

I turn on the light in the kitchen and grab a glass that I fill with water. I feel hungry and open the refrigerator. I grab the leftovers of the stew I had made for my dad and me before I went to do the search. I never got to eat much of it, but I can do that now.

I eat out of the pan and don't even bother to heat it first. It tastes great even cold. Then I move on to the more comforting stuff. I pull out a bucket of Mint chocolate ice cream from Fat Donkey, the ice-cream place off Minutemen. It's the best ice cream in the world and I save it for when I feel especially down. I do now. Because I worry about Salter, because I worry about Paige Stover, and the disappeared women and children.

As I dig into the ice cream with my spoon, I hear a sound. It sounds like it is coming from my dad's room.

That's odd?

I put the ice cream back, then close the freezer. I walk towards my dad's room with my heart in my throat, Snowflake at my heels. Unfortunately, he is not much of a guard dog. He is even more easily scared than I am. During every thunderstorm, he creeps under my bed and shakes for hours afterwards.

I grab the door handle, turn it, and walk inside. My heart is pounding. My dad is still in his bed, on his back, snoring lightly, calmly. I relax my shoulders and walk closer to him.

That's when I notice the window is open and a vase has fallen down from the small table next to it. It isn't broken, but the flowers have fallen out, and the water has run out on the floor. I wipe it up and put the flowers back in, then look out the window before I close it.

Probably just forgot to shut it earlier today.

I feel like a fool, even though I can't remember opening it. I might have done it to give him some fresh air. I am too tired to remember.

My dad is lying peacefully, until he starts to move his fingers and hands excessively. I stare at them, remembering his physical therapist telling me this would happen, that he would experience spasms at night, in the parts where he has recently regained mobility. But then I see something that makes me tear up. His foot.

His right foot is moving too!

I gasp and pull the blanket off. I can't believe what I am seeing. My father's right foot is twitching and turning in small, almost rhythmical spasms.

"Oh, my God," I exclaim, tears streaming from my eyes. "You're actually moving your foot in your sleep, Dad."

Before I leave him, I grab my cell phone and start recording it. My hands are shaking and it is hard to hold the phone still. I can't stop crying and take several videos both of his hands and his foot.

Finally, I leave him and walk back into the hallway. On the way back towards the stairs, I pass the picture wall I have made of us of the few pictures I had left after my dad's house burnt down. Luckily, I had some copies among my things; otherwise, all my childhood pictures would have been lost.

I almost walk past it when I suddenly stop and walk a few steps backwards.

Something is different.

One of the frames is empty. The picture of me with my surfboard that I got when I was seventeen, is gone.

61

April 2016

I show my dad the video the next morning when we're eating breakfast. He too has tears in his eyes when he sees it.

"It's moving. It's really moving!"

I sniffle with joy and cut up some more fruit for him and help him get it on his fork. "I know. I can't believe it either. But there is definitely movement going on down there."

"I can't wait to tell Jack," he says.

"He'll be here tomorrow," I say. "I'll make sure he sees it."

My dad smiles widely. I know how badly he wants to walk again. For the first time, I have a real feeling that it is reachable, that he might be able to walk at some point again, even though I also know there is still a long way to go. Seeing how slow it has been with his fingers and hands, I know we need to brace ourselves with all the patience we can muster, but the hope is there. It is definitely there.

"I had the strangest dream last night," my dad says, after a few minutes of silence. He is chewing his fruit. I know he hates the fruit, but Jack has told him he needs to watch his weight. Being heavy makes it harder on his legs, should he ever get up on them again, since he has no muscles left in them. I am completely to blame for his weight gain, since I constantly feel so bad for him that I always make the best food. It is, after all, the only thing he can really enjoy these days, so why not get the best of the best?

Well, not anymore. I am eating the fruit with him, since I could lose a few pounds myself. Even though breakfast probably isn't my biggest problem.

"Oh, what was it about?" I ask.

"Blake," he says, his face turning very serious all of a sudden. "I dreamt about Blake."

"I dreamt about him too," I say. "What a weird coincidence."

My dad looks speculative. I try to shut my hunger up by eating a banana. I am more in the mood for pancakes, but this will have to do for now. I can't be eating pancakes in front of my poor father.

"That is odd. I woke up with the strangest feeling," he continues. My dad looks at me. "I think he's here."

"Blake? Bah. Nonsense. He and Olivia went to Naples, where he killed her. He's wanted all over the state of Florida. He's probably long gone. Out of the state. He's not stupid enough to come back here."

I help my dad get a strawberry in his mouth, while I think about the missing picture in the hallway and the open window. I shake the thought. Maybe Salter took the photo. Or it fell down or something.

My dad sighs. "I guess you're right. It is just so odd. I have this feeling that…that he is very close. It was like he spoke to me last night."

"You were just dreaming, Dad," I say. "Dreams can get so vivid sometimes."

He nods and I put a piece of watermelon on his fork. He misses his mouth and it splashes on his cheek instead.

"Ugh!" he exclaims. "I hate this! I want some real food!"

I nod. "You know what? So do I." I get up, walk to the kitchen, and open the refrigerator. I pull out bacon and a carton of eggs. "How does bacon and scrambled eggs sound?"

"Like heaven," he yells from his chair.

"Heaven it shall be. It is, after all, Sunday and the good Lord knows we deserve it," I say, and crack an egg and drop it into a bowl.

62

April 2016

We finish our meal and I finally feel full. My dad is also satisfied and asks me to take him out on the porch. He wants to listen to the ocean and feel the breeze on his face. After eating, that is his favorite thing to do.

I place him in the shade with a hat and sunglasses on and he sighs, satisfied, while watching the beachgoers fight with umbrellas. It's very windy today and the waves are completely blown out. A woman loses her hat and starts to run after it as it rolls across the sand.

"Thank you, sweetheart," he says, and takes in a deep breath of the fresh air. "Nothing beats this air."

"I know," I say. "It's the best place on earth."

I take Snowflake for a walk on the beach, thinking the local police force has enough going on today as it is, enough to not care if someone walks their dog on the warm sand.

I walk all the way to downtown and the restaurant, Coconuts on the Beach, where all the tourists lay almost on top of each other, then turn and walk back. When I return to the house, I find Detective Fisher waiting on the porch for me. He is engaged in a chat with my dad.

"Okay," I say, throwing out my arms. "You caught me. I was walking my dog on the beach. You can take me away now. But, I tell you this one thing, it was totally worth it. Please, just spare my dog. He has done nothing wrong."

"Quite the comedian," Fisher says, addressed to my dad.

"Always has been," he says. "Part of her charm."

Fisher chuckles.

"If you're not here to bust me and my dog, then why are you

here?" I ask, and let Snowflake back into the house. He runs to the water bowl and starts to drink, dragging a heavy load of sand with him inside.

"I thought we could chat," he said.

"Sure. What about?"

"Maybe we should do this inside?" he says, and nods at my dad.

"Don't mind him," I say. "I'll tell him everything after you leave anyway. He knows everything that goes on."

"I don't watch soaps," my dad says. "What I hear around here is so much better."

Fisher laughs lightly. He grabs a chair in the shade and sits down. "All right, then. But this can't leave the house, all right?"

"I can't even leave the house," my dad says.

"Anyone want some coffee?" I ask, mostly because I really need some after the night I had.

"It's too hot for coffee," my dad says.

"I can make it ice-coffee if you ask me nicely."

"Then, yes, please," Fisher says. "I would like that."

My dad nods in agreement and I walk inside to make it for all of us. I put straws in the cups and walk back out.

"Quite the view you have here," Fisher says, as I serve it to them. "I wonder how you ever get anything done around here."

I chuckle. "Who says I do? But I can't blame it on the view. Just a lot has been going on lately."

Fisher nods, pulls out a file, and places it on the table. "Yeah. That's what I wanted to talk to you about. Those bodies…that we pulled out of the canal…"

"What about them?" I ask.

"Well, you knew about them. It's two of your girls."

"What do you mean they're my girls?"

"The ones in your articles, remember? The ones you gave to me when we were drinking coffee."

I sink back in the chair. "Really? I mean, I can't say I didn't think the thought, but still. Which ones? Please tell me it isn't Tara and Maria; please say it's not them."

"It's not them."

"Phew." My heart drops. "Then who is it?"

63

April 2016

"KIM AND CASEY TAYLOR!"

Boxer yells at his brother, who sits on the couch in his living room, drinking vodka straight from the bottle. Boxer should know better than to yell at him, since it only makes him sick again, but he can't stop. Not since he saw the face of the girl they pulled out of the canal when searching for Paige Stover, has he been able to stay calm. He

recognized her right away as the girl he abducted from the mall one year ago, along with her mother.

Now they've turned up dead?

"Oh, my God," he says, as he walks back and forth. "They're going to come here, aren't they? They're going to get me for this even though I didn't kill them, aren't they?" he groans.

"Maybe they won't," his brother says and lights up a cigarette.

Boxer can't stand cigarette smoke, especially not in his house, but he also knows his brother is in a fragile mental stage right now, and if smoking helps him, then he'll have to endure it. Boxer stares at his brother as he smokes, holding the cigarette between his shaking hands, eyes closed, and he wonders what he thinks about, worries that he'll get sick again.

PTSD they told them it was once they came home from Afghanistan. They both have it, but his brother is worse than him. Boxer never understood why his brother got it worse than him, since they were both there when the bomb went off, when that little kid blew herself up.

Boxer's brother shouldn't be feeling as guilty as Boxer does. He wasn't the one who was supposed to have shot the kid; he wasn't the one who could have saved another man's life. Still, he suffered more mentally afterwards. He took it harder somehow. Boxer never understood why. Yes, Boxer was tormented by it every day and still sometimes at night as well, anguished by those small brown eyes staring at him from a face so innocent and harmless. But he has learned to live with it. Taking care of his family makes him forget. It helps him to push it back and not worry about it.

Why can't his brother do the same? He has to move on at some point, doesn't he? It's all about not thinking about it. Like with the girls. Don't get attached to them, don't like them, don't worry what happens to them after the delivery. It's not your problem. You don't have to care.

Boxer walks to the back of the house and opens the door. He kneels in front of the dog crate, where Paige looks back at him. She is still sobbing, her lips vibrating.

"Please, let me go home," she whispers.

Boxer stares at her, looks deep into her eyes, and when he does, all he sees is that kid, that little girl on that dusty road, staring at him softly like her eyes were asking him to like her, reeling him in, telling him not to shoot. And that was the reason someone had to die, that was why it all went wrong, because Boxer believed those eyes, because he allowed himself to hesitate for just one second.

It'll never happen again.

"Please. I want to go home. Why are you doing this to me? Why?"

Boxer remains motionless. He is not moved by her pleas. She is not important. She's nothing but a means to an end. And it's only fair to make these little girls pay for what Boxer and his family have had to go through, since he was a kid, just like her, that brought them into this situation in the first place. A kid, just like this young one with big brown innocent eyes just like these, destroyed everything.

"What are you going to do to me?" she asks, her voice shaking in fear. But he doesn't fall for it.

I don't owe you an answer. I don't owe you anything, you little monster!

64

April 1975

Danh hardly feels it when he is lifted up and taken aboard the ship. His eyes open a few times and he thinks it is just a dream, that he is floating in the air. Maybe he is dead? Maybe this is what it feels like?

He doesn't fully wake up till three days later, when someone presses a water bottle in between his lips and he feels like he is drowning.

When he opens his eyes, he realizes it is Long holding the bottle. She is smiling. She even has a sparkle in her eyes. She is still small and skinny, and he can see her collarbone sticking out above her shirt, but she's alive. She's alive and well.

How?

Bao is sitting next to him. When he hears him cough, he turns his head. "He's awake? Finally! That took you some time, brother. Even Long came around before you did."

Danh wipes his mouth and sits up straight, covering his eyes from the brightness of the burning sun above them. He grabs the bottle and drinks greedily. He drinks too fast and chokes, then coughs and spits some of it out on the deck.

"Don't spill it," Bao scolds. "They have given us water, but not so much we can just spill it."

"Sorry," Danh says. He leans his head back against the wall behind him. He is exhausted. "Where are we?"

"On another ship. A much bigger one," Bao says. "They found us drifting in the middle of the ocean and picked us up."

Danh looks around. He spots a man with a machine gun walking by. The man glances at them shortly and he smiles, showing off a couple of gold teeth before he continues his walk. He approaches another guy who looks just like him and who is also heavily armed.

"Who are these people? They're not Vietnamese," Danh asks.

"No. We don't know where they're from. We try not to ask questions. They picked us out of the ocean and had medicine for Long. Her fever is gone already. It's a true miracle."

Danh looks at his baby sister and his heart goes soft. Her eyes are back to their sweet selves, the most beautiful sight Danh could imagine seeing. Hearing her small voice is music to him, so soothing.

"Do we know where they're heading?" Danh asks Bao.

"They haven't spoken to us much," Bao says. "They just gave us water and medicine and some bread and rice to eat." Bao grabs some bread and hands it to Danh. "It's not much, but enough to keep us alive. Now eat."

Danh pulls the bread out of Bao's hand and starts to eat, stuffing his mouth with it. He hardly chews it, but he swallows big pieces before he eats more, groaning and grunting like a wild animal.

"Take it easy, Danh," Bao says. "It takes a while for your stomach to get used to food again."

But Danh doesn't care. He eats everything Bao gave him and asks for more, but Bao tells him he can't take too much at a time, it's not good for him, and besides, they need to ration the food, they don't know when or if they'll get more.

Danh understands. He is happy with what he has gotten so far and just the fact that his sister survived this and is now playing in front of him, turning in the sunlight on the deck, dancing and humming the song their mother used to sing for them, means the world to him. Nothing could make him happier.

"That's it, your majesty," he says and claps his hands. He never thought he was going to see her dance again.

It's the best moment of his life.

Danh looks at his sister as she does her dance just like she used to back home. It's not until halfway through that he realizes her little dance has gathered a crowd. A crowd of men staring at her, wearing hungry smiles and machine guns.

65

April 2016

"BUT THEY MUST HAVE BEEN KILLED RECENTLY, am I right?" I ask, as I place a plate of cookies in front of Detective Fisher.

"I mean, the bodies were pretty intact, even after lying in the water. If they had been there long, they would have been in more of a state of decay and animals would have eaten from them, am I right?"

Fisher grabs a cookie. "The bodies were exceptionally intact, yes. You're right about that. We haven't received the autopsy yet, so there really isn't much I can say on that account."

"But, where have they been? They've been gone for a year," I ask, wondering about Tara and Maria, wondering if they are in the same place as Kim and Casey Taylor were before they were killed.

"I wish I could answer that," he says.

"Of course."

Fisher clears his throat. "So far, we need to wait for the autopsy to be finished, but I felt like I needed to address this with you, since you were the one who knew about these girls disappearing. What else do you know?"

"Well, actually it wasn't me," I say and sip my coffee.

"Then who was it? Chloe?"

"No. Danny."

"Danny Schmidt?"

"Yes. He was the one who found out that Tara and Maria were missing and then started to research this and found all the other single moms that had gone missing with their daughters."

Fisher nods pensively. "All right. I guess I'll have a chat with him, then."

"I think he's working today," I say.

"I'll grab ahold of him later, then," Fisher says, and gets up from his chair. "Thanks for the coffee and the delicious cookies. You make these yourself?"

"Well, yes, I do."

"She's a magician in a kitchen," my dad says from his chair in the corner, where he has been sitting with his eyes closed during my talk with the detective.

"I thought you were sleeping," I say.

My dad answers with a wide smile. I give the detective my hand.

"Let me know if you come across anything that you think might be of importance to this case," he says.

"Sure. Let me walk you out." I open the sliding door, but the detective refuses to go first, so I do. "Have you thought about a possible link between these disappearances and Paige Stover's?" I ask, as we approach the front door.

He nods. "Naturally, I have."

"It could have gone wrong for the kidnappers," I say and open the door for him. I can tell he doesn't like me doing that. Down here, men hold the doors for the ladies, not the other way around. After living in New York, I have almost forgotten my southern etiquette. It amuses me a little. "Maybe the fact that she was in an accident threw them off?"

Fisher nods, holding his file under his arm. He walks outside towards his car, then stops.

"Just one more thing," he says.

"Yes?"

Fisher takes a step back towards me. "Why was Danny Schmidt so interested in Tara and Maria Verlinden in the first place?"

I shrug and pretend I don't know. "You'll have to ask him about that."

Fisher points at me. "I think I will. I think I will." Then he waves, turns on his heel, and walks to his car.

66

April 2016

WHERE IS SHE? Where is my daughter?

It's bad enough that she has been hit by a car, that both her legs are broken and several bones in the rest of her body are too, that she can hardly move and has to lie in this hospital bed that is way too soft for her back. That's all bad enough. But the fact that she has no idea where her daughter is, is devastating.

Nicky stares out her window from Cape Canaveral Hospital. The view from her room is stunning. Intracoastal waters as far as she can see. The hospital is on a peninsula and has water all around it. It's gorgeous, but there is no way Nicky can enjoy all that. All she wants is to get out of this room and look for her daughter.

Where are you, my sweetheart? Where are you?

The nurses and doctors only focus on Nicky's health and only come in to give her medicine or to have her sign papers. Sometimes a doctor comes in and tells her how she is doing. As if she cares how her body is healing? As if she cares about any of that when her daughter is out there somewhere scared, terrified with fear because her mother is not there with her. Nicky just knows she is. She can feel it.

Nicky cries in the bed. The tears soak her pillow, while all she can do is stare out at the stupid water, the same water they just fished two bodies out of yesterday. Nicky saw it on the news last night, where she also saw the story of her own daughter gone missing and saw her picture above the phone number you could call if you saw her.

Her own daughter! Paige on TV because she is missing!

The police have been to her hospital room twice since the accident and asked her a ton of questions. They wanted to know all about the child's father, if he could have taken her, if they had any unsolved disputes between them and so on. Nicky answered all of them, telling them the father wasn't in the picture at all, that he is gone and never was interested in Paige, that she hasn't seen him in twelve years, so why would he suddenly care now?

They told her it's not unusual, so now Nicky wonders if Mike is actually out there somewhere holding the hand of their daughter. She imagines the two of them on the road together, eating burgers and milkshakes, with Paige asking him to take her back to her mother.

She must be so scared, the poor thing.

Still it is more comforting for Nicky to think about Paige being with her father than in the hands of some stranger, some pedophile who wants to harm her. Of course, she has thought about that as well. Who wouldn't?

"Nicky Stover?" A voice says and pulls her out of her nightmarish reverie.

"Yes?"

"I'm detective Fisher with Cocoa Beach Police Department." He shows her his badge.

Nicky starts to cry again. "Please tell me you found her."

His eyes tell her they haven't. "I'm sorry."

Her heart drops. "I didn't think so."

"But I want you to know that we are working as hard as we can to find her. We have called in extra help from the surrounding cities, and everyone is on the lookout for your daughter."

"That's good," she says. "Tell me you won't give up."

"I can promise you I'll do everything in my power. But I need a little help, so if you could just answer some questions…"

"Sure. Anything," Nicky says. "Just bring my baby back to me."

The detective nods. "Like I said. I'll do all that I can." He reaches into his files and pulls out a picture of a man.

"Do you recognize this man?" he asks.

Nicky nods. "Well, yes. I do."

"Does he know your daughter?"

"Yes."

"Where from?"

"From basketball, from the rec center."

The detective writes it down, then nods. "I see. Good. Thank you."

"You don't suspect *he* has taken Paige, do you?" she asks, surprised.

"Right now we're looking into all the angles we can," he replies and closes the file with the picture.

He lifts his cap as he is about to leave. "Thank you for your answer. I'll be in touch."

67

April 2016

Monday, just before noon, Danny returns to his house after his twenty-four hour shift. He turns his key in the lock and walks inside. He puts his backpack on the couch, walks to the kitchen, and grabs a glass of water.

He sighs, looking over the river, thinking about the mother and daughter that were pulled out of that same water the day before yesterday. He was so scared that it was Tara and Maria they had found. Terrified when he helped them pull the kid's body out. Until he saw the face and knew it wasn't her.

Danny drinks his glass and empties it. He hears a sound and turns to look. It sounds like the TV is on in Junior's room. He walks down the hallway, opens the door, and finds Junior inside, still in his bed.

"Why aren't you in school?"

"What's it to you?"

That's the most Junior has spoken to him since he told him about his sister and the affair.

"Well, it's quite important actually. You have that exam today, don't you?" Danny asks, trying hard to keep his cool and not explode in a fit of rage. Junior is graduating in just a few weeks. How can he skip school at an important time like this?

"I don't know," he grumbles.

"Yes, you do know. You never miss school. Are you at least sick?"

Junior doesn't answer. He stares at the TV and pretends Danny isn't there. "Come on, Junior," Danny says. "Don't do this to yourself."

"What do you care?"

Danny sighs deeply. He walks in and sits on the edge of the bed.

Junior doesn't even look at him. "Son. You must know I care. I care a lot about you. I care that you are well, that you get a good education and don't throw everything you've worked for away like this. I care a lot."

"Not enough to not cheat on Mom," he says.

"Ouch. Guess I deserved that."

"Yes, you sure did."

At least he is talking to you. At least he's opening up now. Don't ruin it by getting mad.

"All right. You're right. I have been a terrible father. I cheated on your mother and I had another child. But at least I cared enough about you to stay here. Yes, that's right. I stayed for you, Junior. Because I felt you deserved to have a father. Meanwhile, Tara grew up without one. Meanwhile, I let the woman I love…"

"The woman you what?" Junior asks and sits up straight in the bed, eyes wide, nostrils flaring.

Danny pushes back tears, thinking about Maria and how badly he wanted to be with her back then, how he dreamt about leaving everything, leaving Jean who never loved him, who treated him like dirt, and going to live with her and their daughter.

"You heard me. I loved Maria. I was in love with her. And now she's…she's…I don't know what happened to them."

Junior stares at Danny, biting his lip. "You really loved her?"

Danny nods. "Yes. But I stayed here. To be with you. To make sure you were well taken care of."

Junior shrugs. He doesn't seem as angry as he was before. "So what? Now you want a medal?"

Danny chuckles. "No. No. I don't want that. I don't even expect you to understand, at least not till you're way older, but I think you deserve to know the truth."

Junior doesn't say any more. His glare returns to the TV and he shuts Danny out again. Danny sighs, gets up from the bed, and walks to the door. "Now I need to take a nap. It's been a long shift."

"Wait…" Junior says.

Danny pauses, hand on the door, and turns around.

"Thanks."

The look in Junior's eyes warms him. "Don't thank me," Danny says. "Just promise you'll go to school tomorrow, okay?"

He walks out of the room and down the hallway. As he grabs his phone from his backpack, there is a knock on the front door. Danny opens it.

"Detective Fisher?"

68

April 2016

"So, where were you Saturday morning between eight and nine fifteen?"

Detective Chris Fisher stares at Danny across the table in the small room at the police station. Danny is not sure he understands what is going on. They haven't told him anything. All Fisher said when he came to Danny's house was that he needed him to come to the station with him. Now he's looking at Danny in a way that makes him very uncomfortable in his chair. His hands are getting sweaty. He has known Chris Fisher since they were children, and as the captain of the fire department, Danny has worked together with the Cocoa Beach Police and Fisher for many years. But never has he seen that look on his face when speaking to him.

"I was at home. Why?" Danny answers.

"You weren't at the rally like everyone else?" Fisher asks.

"No. I was at home."

"Can anyone confirm that? Were you with someone?"

"Wait. Am I being accused of something here?"

"Just answer the question, please."

Danny thinks about Junior. Saturday morning was the time when he told him about his sister and the affair. He really doesn't feel like he can tell Detective Fisher about it. Junior got so mad, he ran out of the house, and didn't come back till the afternoon. He doesn't provide much of an alibi anyway. They were only together for maybe half an hour that morning.

"My son was home, but only early in the morning. We had breakfast together, but he left in the middle of it," he says, staying as close to the truth as possible. Then he adds, "We had a fight."

Fisher nods. "You had a fight, you say. About what?"

"Is that really important? It's kind of private."

Fisher looks seriously at him, then down at his papers. He gets up from the chair and walks around. "All right. Then tell me, what did you do after your son left?"

"I..." Danny pauses, thinking about how he broke down and cried. Danny never cries. He takes in a deep breath. He can tell Fisher notices how nervous he is. "I had a cup of coffee and sat out in the back."

Fisher walks behind his chair. "All morning? That's all you did all morning?"

"No. I went on my iPad and read a couple of articles in *Florida Today's* online paper, then went on Facebook."

Fisher walks up in front of him. "Did you post anything?"

Danny shakes his head. "No."

"Did you write any emails? 'Cause that could verify the time and date."

Danny shakes his head. He remembers sitting on the back porch with his coffee and iPad, but not really looking at it. All he did was think about his life while staring at the canal. Crying about how he had wasted his life, how all the choices he had made no longer made sense, how they had ruined so much. Worrying that he might alienate and maybe lose his son now as well, and be left with nothing. But he can't explain that to the detective. They all know him as the tough guy, the firefighter, the captain of the fire department, and the man who's saved more people with heart failure than anyone in the history of the station.

They used to look at me like a hero. Now all I see is contempt in his eyes.

"What is the nature of your relationship with Paige Stover?" Fisher asks.

Danny's eyes widen. "Is that what this is about? Paige Stover?"

"Just answer the question, please. How do you know Paige Stover?"

"From the rec center," he says. "She plays basketball down there. You know I work there as a volunteer for the basketball team and have for years. Is this really about her?"

Fisher clears his throat. "Yes. She disappeared on Saturday morning. Last seen just after nine o'clock when a car drove into the crowd at the rally."

Danny feels so confused. How can he think these things about him? "But...but I don't know anything...I didn't...you think I might have done something to her, don't you?"

Fisher sits down and rubs his stubble. He opens a file, finds a piece of paper, and slides it towards Danny.

"You were arrested recently at the airport, right?"

Danny's heart drops. So this is what this is all about. "You think because I was arrested, then that means I took Paige Stover, is that it?"

Fisher gesticulates. "You were trying to purchase a child!"

Danny leans back in the chair with a deep sigh. "I think I need a lawyer."

69

April 2016

TOM STOPS BY MONDAY AFTERNOON. We decide to go down to the beach and hang out for a few hours while my dad naps on the porch. I don't feel too comfortable letting him see me in a swimsuit, but I decide he has to take me as I am. It's not like I can do much about it. I wear a one-piece and a cover-up dress that I only take off when we go in the water. We jump in the waves and I even take him out on a surfboard. I try to push him into a couple of waves, but he nosedives every time and never gets to even stand up before he finally gives up.

"I'm sorry," I say, when we get back on land. "I forget how hard it is to learn. When you've been surfing since you were just a kid, you tend to forget."

He laughs while shaking his wet hair. He grabs a towel and wipes his face. "Don't feel bad. It was fun. We'll try again another time. Makes me even more impressed that you can do what you do. Plus, it was great to just get out in the water. I kind of needed it. Get my mind off the latest events around here."

"You mean Paige Stover?" I ask.

"Yeah. Can you believe that she would just disappear like that?" he says.

We sit down in my beach chairs. I shake my head. "It's odd," I say. "Did you know her well?"

"Not really. She was mostly with Coach Joe, who gave her private lessons, but of course I knew her a little. She was on the team."

I think about Tara and Maria and the two bodies found in the canals on the same day that Paige disappeared. I can't stop thinking that it might all be connected somehow. I just don't see how. I wonder if I should tell him what I know, but then I remember that I promised Chris Fisher to keep it between us. If word gets out, it might spoil the investigation when people start talking. And they will talk, he said. The more people who know things, the higher the probability that someone will spill the beans at some point. I can't risk ruining anything. I don't know Tom that well yet and have no idea if he can keep a secret like that or not.

"What do you think happened to her?" he asks with a sniffle, as water comes out of his nose. I hand him a towel, knowing the feeling all too well.

"I don't know," I say. "But the more time that passes without her showing up, the more anxious I get."

"I think that goes for everyone around here. I'm glad I took today off from the cape. I can't help feeling a little guilty, you know?"

"You? Why?" I ask, surprised.

He shrugs. "I don't know. Because she was supposed to come to the rec center and play in the tournament, and when she didn't, we just went on with the game. I felt awful, but kept telling myself she would turn up at some point, that she was all right. I should have been out looking for her instead. It wasn't until later I realized she still hadn't shown up."

"You did what you could do. How could you have known?" I say, thinking about how guilty I have felt myself. "I'm the one who could have done something. I was there. I saw her; I photographed her with her friends right before she went missing. I was supposed to have brought her to her mother in the hospital. I keep going over that afternoon again and again, wondering if I could have done something differently, if there was anything I saw that can help the investigation, but I can't seem to come up with what it should be. I have told the police everything I know and remember, but none of it helped."

Tom places a hand on my shoulder. I look at him. He looks very cool with his sunglasses on, but he is so pale he almost looks like he's one of the tourists. I am guessing he doesn't go outside much.

"I think maybe you shouldn't beat yourself up like that. You've done what you could do."

"I sure hope so," I say, when my phone starts to ring from the side pocket of my chair. It's an unknown number. I pick it up. Danny is on the other end.

"I need your help, Mary. I think I got myself into some deep trouble."

70

April 1975

Days pass and they get no more food. Only water is brought to them, and soon they start to starve again. Danh tries to ask some of the guards with the machine guns, but they only point their guns at him and yell in a language Danh doesn't understand.

A week after they were picked up, Bao starts to run a fever. Soon, he is burning up. Danh recognizes the signs from when Long was sick, and it is with terror that he watches his older brother weaken. Without food and strength, it goes fast.

Danh starts to beg and plead with the men onboard for food and medicine. He knows they must have something, like what they gave to Long, but now they don't seem to want to help them anymore.

"No more," they tell him in Vietnamese. "No more!"

Disappointed and scared, Danh returns to Long and Bao on the deck, where they lie uncovered in the burning sun. He tries to cover Bao up with his jacket, like he did with Long, but he is so hot now that he has to remove it for him again.

Long starts to cry. "What are we going to do?" she asks.

Danh shrugs with a whimper. He is scared. Usually in a situation like this, he would do anything he could to make sure Long wasn't scared, to shelter her from the gruesomeness, but not this time. This time, he is angry with her for whining, for crying. He needs her to be strong.

"Stop crying, you baby," he says and gets to his feet. He walks away. He needs to get away.

"Danh?" she says, tears springing from her eyes.

He ignores her. Afraid of what he might say to her, he walks to the other end of the deck and stares out at the water. He feels tears on his face, but wipes them away. There is no time for this now. Crying is useless.

A guy is standing next to him. A man with a machine gun. He is watching the ocean as well. Danh turns to look at him and spots a necklace around his neck that he recognizes.

"Where did you get that?" he asks.

The man smiles, showing off some very bad teeth. He grabs the necklace and pulls it out, then he laughs.

"It belongs to someone I know," Danh says. "See, it says his name on it, right here. He was the captain of the boat I was on. What did you do to him?"

As the realization sinks in, Danh walks backwards, away from the man and his gun. He hurries back to Long and Bao, sits down, and pulls his legs up underneath himself.

"What's wrong?" Long asks.

He looks at her. Usually, he wouldn't have told her anything, but this time he decides she is grown up enough to know. "I think they killed them."

"Killed who?" she asks, sounding innocent and naïve.

"Everyone on our old boat. The captain, everyone. I remember that necklace. He used to rub it between his fingers when he spoke. It's gold. He would never have let go of that willingly. They must have killed him first."

Long doesn't speak. She stares at Danh. Bao is groaning next to them. He's barely awake.

"You think they'll kill us too?" she finally asks anxiously.

Danh looks at her and wonders if he should tell her a lie, tell her it is all a game or part of a play or to look for pirates or dance like he used to, but he decides not to. He looks into her beautiful eyes, and then shakes his head.

"I think they want to do something much worse to us."

71

April 2016

I GET ahold of my lawyer James Holland and make sure he takes care of Danny. As it turns out, the police don't have any evidence pointing at Danny, it's all suspicions based on the fact that he was arrested in Orlando recently trying to purchase a child, something he hasn't even been convicted for. Holland quickly makes sure Danny gets home, and the next day I go to talk to him.

"I got suspended," he says, as he opens the door.

"Oh, no, Danny. I'm so sorry."

He walks away from the door and lets me inside. "Everyone at the station knows I was in for questioning. My superior called and told me I was suspended. I asked him if he thought I was guilty, and even though he didn't say it, I could tell he believed it. It was all in his tone of voice. I'm afraid to go downtown now, since I have a feeling the rumor is all over town that I am a suspect in Paige Stover's disappearance."

Danny throws himself on the couch with a sigh. He hides his face in his hands. "I don't think I can take any more."

I sit down next to him. I put my arm around his shoulder and pull him closer to me. "We'll figure this out somehow," I say. "We'll get to the bottom of it."

"Come on, Mary."

"I'm being serious here!"

"So you're going to do what the police haven't been able to yet?" he asks skeptically.

"If I have to. I have spoken to the others and they're behind you as well. All of them. None of us are going to let you go down on this, you hear me?"

He looks up at me. I touch his cheek. "We're here for you, Danny. Come rain or shine. Like you always have been for us."

"Are you trying to make me cry?" he asks.

"Not really," I say with a chuckle. "But if you feel like crying, then be my guest."

"They called me Boxer," he suddenly says.

"Who did?"

"The police. Chris Fisher."

"Oh, that little brat. I can't believe he would arrest you. I thought we were making progress, that I was helping him with the case. Instead, he took one look at you and believed you were his guy. I could just…" I groan and pretend to be strangling Fisher between my hands.

"He always was annoying," Danny says with a light laugh.

"I know, right? But why do you think they called you that?"

"Apparently, they've found a lot of chats going between this Boxer and Paige Stover on her computer. They showed me a transcript of it and told me they believed I had written it. I had never seen any of these messages in my life, I said, but they didn't believe me. Thank God for James Holland, that he got me out of there. I told them I would cooperate the best I could, but they would have to ask me about things I knew about, not just throw accusations at me."

I get up from the couch and find my phone in my pocket. I call Chloe. "Hey. It's me. Do you remember the name of the guy that you found had chatted with Tara on her iPad? You remember? You had a hunch about him, but I didn't believe you."

"Yeah. He was called Boxer, why?"

"I thought so," I say. "I think we need to take another close look at this guy. And most importantly find out who and where he is."

72

April 2016

BOXER HAS JUST HANDED over the girl to her new owner when he enters the police station. He greets Detective Fisher in the hallway and he shows him back to his desk. Fisher folds his hands on top of his stomach and leans back.

"Thanks for coming down here. We really appreciate it. You say you saw something on the day when Paige Stover disappeared?" he asks. "Something you believe is important?"

Boxer nods. "Yes. At the rally."

"So, you were at the rally?" the detective asks.

"Yes. I was there with my brother to protest against the fish-kill. It's truly awful how our river has been destroyed."

"Yes, we all believe so, but let's get to the point here. We are interested in talking to anyone who was at the rally, as you probably know from the newscasts on TV. What did you see?"

Boxer clears his throat and tries to sound sincere. "I saw Paige Stover at the rally. She was with her mother at first, then walked with some of her friends."

Detective Fisher writes on his pad. Boxer can't help feeling a thrill go through his body as he watches him. He tries to hide it.

"So you saw her at the rally," the detective repeats.

"Yes. She was walking down Minutemen Causeway with her friends."

"And where were you?"

"Me and my brother were not far behind them. And that's when I saw him."

"Who did you see?"

Boxer clears his throat again and sits up straighter in the chair. "I don't know his name, but he was also there in the afternoon when

181

we searched for her, walking hand in hand. I should have known something was fishy."

"Wait, wait a minute. Who did you see?"

"He's the captain at the fire station. That's all I know. He's got one of those faces you don't forget, if you know what I mean, Detective."

"Are you talking about Danny Schmidt?" the detective asks. He leans back and grabs a photo from the drawer, then places it in front of Boxer.

Boxer nods. "Yes. That's him. That's exactly who I saw."

"So, you say you saw Danny Schmidt at the rally?" he asks, while writing on his pad.

"Yes. He was there. He was elbowing his way through the crowd and pushed me aside as he did. I saw him approach the girl after the panic erupted and everyone was screaming and running around. He walked up to her, grabbed her arm and talked to her, then they left together."

Detective Fisher stares at Boxer like he doesn't quite know what to say. "And you're sure it was him?"

Boxer nods. "Yes. One hundred percent. I can't have been the only one who saw them talking."

"As a matter of fact, you aren't," he says. "We have another witness that says she saw a man talk to Paige and grab her arm, but she didn't see his face."

Oh, really?

Fisher rubs his stubble and clears his throat. "Did you see anything else? Like, did they get into a car?"

Boxer shakes his head. "I don't know. I went back to look for my brother and then we drove home."

Detective Fisher gets to his feet and reaches out his hand. "Well, thank you for being such a good and concerned citizen and bringing this to our attention."

"I am just glad to be of help," he says and gets up as well. He shakes the detective's hand.

"Oh, you were a great help," detective Fisher says with a smile. "A great help."

73

April 2016

I PARK the car in front of Joey's townhouse and walk up to the entrance. The light is on inside and I hear voices. I take a few deep breaths to calm myself down a little.

I have spent the entire day with Chloe and Danny, trying to figure out who this Boxer is. Well, it was mostly Chloe who did the work from what she could get out of Tara's iPad. But so far, we still have no idea who this guy is. Only that he has chatted with both girls in chatrooms of several games and social media sites. Chloe went into the police file and found all the info they had extracted so far from Paige's computer and now we hope that she can use that to track this guy down.

Meanwhile, I have no idea how she does any of it, so I have been drinking coffee and talking to Danny and Chloe's mother, Carolyn, who I always try to chat with whenever she's awake and I am visiting their house. I think it helped Danny too to take his thoughts away a little. Carolyn was in a wonderful mood for once and told us amazing stories from her youth.

When we were about to leave, she said something I still can't get out of my mind. She is an old, very sick woman, but there was something about the way she said it. Like it was urgent.

"He misses them," she said. "That's why he keeps looking for them. Over and over again."

What on earth could she be talking about?

I shake my head, then raise my hand and knock on the door. I have Snowflake with me, since he misses Bonnie and Clyde so much, well mostly Bonnie, I think. He can smell the pig on the other side of the door and goes crazy. I can barely hold him.

The door opens and Salter looks at me. "Mom? What are you doing here?"

When Snowflake sees Bonnie, he pulls so hard on the leash I let it go and he storms inside. "What happened to, 'Hi, Mom, so good to see you, Mom; I missed you, Mom?' I'm here to pick you up," I say. "Remember?"

He looks like he doesn't understand. I continue:

"It's Tuesday. You're supposed to be with me from Wednesday till Sunday evening this week."

"I...I...we didn't think that was until tomorrow?" Salter says.

"Who is it?" Joey appears in the doorway. "Mary? What are you doing here?"

I hear loud voices coming from the living room and look in to see a couple of familiar faces. Joey's parents' faces to be exact. Both of them engaged in what looks like delightful chat with Jackie.

"You're introducing her to your parents now? That's nice," I say. "Mary..."

"No. No. It's okay. It's your life. Even though things are moving a little too fast for me, it doesn't have to affect you in any way. I'll keep my mouth shut now. Are you ready to go, sweetie?"

"But, Mo-om, Grandpa and Granny are here."

"Come on. It's my turn to have you now. I've missed you so much and I'm not leaving here without you."

"Go get your stuff, buddy," Joey says, placing a weighty hand on his shoulder.

Salter leaves, shoulders slumped.

"I'm sorry about that," Joey says. "I didn't keep an eye on what day it was. And I'm sorry about...*that*," he nods in the direction of his parents. "I just figured, since she has moved in, they might as well meet."

"Right." I feel very uncomfortable and hope Salter is hurrying up. I don't want to say anything I'll later regret.

Salter finally comes out wearing his new clothes that Jackie bought for him. He looks ridiculous. Who buys a leather jacket for a ten-year-old? A ten-year-old in Florida? And those shoes? What the heck are those? They blink every time he walks, constantly changing colors.

His teacher called me earlier to tell me he can't wear those to school anymore, since they disturb the other students. At first, I thought she was overreacting a little, but now I understand. What's worse is, I am going to have to be the one to tell him and be the bad guy...again.

74

April 2016

"MOMMY?"

Paige Stover tries to open her eyes, but her eyelids feel so heavy. She blinks several times before she succeeds in waking up and looking around. Her mommy is not there. She is not in the dog crate anymore in that awful man's house. But where is she now?

"Mommy?" she repeats and sits up. She is on a bed in a small room with nothing but the bed and a dresser. There is a window, but the curtains are pulled.

Paige gets up and walks towards the window, feeling slightly dizzy. She pulls the curtains and looks out. Water as far as the eye can see. And she is up high. Not in a condominium, but like the third floor of what looks like a house. A big house. A mansion. Below her, she can see a tennis court, a basketball court, and a lap-pool. It's all surrounded by lots and lots of palm trees. The water is not the ocean, she knows that much. She can see land on the other side and a bridge far away. It must be the Intracoastal waters, or the river, as most people call it. It all looks very familiar to her.

Paige grabs the sliding door and tries to open it, but she can't. It's locked. She looks for a way to open it, but can't find it.

"You'll need a key," a voice says behind her.

She gasps and turns. The face looking back at her smiles. "Hello, Paige."

"Who are you?"

"Well, who am I? I'm your new best friend; that's who I am."

"I'm not allowed to talk to strangers," she says. "I want my mommy. Where is she?"

The man sits on the bed. He sighs. "I'll tell you something. I wanted your mom to be here too. But they tell me she couldn't make it. Not this time. Something happened to her."

Paige starts to shake. She fights her tears. "What do you mean something happened to her?"

"Well, last thing I heard was that she was run over by a car."

Paige stares at the man. She had thought it was all a lie. While lying in the crate, she had been certain that Boxer had only told her it to make her go with him. She didn't think it was the truth.

"I want to go to the hospital and see her," she says.

The man shakes his head. "Now, I can't let you do that," he says. "But we can do something else."

"What?"

"How about we play a game?"

"I don't want to play a game. I want to see my mommy!" she yells.

The man gets up from the bed, walks to her, then slaps her across the face. It burns like crazy on her cheek. But it makes her stop crying. She stares at him, baffled, her cheek red and burning.

"There'll be no crying, do you hear me? No crying, no screaming, no trying to run away. You can't get out of here. All the doors are locked and I am the only one who can open them, so you might as well not try. I'll spare you the trouble right away. So you can't run, all right? But you can do something else. Something a lot more FUN."

"W-w-what's that?" she asks, still startled by the slap. She is terrified the man might hurt her again and her voice is shaking.

He leans over and whispers in her face, spitting slightly as he speaks. "You can HIDE!"

75

April 2016

SALTER IS HARDLY SPEAKING to me. The next morning, I send him off to school by bus. His dad lets him bike to school, but I feel more safe with him going by bus. I don't feel like he is safe on that bike, and especially these days with the disappearance of Paige Stover, I am not comfortable with him biking to school.

I explain it to him, but he just gets mad at me. Again, I am the bad guy and he is angry at me all morning.

I feel awful as I take care of my dad. He tries to cheer me up by moving his toes that he is now capable of moving back and forth. It does cheer me up a little, and I can't help smiling when Jack, his physical therapist, arrives.

"He's doing so well," Jack says. "The video you made in the middle of the night helped him believe that he can actually move his feet, that he can regain mobility in his feet and legs again. You have no idea how much hope means for a patient like your father."

"Thank you," I say, feeling slightly overwhelmed with emotion.

He smiles. "Just thought you should know."

I leave my dad in Jack's hands and grab my bike to go to Chloe's house. She's in the kitchen as I knock and walk in.

"Coffee?" she asks.

I nod and she pours me a cup. I sip it and look at her. She looks awful. Her hair is a mess, her clothes the same as yesterday. "You been up all night?"

"Yup."

"Anything new?"

She nods. I feel relieved.

"I have a lot for you to look at, come."

I follow her to the back of the house where all her computers are lined up. It's dark and cold in there. I pull out a chair and sit next to her, my cup between my hands.

"Look at this," she says and hands me a stack of papers she has printed.

I flip through them. First is a case file for the missing persons report for Paige Stover. There are interviews with all the people who have daily contact with her, like her teacher at school, her basketball coach, her swim teacher, and her math tutor. "What am I looking for?"

"Look at the last page. A statement they took yesterday," she says, turning her chair to face me.

I find the last statement and look through it. "What the heck?" I exclaim, after reading a few lines of this guy's testimony. "He says he saw Danny talking to Paige at the rally? That he grabbed her arm and they left together? That's ridiculous. Danny wasn't even at the rally!"

Chloe nods. "Exactly, but the police are all over this. Your friend Fisher is determined Danny is the guy they're looking for."

"He is not my friend," I complain. "I just tried to help him with the case. I thought he took me seriously, but he's just interested in busting Danny."

"And now they have the eye-witness to back up their theory," she says.

"Who is this guy anyway?" I ask and look at the head of the file to see his name. "Joseph Barrow?"

"According to this, he's Paige's basketball coach, Coach Joe," Chloe says. "But check this out. It gets a lot better."

Chloe puts a stack of papers in front of me. "These are all the case files from the missing mothers and their daughters. I have pulled all of the missing persons reports. I went through all of them and this is what I found." Chloe leans over and points at the first report, Kim and Casey Taylor's file. She rests her finger on a name in the heading. "Look who showed up as an eyewitness? Stating he saw them at the mall right before they disappeared?"

76

April 1975

"I'M SCARED, DANH."

Long looks at him with her big moist eyes. Bao is sleeping, his breath uneven and weak.

"Me too," Danh says.

"You think he'll die?"

"Stop saying that. Stop! Now, go to sleep!"

Danh looks around while his sister does as she is told. Three men are watching them, big grins on their faces, machine guns over their shoulders. Danh hasn't slept in two days; he has been watching over his brother and sister night and day, especially keeping an eye on the men on the ship who look at his sister in a way that terrifies him.

He has been begging them for medicine and food for days, but all they've given them is water and very little of it. It's not enough, and Danh is on the verge of breaking down. He is so hungry he can't even feel it anymore and so thirsty he hallucinates, seeing his dear mother coming towards him. She looks angry. Is she angry with him?

I am sorry. I failed you, Mother. I miss you so much. I don't know what to do anymore. I can't save him. I can't save Bao.

"I can help you," a voice says.

Danh opens his eyes. The sun is burning his face. The silhouette of the man standing in front of him is moving closer.

"What?"

"I have medicine," he says and kneels in front of him. Danh can now see his face properly. It's the guy wearing the captain's necklace around his neck. Danh gasps.

"I have medicine for your brother," the man says.

Danh sits up straight. Is this true? "You have medicine?"

The man nods. He reaches into his pocket and pulls out something in his closed fist. He shows it to Danh. A small bottle with the word penicillin on it, curled up in the palm of his hand. Danh looks at it with a small whimper. He knows what this is. He remembers having seen it once before, when one of his brothers was very sick. The doctor came to their house carrying a bottle just like this.

So many sleepless nights, he has been hoping and praying for medicine for Bao. But they told him there was no more onboard the ship. Long got it all, they said.

Danh reaches out to grab the bottle, but the man closes his fist and pulls it back. He is grinning from ear to ear.

"No."

"No?"

"We make a deal."

"What do you want? I'll give you anything, but I don't have much. I don't have anything of value."

The man nods. "Yes, you do." As he speaks, his eyes fall on the sleeping Long next to Danh.

Terrified, Danh shakes his head. "No. No. NO."

The man rises to his feet. The medicine disappears into his pocket again. "As you wish."

He turns and walks away. Danh grabs Long and pulls her closer. He holds her in his arms till she wakes up.

"I heard what the man said," she says, when she opens her eyes.

"What do you mean? Don't talk nonsense," Danh says.

"I want to do it," she says.

"NO! Never!"

"Bao saved my life when we were on that other boat. He refused to let them throw me overboard. Both you and he chose to get into that small boat for me. I owe him, Danh. I can do this."

77

April 2016

I STARE at the name on the file. "Joseph Barrow, Joseph Barrow… who are you?"

Chloe is on the computer when Danny knocks on the door and pokes his head in.

"Hello? Anyone home?"

"In the back!" Chloe yells.

"What's up?" I ask as he comes inside. He has already helped himself to a coffee in the kitchen. He looks so tired and I am guessing he hasn't slept all night.

"The police called. They want me down for more questioning."

Chloe turns her chair to look at him. "I might have an idea why," she says, and shows him the file. "This guy walked in yesterday and told them he saw you with Paige Stover on the day she disappeared. He says you and she left the rally together."

Danny almost drops his cup out of his hand. "What? But I wasn't even there. I told them I wasn't."

"I'm guessing they aren't going to believe you after this," I say.

"Who is he?"

"His name is Joseph Barrow," I say.

"Joe?" Danny asks.

"You know him?"

"Well, of course I do. He's one of the coaches at the rec center. I've known him for years. I helped him get the job; I recommended him because he didn't have anything else when he was fired from Disney two years ago. I've known him since we were in the army together. We were deployed together in Afghanistan in '04. His brother was with us too. Terrible thing. A kid with explosives blew him up. Joe had her, could have shot her, but he hesitated and the kid exploded herself and took Joe's brother. Joe was never himself again after that."

"His brother? But it states here that he was at the rally with his brother. That's what he told them," I say.

"Yeah, he would say that. Joe went kind of cuckoo after what happened. Kept talking about his brother like he was still alive. Kept claiming he was with him everywhere. It was awful. He refused to realize his brother was gone. Hard to understand why he was so attached to him, though. The brother was a heavy drinker and gambler who cheated Joe out of a lot of money, always had him pay off his debts. As far as I know, all Joe has left is his mother who is dying from cancer."

Danny hesitates. He looks like he just remembered something. "Wait a minute."

"What?" I ask.

He looks at me. "Boxer? That's the name of the guy who we believe chatted with both Paige Stover and Tara, right?"

"Right," Chloe says.

"Oh, my God. It's so obvious. Why didn't I think of it sooner?"

"What?" I ask.

"Joseph Barrow is his name."

He looks at us like it's the most obvious thing in the world. I have no idea where he is going. I look at Chloe, who doesn't seem to have a clue either.

"Joseph Barrow," he repeats. "As in Joseph Louis Barrow, as in Joe Louis." He looks at us again. "Ah, come on, get there faster!"

"I have no idea what you're talking about?" I say.

"The boxer. The famous boxer, Joe Louis. He shares his name with him. I should have seen this from the start when Chloe told us about The Boxer."

Chloe looks at me, then at Danny. Danny looks like he isn't really sure he understands this properly yet, like he is still piecing things together in his mind.

"Oh, my God, Joe has taken Paige? And Tara?" he says. "But... he was just there the other day...helping us...you remember him," he says, addressed to me, "you held his hand when we searched for her at the school."

My heart stops. Literally. The very thought makes me sick to my stomach. "That was him?"

"Yes. I can't believe it. He was right there all the time. We've got to tell someone. We've got to tell the police."

"Who is going to believe us?" I ask.

Danny sinks into a chair. "You're right. Fisher knows all of us. Even if you do it, he'll think you're just protecting me."

"How about an anonymous tip?" Chloe asks. "Tell them we

heard screaming from his house. That would give them a reason to go in and find Paige, but then again...what if he's not keeping her at his house? He might have her somewhere else."

"Chloe's got a point," Danny says. "We need to somehow figure out if he has her at his house."

Part IV

COME OUT, COME OUT WHEREVER YOU ARE

78

April 2016

As the school bell rings, hundreds of children run out the doors. Lots of them grab their bikes, other go in the pick-up line, while the rest go to the buses.

Blake watches them as they walk in a nice line to the yellow buses and disappear inside of them. He especially watches bus C26, carrying his dear nephew Salter.

As the bus sets off from the school grounds, Blake drives after it, keeping a distance of one to two cars between them.

The road is still blocked off on parts of Minutemen where they pulled the bodies out the other day. The police tape is still in the bushes, being tossed by the wind.

The bus stops every few minutes as it drives down A1A towards the Patrick Airforce base. It turns just before the base and goes back to A1A northbound, towards Blake's childhood home. He remembers riding in that very same bus himself as a child. Even the bus driver, Mrs. T., is still the same.

Nothing ever changes in this town.

Blake especially remembers coming home after school, being greeted only by his stepmom, Laura, who would look annoyed at him and wish him long gone. She never liked either him or Mary, but most of all she loathed him, because he was there, a constant reminder of the love that her husband lost, when his mother was shot in that very house.

Blake reminded his father of her constantly. It was almost unbearable for his father. So much that he would pay him money to leave the house, pay for anything he wanted, as long as he didn't bother him or Laura.

When Blake turned sixteen, he got a Corvette, the newest one.

But his dad wasn't there to give it to him. It was just parked in the driveway, his name on a card placed underneath the windshield wipers.

HAPPY BIRTHDAY was the simple message. Not even a *Love from Dad*. Blake took it for a spin that day and drove so fast up I95 that he almost crashed. As the car spun around and he missed the tree, he couldn't stop thinking that maybe this was exactly what his dad wanted. That was why he bought him the car, so he could go and kill himself on the highway.

He wasn't going to give him the pleasure.

The bus stops in front of 7th Street and three kids get out. The last one is Salter. Blake drives his rented car into a parking spot, then gets out.

"Salter!"

Salter stops and Blake runs to him while the bus sets off and disappears. Salter looks at him as he runs towards him, his arm lifted. "Salter, wait up."

"Who are you?" Salter asks, as he approaches him.

"Don't you remember me?" Blake asks, smiling widely. He is standing right in front of him now.

Salter's expression changes drastically. He takes a step back. "You're my uncle," he says, his voice shaking.

"That's right, my boy, I am."

"W-w-what do you want?"

Blake shrugs and takes a step even closer to him. Salter is visibly intimidated by his closeness.

"Just to chat. Aren't I allowed to talk to my nephew anymore?"

"You're wanted by the police," Salter says fearfully. "My mom told me you killed someone."

Blake tilts his head. "What do you think? You think I killed her?"

"I…I never said it was a her."

Blake points his finger at him, pretending it's a gun. "Smart kid, huh? Well, I'm even smarter."

In one swift move, Blake reaches out and grabs Salter around the neck. He turns him around and places a cloth over his mouth, then counts backwards from one hundred until the boy stops fighting and becomes lifeless in his arms. As he helps Salter to the car, Blake throws a glance at the house, where he knows Mary will be waiting for her son. But she's going to wait for a very long time.

That's 2-0, dear sis.

79

April 2016

I LEAVE Chloe and Danny at Chloe's house. We have planned to go to this Boxer's house later today, but I have to get back to Salter first. It's early release today, so he is home earlier than usual and he needs to do his homework. He's got a big project he should have done last week, but since his dad thought it was more important to go paddle boarding and hang out with Jackie, he hasn't done it, and now I have to make sure he starts it. I have called Sandra and asked her to come over and stay with him later today so I can go with Chloe and Danny.

It felt strange asking this of her, since I haven't spoken to her in quite some time and since I am still a little angry with her for cheating on Ryan, but you do what you have to do, right? This is important and so I have to swallow my pride.

I park my bike in the driveway and look at the clock. I still have half an hour before Salter comes home on the bus. I decide to bake a cake for him…his favorite banana cake. I am sick of being the bad guy when it comes to my son and I need to win him back somehow. Starting with a cake.

Snowflake is all excited and I let him out in the backyard. Ever since we left Joey's house, it has been hard for me to keep him busy and exercised enough. When he was with Bonnie and Clyde all day it was no problem. Now he's all over the place, especially if I am not home.

I check on my dad, who has fallen asleep in his room in front of the TV, probably exhausted from this morning's physical therapy. It tends to wear him out completely, which is good. I turn off the TV and sneak out. I throw the cake together and put it in the oven, then look at the clock.

The bus should have been there by now.

I shrug and grab a magazine while I wait. I read about how to make a cheesecake with strawberries and soon the timer buzzes on the stove. I look at my watch and wonder why Salter hasn't gotten here yet.

Maybe the bus is just late.

It happens sometimes that Mrs. T. runs late. A couple of weeks ago I freaked out because she was twenty minutes late. Turns out the bus had broken down half way and they had to wait for another one to pick them up. These things happen from time to time. I decide I don't want to allow myself to get all worked up about this like the last time.

I take out the cake and place it on the counter to cool down. It smells divine and I am certain Salter is going to absolutely love it.

Where is he?

The nagging feeling won't leave me alone and I walk to the window to look out at the road. I can't see the bus or Salter anywhere.

It'll be here in a few minutes. Relax. Will you?

I stare at the road, my heart pounding in my chest. No, I can't relax even though I'm trying to. Where is my son? It's now thirty minutes since he should have been home.

I decide to walk out to the road. The bus stops almost right outside my dad's house. It usually doesn't take him more than ten seconds to run inside.

Where the hell is he?

I spot another kid that I recognize from Salter's school. He is crossing the street with his dad. They're walking towards the beach.

"Hey," I yell, and run to them. "Did you come home by bus today?"

The kid nods. He's holding a fishing pole in his hand and so is his dad.

"Was Salter on the bus?" I ask, trying to keep calm, but freaking out completely inside.

"Yes. He got off when I did. We always do."

80

April 1975

DANH'S HANDS are shaking as he grabs the syringe and the small bottle from the man. He watches with tears in his eyes as he drags Long away. She is looking back, trying to comfort him, telling him it'll be okay, not to worry.

He wants to stop her, to stop the man from taking her, but he doesn't. Instead, he looks at the medicine that has been given to him, wipes away his tears, turns around, and faces Bao.

He kneels in front of him, grabs Bao's skinny body, and turns him around. He pulls down his pants, fills the syringe, and places it to his bare skin.

"I sure hope this will help you," he whispers, as he pushes the medicine into Bao's body.

Danh sinks back on the deck and cries. Exhausted, he falls into a deep sleep and doesn't wake up till the early morning hours, when the sun is rising above the horizon.

"Long?"

Bao is next to him, blinking his eyes like he's seeing the world for the first time. "Danh?"

"Bao. You're better. You're not burning up anymore."

Bao tries to smile, but is still too weak. Danh gives him some water, the last bottle they have. He helps him drink.

"You need to rest," Danh says. "Regain your strength. I'll see if I can get you some more water and maybe steal some bread from the trash can. I did that the other day and fed me and Long."

Bao puts his head back down on Danh's jacket. "Where is Long?" he asks, lying with his eyes closed.

Danh wonders about that himself. Why hasn't she come back yet? How does he explain to Bao what has happened? What they had to do? Danh feels the tears building up in his eyes again, but he manages to push them back.

"I'll go look for food and water," he says, avoiding having to answer Bao's question. Danh gets up.

Bao doesn't say any more. He's sound asleep again, but this time with a little color to his skin and a smile on his face. At least the medicine helped. Now all he needs to do is find out what happened to his precious pearl.

Heart in his throat, Danh walks around the ship, avoiding being seen by the men with guns. He hides under stairs, behind trash cans or bags, then sneaks to the living quarters downstairs.

A long row of doors meets him down there. He hears voices coming from behind the doors, people, men laughing, some arguing. He sneaks past the first open door leading to one of the rooms and peeks inside without being seen. In there he sees beds, four beds, and a table with four men sitting around playing cards, their guns hung on the back of their chairs. There's money on the table. Danh looks to see if he can spot Long anywhere, but she's not in this room.

He keeps walking till he reaches another open door. Inside lies a man. He's sleeping, snoring, his gun with him on the bed.

Where are you, my flower? My dancing princess?

His quest leads him to yet another open door and he sneaks close to it before he peeks inside. In there, on one of the beds, he finds her. At first, he lights up, but then everything inside of him freezes.

"Long?" he says, thinking at first she could be sleeping. "Your majesty?"

As he approaches her, he begins to fear the worst. He reaches her and bends over her tiny body.

"Your majesty?"

And that is when he sees it. Danh gasps and tears spring immediately to his eyes. Long's clothes are ripped and she is bruised all over her little body. Her tiny face is pale and blood is running from her mouth. Her eyes are staring, lifeless, into the ceiling. The sight makes Danh sick with sorrow. He puts his head on her chest and starts to scream.

81

April 2016

"THIRTY-FOUR, THIRTY-FIVE, THIRTY-SIX…"

Paige is running down the stairs. She goes for the double front doors first, but just as the man had told her, they're locked. Yet she pulls and shakes both handles desperately and turns all the locks, thinking she can unlock it, but it doesn't work. Next, she's running towards a set of sliding doors leading to the pool area.

"Forty, forty-one, forty-two…"

Paige is crying as she pulls the handle frantically, but the door doesn't open. She sobs, then moves on to the next door, then a window, but they're all locked. She slams her hand into a window, hammering on it while screaming for help.

"Fifty-three, fifty-four, fifty-five…"

The sound of his voice feels like knives on her skin. She runs desperately to the kitchen, but there are no knives or even pans that she can use as weapons. She runs across yet another living room while the voice of the man counting cuts through the air. She spots another set of stairs and decides to run up them.

This house is big. It's enormous. If you want me to hide, then I'll hide. I'll hide so well you'll never find me.

She realizes he is right. The only thing she can do at this point is to hide and to do it well.

"Sixty-five, sixty-six, sixty-seven…"

Hurry Paige. Hurry.

Her hands are shaking, her body trembling in fear as she opens a door upstairs and runs into a bedroom. She looks under the bed, her knees in the soft carpet. She crawls on her belly across the carpet and manages to squeeze herself in under the bed.

"Sixty-nine, seventy, seventy-one…"

This isn't good enough. He'll find you right away! As soon as he steps inside the room the first thing he'll do is look under the bed.

Paige squirms out, gets back on her feet, and looks around. There's a closet. She runs to it and opens it, remembering the time she played with the neighbor's son and she hid behind hanging coats with her feet in a pair of boots at the base of the coats, making it seem that they were just stored objects. He never found her.

But there is no room for her in there. She closes it again, her heart throbbing in her chest.

Please, help me, God. Help me hide.

Paige storms out of the room and runs further down the hallway. Her feet are soundless on the thick carpet.

"Seventy-eight, seventy-nine, eighty…"

The man is counting very loud, probably to make sure she can hear him, she thinks to herself, as she finds another door and rushes inside. She is breathing heavily, desperately, frantically letting her eyes scan the room for possible hiding places. She doesn't want to think about it, but she can't help wondering what he'll do to her if he finds her.

When he finds her.

Oh, my God, he's gonna kill me, isn't he? He's going to find me and kill me.

The look in his eyes had scared her senseless. It was the look of a madman. Paige had seen it before, in that woman from across the street, in the days before she was taken away. Paige's mother had told her she had gone crazy, because she lost one of her children, that she couldn't take care of herself or her other children anymore, and now the hospital would take care of her. Paige heard the rumors about her from the other kids. They said she tried to drive into the ocean with her kids in the car. Her eyes had the exact same look in them.

Like they were lost.

"Eighty-seven, eighty-eight, eighty-nine…"

Panting, Paige looks around this room that appears to be another sort of a living room. There's a fireplace at the end of it. The floors are wooden and creak as she walks across them. Sweat is springing from her forehead.

"Ninety-seven, ninety-eight, ninety-nine…"

Oh, my God. You've got to find a place NOW!

Paige walks fast to the fireplace and the stone chimney. She pokes her head in, grabs the sides, and starts to climb.

"ONE-HUNDRED! READY OR NOT, HERE I COME!"

Paige whimpers and continues to scoot herself upwards until her fingers touch something. She gasps and looks up. A set of eyes in a dirty face look back at her. A girl about her age.

"Who are you?" Paige whispers.

The girl doesn't answer. She lifts her pointer to her lips to signal for Paige to be quiet. Paige holds on to the walls of the chimney and places her feet on both sides to make sure she won't fall down. She clings desperately to the rocks with her fingernails, as the door to the room is blasted open.

82

April 2016

WHERE THE HELL is my son?

I call Joey and, of course, he doesn't answer right away. I leave a voicemail asking him if Salter accidentally went to his house instead, forgetting he was supposed to be with me till Sunday.

I can't wait for him to answer, so I grab my bike and ride it to his townhouse and knock on the door.

"Salter? Joey?"

I can hear Bonnie and Clyde on the other side of the door, but no one opens the door. I grab my phone and call Joey again. Still no answer. I gnarr and knock again, before I decide to go back to my dad's place to see if Salter has come home. Meanwhile, I keep calling Salter's phone, but it goes directly to voicemail. He is not allowed to have it turned on at school, so I figure it's still in his backpack. I leave message number eight, then hang up.

Calm down, Mary. He probably just went to a friend's house and forgot to tell you. You know how distracted he gets sometimes. Maybe Joey even made arrangements with the parents and everything, but forgot to tell you. You've got to stay calm. Can't get yourself this worked up all the time.

It doesn't help.

I am officially freaking out now. While riding my bike back to the house, I try breathing exercises; I try thinking about surfing and the ocean, which usually calms me down, but that doesn't help either.

I throw the bike in the grass by my dad's house, and then run inside. "Salter? Salter, are you here?"

"What's going on, Mary?" my dad's voice asks from his bedroom. I run in there. "I can't find Salter. He didn't come home from school."

"Have you tried calling the school?" he asks.

"Ten times at least. They say he got on the bus as planned. I even met a kid who said he was on the bus with him and that they both got off at 7ᵗʰ Street."

"That's odd," my dad says. "It's not like Salter to not come home."

I sigh nervously. "I know. I don't like this, Dad. I've had a bad feeling all week. I knew something bad was going to happen."

"Now, we don't know that something bad has happened yet," he says. "Let's try and stay calm for now, all right? There could be a lot of explanations for this."

I bite my nails, even though I practically have no nails left. I look at my phone again and again. Then I call Chloe up.

"What's up?" she asks.

"Salter didn't come home from school. I'm scared, Chloe."

"Well, with everything that has been going on lately, I can't blame you," she says. "But don't you think he might be at a friend's house or something?"

"I don't know," I say.

"I'll be over in a sec."

She doesn't exaggerate. I have barely hung up before she knocks, then walks in. She gives me a hug. "Are you all right? Now, don't freak out, okay? Stay calm. It's probably nothing. You hear me?"

I bite the inside of my mouth, while I nod. "Where is Danny?" I ask.

"He went to the police station for more questioning," she says.

I try really hard to not break down and cry. My stomach is turning. It's the worst feeling in the world to not know where your child is.

83

April 2016

A COUPLE OF HOURS LATER, he has still not shown up, and I am getting really anxious now. I call the crew and everyone shows up, except Danny, who we are guessing is still being questioned by the police. Even Joey finally shows his face, dragging Jackie along with him.

"Where were you all day?" I yell at him as he enters. "I've called and called and you didn't answer. Our son is missing, in case you didn't know!"

There you go. Take it all out on Joey. That'll help.

I hide my face in my hands. "I'm sorry," I say. "I'm freaking out here."

"Me too," Joey says and grabs me in his arms. He hugs me for a long time and I let go and cry. Jackie is standing awkwardly behind us, not knowing what to do with herself. Joey looks me in the eyes.

"We'll find him, okay? I promise you we'll find him."

Jackie walks closer and puts a hand on my shoulder. "Yes, Mary. He'll show up eventually. It's a small town."

She's being nice. I know she is, but I can't stand it. I can't stand her in my presence. I force a smile and nod.

"The others are in the kitchen."

They follow me there. Everyone has a phone to his or her ear. Alex looks up and nods at Joey, so does Sandra, while Chloe and Marcia are both way too engaged to notice him.

"Marcia's boy Mark is out on his bike searching the area," I say, filling him in on where we're at. "He knows all the places the boys hang out around here, like the skate park, the bike trails, and so on. If Salter has taken off with some of his friends and just decided to not tell us, he'll find him. He has even enlisted some of his friends from eighth grade to help him out. These boys know the area."

Joey nods. "That's good. That's real good."

"Marcia has also asked Mark to send out texts to everyone he knows at the high school, asking for their help and seeing if they've seen anything. Alex's daughter, Ava is the same age as Salter and she knows everyone at the school. They're busy calling people and getting them involved."

Joey nods again.

"Chloe is trying to get ahold of the bus driver who drove the school bus home, Mrs. T., to see if she knows anything, like if Salter met some friends when he got off the bus or…well, you know…" I am about to tear up, thinking about Salter meeting some creepy guy who kidnaps him, but decide to push it back. There is no time to cry now. "Well, basically anything." I pause. "Meanwhile, Sandra is making sure everyone has coffee and banana cake."

Joey smiles softly. "Salter's favorite."

"Don't remind me," I say, swallowing a knot in my throat.

"What can I do?" Joey asks. I can tell he is about to tear up. I am guessing, that seeing this, seeing all these people working like this to get our son back made it all very real to him. He is probably just realizing the seriousness of it all now.

I hand him my phone. "I want you to call the police. It's been four hours now. The sun will set in less than two hours. I need them to start looking for our boy."

Joey grabs the phone with an anxious look. "We gotta do what we can now," I say. "We have to find him before nighttime. We've simply got to."

84

April 1975

DANH CARRIES Long's lifeless body up on the deck. His body is threatening to crumble as he takes one step at a time towards the bright deck, bathed in sunlight. He walks outside and turns towards the place where Bao is sitting. All the while, he is thinking about Long, imagining her dancing for him again, seeing her laugh and smile for his inner eyes, pretending, playing with him like they used to.

Your majesty! Don't leave me this way!

Men on the deck watch him as he walks. He doesn't even look at them. All he can focus on right now is her, her small fragile beat-up body between his hands.

Bao rises to his feet as he spots Danh walking towards him. Danh starts to cry again when he looks at his brother and he sees the realization sink in.

"No!" Bao says as their eyes meet. "No!"

Danh nods. He stretches out his arms towards Bao, so he can better see their sister or what is left of her.

"Please, God, no. Please not Long!"

Danh can't stand anymore. He falls to his knees, Long still in his arms. He is crying and leans forward above her body. Bao falls down on his knees as well and they cry and yell in anger.

"Why her? Why her?" Bao cries out towards the sky.

They stay like that for hours on end. As darkness sinks upon the ship, they finally do what they know they have to. They say their goodbyes, each of them tell a story of their baby sister, from when she was still alive, then in unison, they lift Long over the railing and let her fall into the vast dark ocean.

They sink onto the deck in each other's arms, and cry their way through the night, tired, exhausted, and beaten.

Especially Bao seems to have lost the will to continue. In the coming days, he walks around, not talking to Danh, just shifting between crying and staring at the ocean, and Danh soon fears for him and wonders if he is thinking about ending it all, of jumping into the ocean and leaving Danh.

But that is not what is on Bao's mind.

Three days after Long's death, he finally speaks to Danh. In the middle of the night, he comes to him carrying bread and meat leftovers from the trash can.

There's a new fire in his eyes that Danh doesn't recognize as he speaks to him. "I heard we will soon be close to land," he says, while gnawing on an already half eaten chicken bone. "I overheard two men talking about it. They think we're only two days away."

Danh lights up. There is nothing he is looking more forward to than getting off this ship. He has lost track of how long they have been on the ocean and can't wait to feel the solid ground beneath his feet again. He longs to smell the grass, to see trees and mountains. He never wants to see the ocean again after this. Never. If only Long could have been here to experience it with him. If only.

"That's good news, right?" he says.

Bao bites his lips, then gnaws on the chicken bone until there is nothing left on it. "Depends on how you look at it."

"What do you mean?"

Bao turns his head and looks straight into Danh's eyes. The look in them frightens him slightly.

"It depends on if you think it's alright for these bastards to get away with killing your sister."

85

April 2016

FEET ARE WALKING across the wooden floors. Heavy feet that make the floors creak eerily, while Paige is holding on to the rocks inside the chimney. One of her fingers has already slipped and several others are on their way too.

The steps are coming closer.

"Come out, come out wherever you are," he says. "You cannot hide forever, you know. This house has eleven bedrooms and twelve bathrooms, but I know every corner, and every hiding spot. I will find you. It's only a matter of time."

Paige lets out a small whimper, then closes her eyes, biting her lip so hard she can taste blood.

Did he hear me?

More steps across the wood. Paige can see his shoes now through the opening of the chimney. She holds her breath. The girl above her doesn't move at all. Paige finds it hard to hold on. Another of her fingers slips and she is now holding on with only three fingers. She closes her eyes, sweat springing from her forehead. Her hands are getting clammy and that makes them even more slippery.

"Where are you hiding, little girl?" the man says.

Paige is clinging on to the rocks, barely holding on with her fingertips when her right hand slips and she falls to the side, barely managing to grab on to the wall with the palm of her hand. Her foot is about to lose its grip and she moves it higher up, hoping and praying the man won't hear her.

She holds her breath and waits in the silence for the man to make his move, imagining him reach his arm up the chimney, grabbing her leg and pulling her out. She is shaking with fear. Her eyes are fixated on the black shoes, when suddenly they move. She watches as they turn around and start to walk away. She listens to every step as they slowly disappear. When the door is finally closed, her hand slips again and she falls to the bottom of the chimney. Coughing and panting, she rolls onto the floor. Seconds later, a pair of legs comes out after her and a small face appears. Paige is lying on the floor, catching her breath, trying hard not to panic.

The girl comes out, then sits next to her.

"I'm Tara," she says.

"I'm Paige."

"Just arrived?" she asks.

Paige nods.

"You're good at playing this. It took a long time before I found this spot. He hasn't found me up there yet."

Paige looks at Tara. She is skinny and dirty. She looks tired. "How long have you been here?"

Tara shrugs. "Who knows? I stay hidden and live off food I find in the pantry downstairs when he leaves the house or at night. He keeps Cheerios boxes there. Lots of them. I don't think he realizes any are gone."

Paige looks at her with hope. "He leaves?"

"He does. But he always comes back."

Paige looks around. Her heart is still racing in her chest. She is trembling and can't hold her hands still.

"What does he do with you if he catches you?"

The girl doesn't look at her. She stares out the window where the sun is about to set. The river is glistening and birds are flying low.

"You don't want to know," she simply says, and Paige knows not to ask again.

86

April 2016

NEVER HAS WATCHING the sun set been such a nightmare for me. I stare out the window as darkness settles on the ocean and the shadows grow longer on the beach until they finally vanish.

Where are you, Salter?

Tom has arrived too and now he brings me a cup of coffee. "How're you doing?" he asks.

I exhale and look at the steaming cup between my hands. My stomach is in one big knot. "How do I feel?" I say. "Let me tell you how I feel. I want to scream. I want to yell and scream hysterically."

"Can't blame you," Tom says and sips his own cup.

I look at him. It feels good to be near him. His calmness makes me feel better. Out of the corner of my eye, I spot Joey. He is standing across the living room, his eyes resting on me and Tom. He looks a little like a boy whose toy was stolen from him. It's the first time the two of them have been in the same room together, even though I have told him I was seeing someone. Of all the circumstances in which they could have met, this is the strangest one. I can tell Joey isn't happy about having him here, but since he brought Jackie, I don't have to care.

"Here it comes," Chloe says and turns up the volume on the TV.

Every eye in the room turns to look at the screen as the picture of my son appears behind the anchor, and she, with very serious eyes, says the words 'amber-alert' and 'missing' in the same sentence. That is when I finally break down. Seeing my baby boy on the screen like that, hearing her say that the police in Cocoa Beach want everyone to be on the lookout for this kid, shatters my heart to pieces.

I feel Tom's arm around me, trying to catch me as I fall forward to my knees, crying, weeping helplessly.

"It'll be all right, Mary," Tom says. "We'll find him. We will find him."

Chloe turns off the sound, and hurries to me. She squats next to me. "Salter is a tough kid, Mary. And you're a tough mom. We will get him home, you hear me? I won't rest till we do. None of us will."

I look up and see the faces of the crew. All my friends have approached me. They're surrounding me.

"Chloe is right," Danny says. "You're always there for us."

Marcia nods, tears in her eyes. She clenches her fists and knocks on her heart. "Always, Mary. To the end of the world."

Sandra is there too. She reaches down her hand. I grab it and let her pull me to my feet. She smiles, her eyes damp. Alex is standing behind her.

"You're not alone in this," Sandra says.

We all join in a group hug, only Joey is standing outside looking at us, Jackie by his side. The TV is still on and now the woman presents a new story. I let go of my friends and walk to it, then turn the sound back up.

"What is it, Mary?" Chloe asks.

"It's a piece about the bodies they pulled out of the river the other day," I answer. "The mom and the daughter, Kim and Casey Taylor."

"What about them?" she asks.

I turn to look at her. "They say they were embalmed."

"They were what?" she asks, lifting both her eyebrows.

"Embalmed. She just said they were embalmed before they were thrown in the water. Apparently, they can't determine exactly when they were killed, since their bodies are so pumped full of formaldehyde there is almost no decomposition."

A gazillion thoughts go through my mind as I watch the piece. They show pictures from the canal where they found the bodies, then the police state that they need the public's help in this case. I watch the pictures of Kim and Casey Taylor while they were still alive. It's all churning inside my mind, mixed with images of Tara and Maria, Paige and Salter.

"The sick bastard," I mumble.

"What's that?" Chloe asks. "Who?"

"Boxer. I think it's time for us to pay him a visit."

"You can't do that," she says.

I look at her, making sure there is no doubt that I am being serious here. Very serious.

"Try and stop me."

87

April 2016

HE PULLS out his suitcase and puts it on the bed. He pulls out shirts, underwear, pants, and shoes and throws them in.

"You might need to take your jacket too where you're going," his brother says, standing in the doorway, holding a bottle of gin.

"Stay out of this," Boxer snarls, but grabs the one winter coat he owns that he's never used while living in Florida, and throws it in as well.

"So, you're just going to leave me here?" His brother lifts the bottle and drinks from it, like it was water.

Boxer stares at him and sighs. "I can't stay. I have to go. They found those two bodies and I am afraid it will only be a few days before they trace them back to me. Or they'll find out that I took Paige Stover. Even though I know they have Danny Schmidt at the station, I'm afraid. It's getting too dangerous. I've saved enough money. I'll never have to work again."

Boxer grabs the suitcase and walks out the door. His brother follows him closely down the stairs.

"What about Mom?"

Boxer stops at the bottom of the stairs, closes his eyes, and takes in a deep breath. He had to bring her up, didn't he? He simply had to poke at his guilt. His dying mother. Their dying mother.

"I don't know," he says. "I guess I'll keep paying for her. They'll take care of her at the hospice."

"But who will visit her?" his brother asks. "She'll get lonely."

"That's not my problem," Boxer hisses. "How about you do it for once? How about you do something?"

He manages to calm himself down just as there is a knock on his front door. Not just a simple knock, but an aggressive, hard knock.

Not with authority like the police knock, more like someone in a hurry to get in.

Boxer puts down the suitcase, walks to the window, and looks out from behind the curtain. A woman is out there. Boxer recognizes her face from the day of the rally. She was the one who took the pictures and posted them on Facebook, leading him to Paige. He remembers her name was Mary, Mary Mills or something like that. And when they later had that search party for Paige, he was holding her hand. She had sweaty fingers, he remembers.

What does she want?

"I know you're in there!" she yells. "Open the door. Open it now."

The woman is not alone. She's with another woman. She is small, red-haired, pale, and wearing glasses. They seem harmless, so he decides to open the door.

Boxer smiles. "Hello. What can I help you with?"

He looks into the eyes of Mary Mills and quickly regrets having opened the door. They're filled with what seems to him like obsessed anger and pillars of fire.

"Where is my son?" she asks, spitting as the words leave her lips.

Boxer stares at her. He shakes his head slowly in confusion. "Your son…I…I'm not sure…"

"Don't give me that," she says. "I know you have him. What have you done with him, you sick bastard?"

"I'm not sure…" Boxer looks at the other woman for help. "What is she talking about?"

Mary takes a step closer. It frightens him a little, and without thinking about it he takes a step backwards into the living room.

"You took him, didn't you?" she says. "You took him like you took Paige Stover, like you took poor Kim and Casey Taylor, along with Maria and Tara and all the others, didn't you?"

Boxer stares at her, eyes and mouth open. He doesn't know what to say, how to deal with this.

How does she know all this?

"You did, didn't you? I can see it in your eyes," she says and points at him aggressively. "I know you're the Boxer. I know it's you!"

"Uh-oh," his brother says behind him, in between sips from his bottle. "You're in trouble now, brother. You're in deep trouble."

Boxer closes his eyes. He slumps his head, then turns around and yells at his brother:

"SHUT UP! SHUT UP! You're dead, for crying out loud. Why won't you leave me ALONE?"

88

April 1975

THEY DO it in the middle of the night. Bao and Danh stay awake till everyone else on the ship has fallen asleep, some so drunk they never make it to bed, but simply pass out in their chairs.

They don't talk about what they're going to do. They don't have to. Driven by their anger and lust for revenge, they grab on to the two machete knives that Bao stole the night before and hid underneath Danh's jacket, while they waited for the right time to arrive.

They are close to shore now. All day they have been able to see land on the horizon, and according to what they have heard, the captain plans on making it to the harbor the very next day.

Except he will never set his feet on solid ground again.

They start with the sleeping quarters downstairs, sneaking down one step at a time, sweat springing on their foreheads, holding their breath, stepping lightly so they won't be heard.

Danh gets the honor of taking out the first one. He chooses the man who dragged Long away on that fatal evening, the guy who gave Danh the medicine as payment for his sister.

Danh hardly feels anything when he places the machete on his throat and simply slides it through the flesh and bones without even blinking. Blood gushes out from the wound and soaks the floor. Danh takes in a few fast breaths, watching the body as it is emptied of all life.

Danh is a little disappointed. He thought it would feel better than it did, but he still isn't satisfied. He realizes he really wants them all to die. When Bao started talking about revenge, Danh hadn't been sure that was what he wanted. He knew he wanted to see this guy dead, but the rest? Now he has no doubt in his mind.

They all have to die.

Danh grabs the necklace from around his neck and pulls it off, then leaves the room before he enters the next.

One by one, they slaughter them in their sleep, all the sailors sleeping, even one that is still awake, coming running towards them pointing his machine gun at them, but so drunk he can't find the trigger. Danh watches Bao slaughter him and the headless body falls to the ground with a plump sound.

Danh feels no sadness, no mercy for these men, as they fall by their feet one after the other. He feels completely empty, and as they finally finish off the captain, Bao yells the cry of a warrior, holding his machete high in the air, putting one foot on the body beneath him. Danh stares at him, empty inside, until the second his eyes lock with those of a man creeping up from behind holding a machine gun.

It all goes so fast, he doesn't get to warn Bao before the shots are fired. The bullets hit Bao and his chest soon explodes, his blood hitting Danh's face.

Danh leaps through the air towards the man, cuts both his hands off with the machete, and screams as the man falls backwards before he cuts his throat.

Danh then throws himself at Bao's dead body. He is crying, helplessly trying to revive him. He lies like that for a few hours, while the ship drifts in the deep ocean, being helplessly thrown back and forth by the waves.

It's not until after the sun has set that he suddenly hears voices, foreign voices that are approaching. He doesn't want to let go of his brother's body and holds on to it, even as the ship is filled with army pants with black boots and more yelling surrounds him.

I am never letting you go again, Bao. Never.

89

April 2016

"Leave me ALONE!"

The guy, Boxer, is standing in front of me and is yelling loudly, but he's not yelling at me. Instead, he seems to be addressing his anger at someone inside the house, someone standing behind him, but I can't see anyone, even though I stretch my neck. All I can see is a green suitcase.

I decide I am tired of waiting. I want to see for myself if my son is here or not. I walk in, push him aside, and hurry through the living room, my eyes scanning the area for anything or anyone.

"There's no one in here." Chloe is right behind me. "Who the heck is this guy talking to?"

I shrug and look back. Boxer stays put. He doesn't seem to notice us or even care that we're in his house. He is still yelling.

"You're dead. Don't you understand that? You were killed. I saw you blow up. Stop bothering me! Leave me alone."

We stop for a second and watch as Boxer grabs his head between his hands and falls to his knees, sobbing.

"Please, just leave me alone."

What's with this guy?

I decide I don't care. Meanwhile, I run into the kitchen and look in every cabinet, calling my son's name.

"Salter. Salter, if you're here, yell or knock or something!"

We go through the two bedrooms, looking under the beds, in the closets, and in the bathrooms. We even go to the attic. Chloe lifts me up so I can crawl in. I get very dirty, but I don't find Salter, nor any sign of him or Paige being here.

"There's a room in the back, downstairs," Chloe says. "I saw a door when we came in."

"Let's check it out."

We run downstairs and find the door, then open it. I turn on the light. There is nothing in the room except a big dog-crate placed in the middle of the white tile. It's extremely clean for a room supposed to house a dog.

"Where is the dog?" I ask.

Not a dog toy anywhere in sight, no dog food, no bowl of water, not even dog hair. But there is something else. Where you close the door to the crate, a lock of long black hair is trapped.

I pull it out and hold it up in the light to better study it. "This here, my friend, isn't dog hair."

Chloe looks at it. Her eyes are serious. "You're right. This is definitely not dog hair."

She pulls out her phone.

"Who are you calling?"

"I think it's about time we involve the police in this," she says. "We're in over our heads here."

While Chloe speaks to the police and convinces them to come here, we hear the front door slam shut. Our eyes meet the second before I storm back to the living room only to find it empty, the front door closed, and the suitcase gone as well. I run outside and see a white van disappearing down the street.

90

April 2016

THE MANSION soon grows dark and quiet. Tara crawls inside a closet to go to sleep, and she tells Paige to find a spot where she can sleep hidden and be ready to crawl back up in the chimney should the game start all over again.

"You never know when he'll start counting again," she says.

"Does it happen at night as well?" Paige asks.

"Usually, the nights are peaceful," she says. "So are the times when the man leaves the house. But don't let him find you. You must hide at all times."

Paige creeps under a couch and tries to fall asleep, but she can't. She is too scared and misses her mom so terribly. She still doesn't know if what Coach Joe said was true, if she was really hurt or not.

Paige's back is hurting from lying curled up underneath the couch, and soon she crawls out. She walks to the window, grabs it, and tries to open it, but with no success. She stares into the darkness of the river in front of her, wondering where her mother is and if she'll ever see her again.

She thinks about Tara and how long she has been here, trapped in this house, hiding from the man, and she wonders how long she herself will have to do the same. How long before he figures out to look up the chimney? Will she just be waiting for it to happen? Is that really all she can do?

Paige's stomach is rumbling and she remembers what Tara told her about the Cheerios in the pantry. She decides it can't hurt to sneak there now. She is starving and can't sleep.

Carefully, Paige sneaks out the door and walks down the hallway, hoping she is going in the right direction. The carpet on the stairs helps her to not make a noise. She walks carefully towards the kitchen, which she remembers running through when looking for a hiding spot. She just hopes she won't get lost in this house. She doesn't want to lose Tara or the good hiding spot. She wants to make sure she is capable of finding her way back, so she memorizes details about the rooms and hallways she walks through. A painting, a vase or a sculpture.

Finally, she reaches the kitchen and spots a door she thinks must lead to the pantry. To her surprise, she is right. It's a sight for sore eyes or hungry mouths. An El Dorado of cereal boxes from ground to ceiling. Not just Cheerios, but all kinds of cereal. Any kind, really.

Paige grabs a box of Captain Crunch and opens it. It makes a lot of noise and she stops to listen if anyone could have heard her. She holds her breath until she knows there is nothing, no one in the kitchen, before she sticks her hand into the box and stuffs her mouth with the cereal till she can contain no more.

Full and exhausted, she slides to the ground, leans her head on the box, and closes her eyes.

Just one second. I just need one…

She wakes up with a start. There is cereal on the floor and she hurries to clean it up, then place the box back on the shelf. She opens the door to the pantry and pokes her head out to make sure no one is on the other side before she sneaks out and through the kitchen. As she passes through one more living room, she sees a light coming from underneath a door that is left ajar. She stops and stares at the light, when she hears a still small voice coming from the other side.

"There you go…*your majesty.*"

Curiosity makes Paige sneak closer, till she can peak inside using just one eye. The room looks like a church room…statues and smoking incense sticks placed on a sort of an altar. In the middle sits the man. Paige gasps with fear when she sees him. He is bent over something, holding it close to him while he cries. Paige gasps again when she realizes it is a woman. The woman has long black hair that he caresses and brushes. She isn't moving. Her body is stiff. Paige takes a step backwards, clasping her mouth as she slowly realizes the woman isn't alive.

91

April 2016

"LET ME GET THIS STRAIGHT. You found this hair stuck on the crate?"

Chris Fisher looks at me, holding the lock of black hair that I have given him in his hand.

"Yes. I believe it belongs to Paige Stover. But I have no proof of that. All I know is it isn't dog hair. And Paige has black hair like that."

"And you believe this guy is the same one who chatted with Paige Stover and called himself the Boxer?" he asks.

"Yes." I turn and look at Chloe, who is working with the guy's computer. "I have a feeling she might be better at filling you in on that. Right now, I am only focused on finding my son."

"And the guy, the man who lives here who you believe is the Boxer, who took Paige Stover, where is he now?"

"He drove away. I told you this already; come on, Fisher. We need to move on here. My son is out there somewhere. I need to find him."

Fisher nods, but is not ready to let me go yet. Chloe interrupts him just as he is about to ask me another question.

"I think I might have found something, but…"

Chris Fisher turns around, notepad in his hand. "What is it?"

She draws in a deep sigh. "It's kind of disturbing…I'm not sure…"

Fisher walks to her and looks over her shoulder. "What have you found?"

"First of all, I can tell you that this computer definitely belongs to the Boxer and that he has been in contact with Paige Stover for a long time, chatting with her online. His history alone reveals that he

224

has been visiting her Instagram profile and Musical.ly profile several times a day. He has written messages to her as well, especially in Minecraft, pretending to be a thirteen-year-old boy from Daytona, whose nickname is Boxer. He has downloaded many pictures of her from her mother's Facebook profile, from Paige's Instagram, and even videos from Musical.ly."

"So, he was stalking her," I say. I look at Fisher to make sure he gets it all and understands that this means…that Danny had nothing to do with the disappearance of Paige Stover.

"There's more. There's a lot more," Chloe adds. "First of all, Paige wasn't the only girl he was watching closely like that. I found pictures of Tara and Maria Verlinden as well, and of Kim and Casey Taylor, Jenny and Stacey Brown, and I bet if I look a little more I'll find Joan and Nicola Williams as well."

"So, he was watching all of the women who disappeared with their children, the same that we gave you the names of," I say. "I told you those cases were connected. Now do you believe me?"

Chris Fisher rubs his stubble, which is about to become a real beard one of these days. I am guessing he hasn't had much time to shave lately. A shower would probably benefit him as well.

"All right," he says. "I'll buy into some of your theory here…but what I really want to know is, where the heck are they? I mean, Kim and Casey we have found, but where are the rest? What did he do with them?"

I shrug. "Could they have ended up in the river as well?"

"No," Chloe says. She is staring at the computer screen, looking paler than usual. "The girls weren't for himself."

She looks up at me. I don't understand what she is telling me. "What do you mean, they weren't for himself?"

"I mean, he sold them. Look at this."

92

April 2016

So THIS GUY was kidnapping single moms and their children, and selling them off on the Internet. I can't believe any of this. I am staring at Chloe while she speaks, completely freaked out about this revelation. How could anyone be so cold, so calculated and cynical? To sell people? To sell mothers and their kids?

It's got to be the most disgusting thing ever.

"So what we have here is nothing but a salesman. He's not even the killer?" I say. "He didn't kill Kim and Casey Taylor, he just sold them off to someone else? I mean, who does that? And who buys them?"

"It seems to be the same guy ordering them," Chloe says, still focused on the Boxer's computer. "I don't know how much you people know, but there is a part of the Internet for guys like Boxer, where criminals can buy and sell anything and never be traced."

"The Dark Web," I say.

"I thought it was the Deep Web," Fisher says.

Chloe looks at us, annoyed. "That's what the media calls it, but there is a distinct difference between those two things. I'm not going to go into too much detail, but the Deep Web is distinct from the Dark Web." The Dark Web is the encrypted network that exists between Tor servers and their clients, whereas the Deep Web is simply the content of databases and other web services that, for one reason or another, cannot be indexed by conventional search engines."

She has already lost me and I am pretty sure she has lost Fisher as well.

"Nevertheless," she continues. "I have found and decoded an

encrypted chat in here between him and this guy who calls himself Dr. Seuss. Boxer sends him pictures of the girls, and Dr. Seuss chooses from the gallery."

Chloe shows us the many pictures. I recognize two of the girls from Salter's school. It makes me sick to my stomach to realize this guy has been watching our neighborhood's kids like that, trying to sell them off.

"As far as I can tell, Paige Stover was delivered to Dr. Seuss a few days ago. Her mother was supposed to be with her, but…well you know what happened to her. My guess is Paige is there right now, in the hands of this Dr. Seuss."

"So, who is this Dr. Seuss?" Fisher asks. "And how do we find him?"

Chloe sighs. "That's the problem with the Dark Web. You can't trace anyone. You can't find them. They can do anything they want in here and never be prosecuted for it. There's a lot more to it than just criminal activity, but that's for another day when we have more time."

"So…" Fisher starts, then stops himself. He looks as confused as I feel. "So, how do we find Paige Stover?"

"We don't," Chloe says and leans back in her chair.

"What?" Fisher asks, not accepting the answer.

"At least I don't. I can't do it."

"Didn't they write down a meeting point or anything?" I ask. "How does Boxer know where to drop off Paige Stover?"

"I don't know," Chloe says. "My guess is they had another way of communicating as well when planning the details, things that aren't able to incriminate them, like using a phone. It would help a lot if we could get our hands on Boxer and maybe his phone."

Fisher sighs. "I'll have every man looking for him around here. I'm sealing this house off and will have forensics out here right away. And we'll get ahold of this guy's phone records ASAP."

"What about Danny?" I say, directed at Fisher.

"What about him?"

"You're keeping him at the station. Isn't it about time you let him go?" I continue.

Fisher sighs. "I can't. At least not till I have more to go on. I'm sorry." Fisher picks up his phone and walks out.

Chloe gets up and walks to me.

"What do you want to do now?" she asks.

I shrug. "It's getting late. Maybe we should get back to the house and see if anyone has heard anything."

Chloe nods and we walk back to our car and get in. I start the engine and look out into the darkness in front of me.

"The only thing I don't get is why would he take Salter?" I say. "You didn't find any pictures of him on the computer, did you?"

She shakes her head and I drive into the street.

"It doesn't make any sense," I mumble under my breath, as we drive back and I wonder about my son. "It makes no sense at all."

93

April 2016

HE RUNS the brush carefully through her black hair. Her head is resting in his lap. He likes to pretend her eyes are looking at him, but they're not. They're staring lifelessly into the ceiling.

He has bought her a new dress. A brown dress very similar to the one his mother was wearing the last time he saw her, when she stood in the doorway of their small home in Saigon forty years ago and told him to go, to take his sister, to just leave town and not come back before it had all calmed down.

He never saw her again.

Danh draws in a deep breath and puts the brush on the table next to him. He caresses the woman's pale face gently, while humming the song his mother used to sing for him when he couldn't sleep.

"Now we can be together again. Finally, dear mother, we're together again. You, me, Bao, and Long," he mumbles, while touching her lips and running a finger up the curve of her nose.

Danh's other brothers all made it out of Saigon and Vietnam. Two of them live in Japan, one in Spain, two in Sweden, and one in Germany. Danh is the only one who ended up in the U.S. He hasn't seen them since they left Vietnam. Only written them letters and they have written back. It took many years for him to find out what happened to all of them, and it wasn't until a few years ago that he knew of the fate of his mother. That she was taken by the soldiers who came to town because she refused to tell them where her sons were. In prison, she was tortured, and finally killed. Danh never knew what happened to his dad, and still hopes he'll one day know.

He places his hands under the woman's armpits and pulls her up. He places her in the chair at the dinner table, her hands on each side of the plate like she is about to pick up the silverware. Danh then walks to the other side of the table and sits down across from her. He forces a smile.

"Now, let's eat."

Danh picks up the box of Cheerios and pours some in his bowl, then pours milk on it and starts to eat. It was all he ate on the American aircraft carrier after they picked him up while drifting around in the ocean. They told him they found him on top of his brother's body and that he refused to let go of him. They had to take the both of them onboard their carrier. Danh was introduced to cereal by the soldiers and that was his favorite food ever since. After his retirement he never ate anything else.

When they reached land, they helped him take his brother with him to the United States. They had the body embalmed in Thailand so it wouldn't decompose during the long journey. Danh was supposed to have him buried once he arrived there, but instead he kept him in the small condo that was given to him. He bought a casket for him with a lid of glass and kept him in there for years. He didn't want him to leave him, ever again.

Danh pours himself a glass of orange juice and lifts it to salute Bao, sitting next to him at the table.

"To family," he says.

No one else lifts their glass. Danh looks at them. He sighs and puts down his own glass. "I know," he says. "I know. We're not complete. Long isn't here. I am sorry. We've been playing hide and go seek."

Danh laughs out loud and leans back in his chair. "I haven't had this much fun in years," he says. Then his face freezes. He slams his fist into the table with a loud noise.

"You're right. There is a time to play and a time to eat. I will find her. She needs to be with her family."

Danh pushes his chair out from the table.

"If you'll excuse me, I'll go get her."

94

April 2016

BOXER STEPS on the gas pedal as he drives through downtown. A couple crossing the road jumps for their lives as Boxer's van barely misses them.

"Freaking tourists," he grumbles.

Boxer is sweating, his hands are moist and feel slippery on the wheel.

"You'll get us both killed if you continue like this," his brother says.

Boxer turns his head and looks at him in the passenger seat. "You again? What do you care? I thought you were already dead. Remember the bomb?"

"Vividly," his brother says, as he pulls out a bottle of vodka and starts to gulp it down. "I also remember you not shooting the kid when you were told to."

"So you're saying I killed you, is that it?" Boxer growls and takes a turn so sharp the wheels screech. He almost hits the wall of the Chinese place, Yen Yen on the corner of A1A and Minutemen.

His brother shrugs and keeps drinking. "You said it; I didn't."

Boxer screams and turns the wheel to avoid a street light. "I hate you. Do you know that? I hate you! So what if I killed you? Maybe I wanted to kill you. Have you ever thought about that? With all the gambling and the drinking. It was always my mess to clean up. You always came to me and I had to fix everything. You ruined my life! Do you even realize that? You ruined everything. Mother couldn't cope with it; she couldn't take it, and so I had to. Still, she was heart-broken when you died. And she blamed it all on me. *Why couldn't you save him, Joe? Why didn't you protect him? I told you to protect him when you left. I told you to watch over him.*"

His brother laughs.

"Why the heck is that so funny?"

Boxer is screaming when he speaks. His eyes are filled with the anger and tears gathered from years of frustration. He doesn't look at the road in front of him, only at his brother. His drinking brother who destroyed everything while alive and still does even though he is dead.

"Get out of my life!" he yells, his mouth frothing in anger.

He doesn't see the man in the street until it's too late. He turns the wheel hard and misses the man, but the van spins out of control and crashes into a wall.

At first he is confused and doesn't know where he is. He has bumped his head. It hurts. There is smoke everywhere and flames erupt at the front of the van. Boxer sobs and looks at the seat next to him.

It's empty.

"Peter?"

He looks everywhere inside the car for his brother, but he's not there anymore. Boxer doesn't understand where he is, since he is always there. Always right there next to him, ready to torment him, but now it is quiet. So quiet.

The flames are getting bigger now and he knows he has to leave fast. Boxer jumps out of the van and walks backwards away from the car while flames eat it. Peter is still nowhere to be seen.

Is he really gone?

Boxer looks at the van as it is quickly devoured, then hears sirens in the distance. He throws a glance at the road ahead of him, then looks back at the car, just as the first fire truck turns the corner at the Chinese place. Next, Boxer turns on his heel and starts to run.

95

April 2016

"HE'S NOT HERE."

Joey is the first to announce it to me as I storm in the front door. He can tell by the look on my face that I have been hoping that Salter has returned while Chloe and I were gone. But, of course, he hasn't. They would have called me if he had. I just somehow had hoped that maybe he had.

"I know," I say, my shoulders slumped.

"All police cars on patrol and all firefighters are looking for him," Joey says, as he grabs me by the shoulders and hugs me. "We will find him."

Sandra pours me a cup of coffee and I take a small sip. She sits down in front of me. Ever since the accident, it has been difficult for her to smile properly, and I appreciate her effort in trying to do so now, to try and comfort me.

"How are you holding up?" she asks.

I stare into her eyes. They are still gorgeous. No one can ever take that away from her. The rest is just packaging, if you ask me.

"I don't know. I feel like panicking, but what's the use?"

Sandra nods. She is holding her coffee between her hands. "Did you find anything at that guy's house?"

I nod. "Hair. We found a lock of hair that I think must belong to Paige Stover. She has that type of hair that…"

I pause and look at Sandra without really seeing her. Thoughts and images are flickering through my mind. "Wait a minute," I say and get up.

"What?" Chloe asks and approaches me, a soda in one hand, and banana cake in the other. The sight of the cake makes my stomach turn in worry, but I shake it. I can't let myself be overwhelmed with emotions. Not now. Not when my son needs me more than ever.

"The hair," I say. "All of their hair."

"What are you talking about?" Chloe asks, mouth filled with cake.

"Why haven't we seen that?" I grab my laptop and open the article about Kim and Casey Taylor. "Look at them."

"Just get to the point, will you?" Chloe asks.

"They're all Asian. All of the kidnapped women and their children have Asian features. They all have the same long black hair and eyes. Tara is only half Asian, but she still has the characteristics."

"So, what does that mean?" Chloe asks. "I mean, besides the fact that this guy who calls himself Dr. Seuss is into Asian girls? Lots of men are."

I shrug. "I don't know. But it must mean something, right?"

Chloe bites her lip. I can tell she really wants to make me happy, make me think this will lead somewhere. "Sure. We just don't know what."

I sit down again, and then open my computer. I Google Dr. Seuss, then Asian girls. Shouldn't have done that, since it mainly brings up a lot of porn sites. I go back to Dr. Seuss again. I open Wikipedia and read through his story, thinking maybe there is a reason this guy calls himself that. Maybe there is something in his story about Asian girls or maybe just something else that made this guy choose that name, like Boxer chose his because he shared name with a famous boxer.

Shared a name?

"I think I've got it," I say and stare at the screen.

Chloe approaches me. "Got what?"

I grab my phone next to me, rush into my dad's room, and grab his gun to put in my purse.

When I return, I walk past Chloe, reach for the door handle on the front door, and look at her.

"I know who Dr. Seuss is. Let's go."

96

April 2016

SHE CAN HEAR him on the stairs. She and Tara are sitting in the room upstairs by the fireplace, sharing a bowl of Cheerios that Paige brought back with her, when Paige hears it.

"He's coming," she says.

Tara shakes her head. "He can't be. He never comes up here at night. He stays down there with…"

Tara grows silent. "I call them the zombies. There used to be more. Now my mom…my mom is one of them. He places them around that table and then he has dinner with them. When I came here, there was a little girl there too. And another woman. But now they're gone. Now he sits there with my mom."

"Do you think he wants to do the same to us?" Paige asks, remembering seeing the woman he was with in the library downstairs.

Tara doesn't say anything. She doesn't have to. Paige knows that's what she is afraid of.

"He did it to the other girl," she says with a low voice. "I saw her. She was already stiff and had dead eyes when I saw her the first time."

Paige swallows hard. She listens carefully, but can't hear the steps anymore. Maybe it was just all in her head. Living in constant fear of him starting to count again has made her jumpy and nervous.

Then the sound is back. She gasps and looks at Tara, who has heard it too. Her eyes are big and wide.

"You heard that?" Paige whispers.

Tara nods. "But…I haven't heard him count. He always starts the game by counting so I can hide."

"Ready or not…" they hear him say all of a sudden. The voice sounds like it is very close to the door.

Paige gasps and looks at Tara, who sits frozen.

"Here I COME!"

As the handle turns, Tara springs for the chimney. Paige is on her tail. Tara is fast. She climbs up and makes room for Paige to get in as well. Heart throbbing in her chest, Paige climbs up the rocky walls inside the chimney, her slippery hands failing to get a good grip. She is whimpering and struggling to keep quiet. She stays still to not make a sound and hears footsteps across the wooden floors, the bowl of cereal being turned over, then more steps, and suddenly a hand grabs her leg.

"Found you!"

Paige screams as she feels the fingers surround her ankle and start to pull. Paige holds on to the rocks, but her fingers slip, and soon she is pulled downwards, her face scratching against the walls of the chimney. She tries to get a new grip and to protect herself with her hands, but she can't hold onto anything, and soon her face is smashed into the bottom of the fireplace and she screams in pain.

Whimpering and crying, she is pulled across the wooden floors and into the carpeted hallway. She is screaming for him to leave her alone and trying to kick herself free, but his grip is too strong. She tries to grab ahold of doors or the rails on the stairs. Between screaming and crying, she can hear him singing. She recognizes the song from the movie she always used to watch with her mom, The Lorax. Paige has always hated this song. And hearing it coming out of this creepy man's mouth scares her more than anything.

"How ba-a-a-ad can I be?
I'm just doing what comes naturally,
How ba-a-a-ad can I be?
How bad can I possibly be?"

He keeps singing as he walks down the stairs, banging her head on every step. Paige screams in pain and pleads with him to stop, but he completely ignores her and keeps singing:

"Well there's a principle of nature, principle of nature
That almost every creature knows,
Called survival of the fittest—survival of the fittest."

At the end of the stairs, he turns and drags her towards the library. Paige sees it approaching, the door left open, and soon she is pulled inside and placed on the floor. She screams as she sees what looks mostly like two zombies sitting at a dinner table. The man lets go of her foot, and walks to the door to close it, while still singing:

"And check it; this is how it goes,
The animal that wins gotta scratch and fight and claw and bite and punch,

And the animal that doesn't, well the animal that doesn't winds up someone else's la-la-la-la-lunch — munch, munch, munch, munch, munch."

Paige tries to crawl her way towards the door, but it is slammed shut right in front of her. The man is standing above her. He grabs her by the arms and pulls her back across the floor, kicking and screaming. He leaves her there, grabs a cord, and puts it tight around her throat, still while singing:

"I'm just saying,
How ba-a-a-ad can I be?"

97

April 2016

"HE MISSES THEM."

I am driving down A1A towards downtown while explaining everything to Chloe. "It was actually your mom who said it to me."

"My mom? I'm not quite following you here."

"She looked at me and said to me that he misses them. And it was when thinking about that that I realized how it was all connected."

"Could you please explain it to me, then? 'Cause I don't get anything right now," she says.

"Dr. Seuss. His real name was Theodor Seuss Geisel. It was while reading his wiki page that it hit me. His real name was Theodor. Theodor G."

Chloe turns her head and looks at me. "Are you insane? The football player? The founder of Pull 'N Pork? That Theodor G? The man is a hero around here."

"Yes. I know. But it totally makes sense. I remember reading about him a few years ago in an interview where he talked about his mother and how he had recently discovered what happened to her after he fled Saigon back in '75. Theodor and his siblings all fled the country, but he lost his brother and sister during a pirate attack on the boat they were fleeing on. He never knew what happened to his parents until a few years ago, when he learned his mother had been killed in prison. That's why he's kidnapping girls and their mothers, because he misses them."

"Why doesn't he kidnap fathers and brothers then?" Chloe asks.

"Most of his brothers survived and still live all around the world; his father he never knew what happened to. But his sister and mother died, and now he's finding girls and mothers who look like them."

"That's crazy. He still lost one brother," she says, rolling her eyes. "He should be missing him too."

"I don't know the details, but I think we're on to something here," I say. "It fits with the fact that it was about two years ago that the first disappearance took place. The first Asian woman and her daughter. And then there is the name. Theodor G. It's not his real name; I remember reading that he changed it many years ago to separate himself from his past."

"This is insane, Mary. Let's go back home. You're going to embarrass yourself and me in front of the whole town if you accuse him of this."

I take a sharp turn onto Minutemen, ignoring Chloe. "He might have Salter as well. Maybe he had Boxer kidnap Salter to act like the brother or something. I have this hunch and I have got to follow it."

As we drive onto Minutemen, we see a small fire being put out by a fire truck. A couple of police cars are there too. They have blocked one side of the road. We drive past it slowly.

"What happened?" I ask.

"Looks like a car crashed into the Thai-place. Not much left of it, though. Hope no one was hurt."

I hit the gas pedal once we've passed the accident and accelerate down Minutemen Causeway. "I remember reading that he lives in this huge mansion by the country club," I say. "It has eleven bedrooms. The biggest house in Cocoa Beach."

Chloe grabs her phone and starts to tap on it.

"What are you doing?" I ask, as we drive past the two schools and into the residential area.

"Checking if you're right."

"How do you do that?"

"Wait and see."

98

April 2016

"Bingo."

Chloe exclaims and looks up at me, just as I park the car in front of the big gate to Theodor G's mansion.

"What?" I ask and lean over to better see.

"I think you might be on to something after all," she says. "Look who ordered a tankful of formaldehyde two years ago?"

"Theodor G?"

"Close enough. It was ordered in the name of the company behind Pull 'N Pork, but my guess is it was him, yes. There aren't that many places around here that sell that stuff; it's mostly for funeral parlors. It was pretty easy to break into their records."

"A tankful you say? That's a lot."

Chloe nods. I stare at the huge gate and the cameras. Of course the guy has a fort. I always thought it was to keep people out, not in. I can't stop thinking about Salter and whether he is in there right now, scared to death.

"Why didn't we bring any of the guys again?" Chloe asks. "Or call the police?"

"None of them would have believed me," I say. "You hardly did." I reach into my purse and pull out my dad's 9 mm. "Besides, I did bring one of the boys."

"Maybe we should call Alex or Joey first. Have them come here."

I scoff. "You think they can do a better job than I can? I've been taking lessons at the shooting range for six months now. Besides, there's no time to waste. We can't wait for them to get here."

I get out of the car and Chloe follows me. As I step outside, I hear a scream. I look at Chloe. "You hear that? It sounded like a child."

Chloe nods. "All right. What do you want to do? The place is a fort. I'm guessing he won't be opening the door if we ring the bell."

"Are you so sure about that?" I ask.

99

April 2016

THE GIRL REFUSES TO DIE. Danh is holding onto the cord as tight as he can, but the girl is still kicking and screaming, and worst of all, she is still breathing, no matter how tight he squeezes her neck.

And now there is someone by the gate. Danh sees them on the camera and recognizes the woman as that blogger, the one who interviewed him at the rally about his involvement in the protest.

What does she want now?

Danh holds onto the cord and struggles to keep the girl down, while thinking they'll go away if he ignores them. But they don't. They're still ringing the intercom and the noise disturbs him mentally.

How am I supposed to kill someone with all this noise?

Finally, the girl seems to lose the fight. The kicking becomes more random, and soon it stops completely. The intercom buzzes again and Danh growls. "All right. All right! I'm coming," he yells at the monitors, where the two women are standing looking expectantly at the gate.

He lets go of the lifeless girl, then walks out of the room and closes the door behind him. The girl is ready now and he can begin the injections as soon as she is cold. That should give him enough time to get rid of these two annoying women.

Danh presses the Intercom. "Do you have any idea what time it is?"

"Yes. I am so sorry, Mr. G," the blogger says. "I know it's late, but we were out walking my dog, and suddenly it saw a small bunny, and before we could do anything it chased it onto your property through the hedge over there. Would it be alright if we came inside and looked around for him?"

Danh grunts. He is terrified of dogs. The thought of one being loose on his property makes him very uncomfortable. He won't close an eye all night just thinking about it. And even worse if it finds its way into the house. That would be awful.

"All right," he says and presses the button to open the gate. "But hurry up. And use a leash next time you walk your dog, will you?"

"Sure. Again, I am so sorry about this, Mr. G."

Danh rolls his eyes and turns away with the intention of walking back to the girl, his soon to be new Long. He thinks he finally found the right one. He has gone through several and none of them were quite right, but this one is promising.

When he turns around, he sees a figure standing in front of him in the darkness. The figure walks into the light. He is smiling.

"What the heck are you doing here?" Danh asks, appalled by his ugly face. "You're not getting any more money until you deliver the mother. You know that."

Boxer shakes his head. "No. No. No more. Now it's your turn to do something for me."

Danh rolls his eyes again. He scratches his head. This guy annoys him. "I don't have time. I have things to do."

"You hear those sirens?" Boxer asks. "That's the police looking for me. I have nowhere to go, nowhere to hide. You have to hide me and help me get out of the country when things simmer down out there. I know you have a private jet."

"Have to?" Danh says, blowing raspberries. "I don't have to do anything."

"Oh, yes, you do. Or I'll take you down with me. I've saved everything; every chat, every deal we've made is saved on my computer."

"You did what? What kind of an idiot are you?"

"I was just protecting my future," he says. "It was all going so well. I was going to leave and get out of here. I would have brought the computer with me. But then those women came to my house…" Boxer clenches both his fists.

Danh stares at the Boxer. "What women?" He grabs Boxer by the neck and pulls him to the monitor by the front door. The two women that he let onto his property are walking around, calling the dog's name.

"These women? Tell me Boxer, *dearest*, are these the same two women?"

100

April 2016

"SNOWFLAKE? SNOWFLAKE?"

I am yelling while walking around the huge yard, pretending to be looking for my dog, while Chloe and I are really studying the cameras and trying to find a way into the house.

"I think I might have found something," Chloe says, keeping her voice low. "There's no camera here by this back window. It's locked, but I know a trick."

She takes off her shirt, wraps it around her wrist and hand, then slams it through the glass. I gasp in surprise.

"Chloe! Are you alright?"

"Damn, that hurt. I thought it would be so easy. They do it on TV like it's nothing."

"Chloe, your hand is bleeding!" I grab her shirt and rip off some of the fabric from the sleeve to make a bandage, then help her get the rest of the shirt back on.

"Damn, it was my favorite," she grumbles, when she sees the ripped shirt. Blood from her hand has colored it red in spots.

"I'll buy you a new one," I say, and examine the broken window. I remove the fragments of broken glass so we won't cut ourselves. "You think he heard us?"

"Probably," Chloe says, and climbs inside, careful not to touch any of the broken glass on her way.

I follow her, and soon after we're both standing in a room inside the mansion. It's very dark. Chloe finds a door and opens it carefully, making sure no one is waiting on the other side. When she finds the hallway outside empty, we sneak out. I have the gun in my hand as we find a stairwell and walk up. I keep thinking we might find my son in one of the bedrooms. I go first through the hallway, opening one door after another, gun in my hand, examining every room we reach until I find one where the light is on and I spot two bowls of cereal tipped over on the wooden floor.

"Someone was in here," I whisper and we walk inside. The cereal and milk are scattered all over the floor in front of the chimney. Black ashes from the fireplace are spilled out, which I find odd. I bend down and look up the chimney. A small whimper makes me look further up, and I spot a set of eyes staring back at me. They belong to a little girl. She looks terrified.

"Who are you?" I ask.

She doesn't answer.

"I'm Mary. I won't hurt you."

She still doesn't open her mouth.

"Please," I say. "I can get you out of here."

Finally, she gives in. Slowly, she slides down the sides. I crawl out and help her get outside. I recognize her face from the pictures and clasp my mouth.

"Tara?"

The brown eyes in the dirty face from the soot inside the chimney stare back at me. Then she nods.

I am brought to tears. I pull her close and hug her tight. "Oh, my God, Tara. You're still alive. I can't believe I found you."

I hug her again and close my eyes. As I open them again, Chloe is standing by the door, a gun to her head. Holding the gun is Dr. Seuss. Next to him is the Boxer. Dr. Seuss looks at the girl in my arms.

"Thank you," he says. "I've been looking all over for her."

"Really?" I say. "And you never thought about looking inside the chimney?"

Dr. Seuss's eyes turns to ice. "Hand her over or your friend dies."

I look into Chloe's eyes. They tell me *no. Don't do it.* "Where is my son?" I ask, trying to stall for time.

Dr. Seuss looks confused. "What?"

"My son. Salter. You took him."

"What?"

His confusion makes me angry. I draw my gun and point it at Dr. Seuss. "Where is my son? Tell me or I'll kill you. I don't care if you kill her or anyone else. I demand to know what happened to my son!"

101

April 2016

IT DOESN'T WORK. Of course it doesn't. I should have known. Especially since I have failed to notice that Boxer has his hand on a baseball bat that he now swings and hits me in the side of my head. The blow makes me pull the trigger, but I miss Dr. Seuss and the bullet hits the wall behind him instead, while I fall forward into the floor with the taste of blood in my mouth.

I am not really conscious. Still, I sense that I am being lifted up and carried down the stairs. I feel my body being moved, but I can't do anything about it. I hear loud voices around me and a lot of yelling, but can't really determine if it is real or just part of a dream.

Not until I finally come back ten minutes or so later. When I do, it is all quiet around me. I open my eyes and look into the face of Paige Stover. Her eyes are closed and she is not moving. Her throat has marks from being strangled. I gasp and sit up. That's when I realize I have duct tape covering my lips. I can't scream. I can't yell or even talk.

Where am I?

My arms are tied behind my back with a cord. My legs are tied together too. My head is pounding where the bat hit me. Paige and I aren't the only ones in the room. There's a dinner table with two people are sitting at. I look at Paige. Is she alive? She looks very pale.

Who are the people at the table?

I manage to get up on my feet and jump with my feet very close together towards the table. I jump small bunny jumps to get there, and as I approach, I get a strange sensation in my stomach. Whether it is the strong smell that makes my stomach turn or the sight that meets me, I don't know. But suddenly I feel very sick.

Zombies is the word that comes to mind. Zombies sitting at a table. Dead faces, one of them with very little hair or skin left. Dried up, dead bodies, sitting there like they were waiting to be served, but the waiter never came. Crooked bony fingers on the white table-cloth. I recognize the one body as Maria Verlinden, Tara's mom, and feel even worse.

Did she see it? Did Tara see what happened to her mom? Oh, my God, I hope she didn't.

I panic and my stomach turns so bad I feel like throwing up. But I can't. The duct tape will only make me choke on my own vomit, so I hold it back. The taste in my mouth is awful. I swallow. It burns my throat. I close my eyes and turn away from this strange scene. I jump back to Paige's body and throw myself on the floor next to her. I am crying heavily now. It's all such a mess. Where is Salter if he isn't here? I miss him terribly. I remember the look on Dr. Seuss's face when I asked about him, and I wonder if he was being truthful. Did he really not know? The thought is terrifying, because now I have no idea where to look for him, but it is also little optimistic. It leaves me with the small hope that maybe he wasn't kidnapped after all. Maybe he is just really angry with me and has run away like a normal kid.

I comfort myself with the thought of it, then start to wonder where the others can be. Where is Chloe and what about Tara? Are either of them still alive? Have they taken them somewhere? Where? How am I supposed to get out of here and find my son? Will they kill me next?

How will I ever get out of this alive?

102

April 2016

"WHAT ARE WE GOING TO DO?"

Boxer is freaking out. He is walking up and down Danh's living room, frantically biting his lips. Danh takes a couple of deep breaths.

"What do you mean?"

"What do I mean? What do I mean? Look around?" Boxer points at the red-haired woman tied to a chair, the young girl next to her tied up as well. Both are grunting and gnarling behind the duct tape, struggling to get loose.

Danh looks at them and shrugs. "What about them?"

Boxer groans and pulls his hair. He gesticulates wildly as he speaks. "You have another one in there, unconscious, and a dead young girl. What do you intend to do about all of them? Don't you think someone will eventually come looking for them? Oh, my God, what if they told people they were coming here? I bet the police will be here shortly."

"They won't find anything here when they come," Danh says, while opening the box of syringes.

"What do you mean? Are you planning on killing them? All of them? Hey, man, I'm no killer. I was only in it for the money. That's all. I'm not going to kill anyone."

Danh pulls out a syringe, the biggest he has, and holds it in the air. Yes, that should do the trick. The needle is brutally big, but it will go faster this way.

"I don't have time to kill them," Danh says. He walks to the kitchen, then comes back with two more syringes, which he prepares.

"So…so what is your plan?"

Danh sighs and closes his eyes. Part of him hopes this Boxer will be gone when he opens them again, but he is still there.

"I-I-I…I can't be here…when you, I can't kill…I'm no killer."

Danh tilts his head as he looks at him, the poor thing, getting himself all worked up. "Have you heard of survival of the fittest?" Danh asks, while walking to the table and picking up a syringe. He fills it from one of the big bottles he has lined up on the table in front of him.

Boxer nods his head. "Of course I have."

Danh smiles. "Good. Good. So you understand that the animal that wins gotta scratch and fight and claw and bite and punch, and the animal that doesn't…well, the animal that doesn't winds up someone else's *la-la-la-la-lunch — munch, munch, munch, munch, munch?*"

Boxer stares at Danh. He is at loss for words, it's obvious. Danh finds it amusing. But he has no time to be playing with his little friend anymore. He walks over, grabs Boxer around his shoulders, holds him down so he can't move, then places the needle on his neck and pierces it through the skin. He empties the syringe completely before he lets go of the screaming Boxer.

"What the hell are you doing?" Boxer yells, pulling away forcefully, but it's too late. He's too slow.

"You might say I am preserving you. Did you know that formaldehyde, when injected into your body, turns into formalic acid? When the fluid enters the arteries, pressure builds throughout the veins, which means the fluid is moving throughout the body. You'll notice your veins bulging somewhat. That's your blood trying to get out, the fluid is pressuring it out, so to speak. When I do it to a dead body, I usually have to open the jugular drain tube periodically to allow blood to escape and relieve the pressure. But I have never tried it to someone who is still alive. I am curious as to what will happen. Now, what do you know? The big vein on your neck is already bulging. I didn't know it would go that fast." Danh approaches his neck and touches the vein, caressing it with his finger.

"What the hell have you done to me!?" Boxer yells and pulls away, holding a hand to his neck. He stumbles backwards, looking at his hand, where the veins are now bulging too, screaming in terror.

Boxer staggers backwards through the living room, zig zagging and groaning in pain. Danh leaves him; he doesn't have time for him. He'll have to find him later and throw him in the river with the others. Just like when you kill a cockroach with spray and it runs to hide, it always shows up the next day dead on the floor somewhere. So will he.

Next, Danh picks up another syringe and turns to look at the woman and young girl in front of him.

"Who wants to be next?"

103

April 2016

I HEAR voices coming from the next room, followed by loud scream-ing. It scares me like crazy. Then I hear a sound that doesn't scare me but fills me with relief instead. The sound is coming from Paige's mouth.

She is alive. Oh, my God, she's still alive!

"Paige," I say, muffled behind the tape.

Slowly, she opens her eyes and looks at me. She gasps and is about to scream, but then hesitates.

Good girl. Don't speak. Don't say anything.

I grumble behind the tape and finally she understands. She leans over, grabs the tape, and pulls it off. It hurts worse than getting a Brazilian wax. I only tried that once and I'm never doing it again.

I fight my urge to scream, but instead I take in a few deep breaths. "Thanks," I whisper. "Could you?" I show her my hands and she unties the cord around them. I can tell she is in pain. Her neck looks terrible. She touches it.

"He tried to strangle me with a cord," she whispers, when she sees I am looking at it.

The cord left a visible mark. I don't say anything. I just nod.

"Where is he now?" she whispers.

I nod in direction of the door, then put my pointer finger to my lips to signal that she needs to be very quiet. Meanwhile, I untie my legs. I get up and help Paige get up as well. I can tell she is shaken. The man behind the door terrifies her. We have to move fast now before he finds out we're up and running.

I look around at this strange room we've been placed in, trying to find some sort of a weapon. They took my gun when they knocked me out, and my phone. There has to be something else we can use.

I scan the entire room and finally my eyes land on two machetes hanging on the wall. In the middle hangs an old gold necklace.

Bingo.

I grab a chair and climb up to grab the machetes. I give one to Paige, and keep one for myself.

"We better hurry up," I whisper. "You ready?"

She draws in a deep breath and looks down at the big machete between her hands. "You can do it," I whisper. "If any of them come at you, you swing that beast."

"Them? There is more than one?"

"Yes," I say. "You see a man, you swing it at him. You kill him if you have to. Survival of the fittest, all right?" I say, and lift my clenched fist in the air.

We bump fists before I lift the machete up in front of me and walk towards the door. Carefully, I open it and peek out. I can't see anything, but I can hear a voice. It sounds like Dr. Seuss. He is talking to someone. I signal Paige to follow me and we walk out of the room towards where I hear the voice. I wonder if we can make it through the front door without him noticing it, but realize we can't get through the gate if we do. Plus, I need to find Tara and Chloe.

Seconds later, I find them. As we walk closer, I spot Chloe sitting in the middle of the living room, tied to a chair, Dr. Seuss is in front of her, talking to her.

What's that in his hand? What the heck is he doing to my friend?

The realization hits me like a train wreck. Dr. Seuss is holding a massive syringe in his hand, and as I stand there and watch, he places it on Chloe's skin and presses it down.

104

April 2016

"TOWANDA!!!!"

I don't know why I am yelling exactly that, but the quote from *Fried Green Tomatoes* is all I can come up with as I storm through the house towards Dr. Seuss, the machete held high in the air.

I want to startle him; I want him to stop what he is doing right away. And I succeed. My yelling makes him turn and look, but the syringe stays in Chloe's skin. I swing the machete and hit him right in the face. Dr. Seuss is knocked down, but to my surprise, the knife doesn't cut anything.

Dr. Seuss falls to the ground with a bruise on his head, but is quickly back on his feet.

"What?" I ask.

Dr. Seuss laughs. "Do you have any idea how old these machetes are? Forty years old. They have never been sharpened. They're dull and couldn't cut a banana."

He walks towards me, reaching out to grab the knife, but I pull it back. Dr. Seuss sighs. He pulls out his gun and places it on Tara's head. Chloe is struggling behind the tape. I look at the syringe and wonder how much of that stuff he managed to put in her before I disturbed him. It is only half full now.

"I'm getting tired of you people," Dr. Seuss says, scratching his head with the one hand that isn't holding the gun. I watch his finger on the trigger to see if it moves. My heart stops completely, thinking about Danny and how badly he wants to be in Tara's life.

If she'll live. If any of us will survive this maniac.

"Let her go," I say.

"Or what?" Dr. Seuss says. He scratches his head again, and that's when I see it. I take a step closer.

"You have lice," I say.

He shakes his head. "What?"

"Lice. Right there. All over your hair. They've even infested your eyebrows." I reach out and snap a louse from his eyebrow and show it to him. "See?"

Dr. Seuss stares at the louse between my nails, then reach up to touch his hair, a look of utter terror on his face. While he's touching his hair with both of his hands, the gun finally pointing away from Paige, I spot my moment. I lift the machete and swing it down once again, this time harder, and to my luck it cuts through his skin and leaves an open wound in his chest.

He gasps, drops the gun, and puts both of his hands to the gushing wound. I take a step backwards while blood fills his mouth and starts spurting out. He tries to speak, but no words come out, only thick red blood.

Epilogue
APRIL 2016

"YOU'LL NEVER BELIEVE THIS."

Chris Fisher is at my door. I smile when I see him and let him in.

"After what I've been through, try me," I say. I walk to the kitchen and pour us some coffee. Three days have passed since the insanity at the mansion. I am still exhausted and haven't slept much. Salter is still gone and I have no idea where to look for him. It makes me sick to my stomach. I am hoping that Fisher is bringing me good news, but I have learned to not get my hopes up these days.

I serve him coffee and sip my own. We sit at the kitchen table. Fisher is in Salter's spot.

"So, what is it you don't think I'll believe?" I ask.

"Well…considering with your son and all, I know you're waiting for good news about him, but this is about something else," Fisher says. "I just thought you should know this."

"Maybe it can take my mind off Salter for a few seconds. What is it?"

"We found the cause of the massive fish-kill in the river."

I look at him, surprised. "That's awesome. What caused it?"

"Well, actually, we owe it all to you. That we found it, I mean."

I shake my head in confusion. I am very tired and not sure I am hearing things right anymore. "Me? What do you mean?"

"It was formaldehyde," he says.

"Formaldehyde?"

He nods eagerly. "There was a spill. From the tank at Theodor G's mansion. Salt had eaten away at it and it was rusting badly. It was leaking and had been for quite a while. Right into our river. Killed thousands of fish."

"You're kidding me, right?" I ask.

255

"Nope. We solved it. Now we can clean it up and get back to normal again. A team of specialists is out there right now; they'll flush it out, they say. I don't know how these things work, but hey, they're the experts, right?"

"That is great news. So no spill from a power plant or any other polluting chemical factory, huh? I guess my story is down the drain as well."

"Well, you're the first person I'm telling this to, so maybe if you write it now, you can get some attention on that account."

I shrug. "I'll try, even though I'm not in the mood for writing much these days."

"How are you holding up?"

I shake my head with a deep sigh. "I'm still here, aren't I?"

"Sure. How's Chloe?"

I sigh thinking about her. I can't believe she was hurt like that. Why does everyone around me keep getting hurt?

"They don't know yet. She did get a lot of the formaldehyde into her bloodstream, but they still don't know how much it has destroyed. She's gotten a blood transfusion and they hope that'll save her."

Fisher puts his hand on top of mine and squeezes it. He can tell I get emotional when talking about it. I have been living at the hospital these past days, waiting for news about Chloe and taking Paige to visit her mother.

"How's Paige doing?" he asks.

Paige has been living with me and my dad to make sure she's not alone while her mother is getting better. Nicky should be discharged in a few days, they have told me.

"Getting better," I say. "The psychologists say she is doing really good actually. I have taken her to the hospital every day to be with her mom. And I think we finally got rid of those little critters of hers, using tea tree oil, so she won't spread them to anyone else. I noticed them in her hair back when we found that lock in the Boxer's house. Filled with nits. I'd recognize those critters anywhere, since we went through it with Salter last year. Such a nightmare. But I think we've got it under control now."

"Good. That's really good," he says. I can tell he is eager to move on. "Well, I'd better…it's been a busy few weeks, I'll tell you that."

"I know. Have they found any of the other missing women or children?" I ask.

Fisher gets up and puts on his cap. He shakes his head. "Nope. All we found so far was the body of the Boxer and the embalmed bodies of Maria Verlinden and Theodor G's own brother. But they were all at the house. We'll keep looking in the river, but with all the animals out there, chances are there isn't much left of them if he dropped them in there like he did with Kim and Casey Taylor. But we'll keep looking, searching all areas of the river."

I try to smile, but it doesn't come out right. Fisher sees it.

"At least Danny gets to be with his daughter," he says. I can tell he is trying to make me feel better. "And he is now officially acquitted of everything. Even the trouble he got himself into in Orlando. They decided to drop all charges. It's not all bad, you know. And you saved those two girls. Just sayin'."

I do feel happy for Danny. I can still see that look on his face when he got to meet Tara for the first time. I took him to see her at the hospital, where she was being kept for observation. Danny tried hard, but couldn't hold back his tears as soon as he saw her. Luckily, Tara took it really well. It's not easy to lose your mother and gain a father in the same week. But she was very moved to finally meet him. She threw herself in his arms and they spoke for hours after-wards. I hope he'll be able to get custody of her and that they'll all be a family with Junior too. I am beyond thrilled that everything went so well for Danny. Especially that they never found out he killed that woman. I just hope he'll leave the police work to those who are paid for it from now on.

Well…who am I to talk?

"I know. It's just so hard to…you know be happy when…when your son…" I am tearing up as I speak, thinking about my son, and I am forced to stop. I close my eyes quickly, then look at him.

"See you around, Detective. Let me know if you have any news, alright?"

He nods and walks to the door. He stops just as he is supposed to open it, his hand resting on the handle. He hesitates, then looks back at me, biting his lip, like he wants to say something, but then changes his mind.

"Have a nice day, ma'am," he says, lifts his cap, and walks out the door.

Back in the kitchen, I am left to my own emotional roller coaster. I try hard to not cry, but it still overwhelms me. It shouldn't. I mean, we got the bad guys. They're both dead. No more disappearing single mothers and children.

But we never found my own son. Why is it I can save everyone else, but never myself? I can fix everyone else's life, but never my own?

I decide I want to write the article. Maybe it'll take my mind off things for a little while. I open the lid of my laptop and find my blog, just as an email pops up on my screen.

I open the email with a small gasp when I realize it contains a picture of Salter, sitting on the back of a motorcycle, blindfolded. In front of him, in the driver's seat, taking the selfie, is my brother, Blake Mills.

The picture comes with a message:

Careful little eyes, what you see.

To be continued…
THE END

Afterword

Dear Reader,

Thank you for purchasing *You Can't Hide* (7th Street Crew #3). I hope you enjoyed it. I got the idea for this story from a long post I read on Facebook. A woman described how she was in Target one day and this guy followed her and her daughter and approached her afterwards in the parking lot. She got away, but called the police who told her there is a sex trafficking ring that target moms and their daughters. She wrote the post on Facebook to warn other moms.

The story turned out to be a hoax, but it had me thinking. I was terrified when reading it and so I believed it could make a book. The part about slave-auctions in the airports is true, though. Ugly as it might be. You can read about it here:

http://www.theguardian.com/uk/2006/jun/05/ukcrime. travelnews

Furthermore, I am terrified of what my kids do on the Internet every day, who they meet, what they tell them, and how they could be tricked by some old guy lying to them. It simply terrifies me that I can't control them all the time, which I can't. So I wanted to write about that too.

Then there is the story about Danh. It's based on a lot of true stories I have read. With all that is happening in the world today, especially in Europe, we have to remember that many before them have been refugees, and that they go through terrible trials to get to their destinations, and often they lose their family members on the way. Some might not even find each other again until years later. People flee because they can't stay, and it is horrible what they go through. I wanted to describe that using Danh's story, and a lot of what I wrote is taken from real stories about people fleeing Vietnam in 1975. I made up all the terrible stuff, but what I have read is also horrifying, and many people died trying to flee the communist regime.

Here's an example of one of these remarkable stories:
http://ireport.cnn.com/docs/DOC-443335

About the fish-kill. Well, it is actually going on right now in Cocoa Beach. Thousands of fish have turned up in people's canals and no one knows why. They believe it's from a type of algae, but why it is so bad right now, they still don't know. I came up with the idea of spilling the formaldehyde because it has actually happened once. And it killed a lot of fish somewhere in California. You can read about it here:
https://news.google.com/newspapers?nid=336&dat= 19820326&id=Gv0yAAAAIBAJ&sjid=WoMDAAAAIBAJ&pg= 5537,7427887&hl=en

So now you know a little more about how this book came to be. I hope you'll check out all my other books as well, if you haven't already read them, and don't forget to leave a review of this book, if you have the time for it.

Take care,
Willow

To be the first to hear about new releases and bargains from Willow Rose, sign up below to be on the VIP List. (I promise not to share your email with anyone else, and I won't clutter your inbox.)

GO HERE TO SIGN UP TO BE ON THE VIP LIST :
https://readerlinks.com/l/415254

Tired of too many emails? Text the word: "willowrose" to 31996 to sign up to Willow's VIP text List to get a text alert with news about New Releases, Giveaways, Bargains and Free books from Willow.

Cover design by Juan Villar Padron,
https://www.juanjpadron.com

Special thanks to my editor Janell Parque
http://janellparque.blogspot.com/

**To be the first to hear about new releases and bargains
from Willow Rose, sign up below to be on the VIP List.** (I
promise not to share your email with anyone else, and I won't clutter
your inbox.)

- GO HERE TO SIGN UP TO BE ON THE VIP LIST :
http://readerlinks.com/l/415254

Tired of too many emails? Text the word: "willowrose" to
31996 to sign up to Willow's VIP text List to get a text alert with
news about New Releases, Giveaways, Bargains and Free books
from Willow.

FOLLOW WILLOW ROSE ON BOOKBUB:
https://www.bookbub.com/authors/willow-rose

Connect with Willow online:
https://www.amazon.com/Willow-Rose/e/B004X2WHBQ
https://www.facebook.com/willowredrose/
https://twitter.com/madamwillowrose
http://www.goodreads.com/author/show/4804769.Willow_Rose

http://www.willow-rose.net
contact@willow-rose.net

About the Author

Willow Rose is a multi-million-copy best-selling Author and an Amazon ALL-star Author of more than 80 novels. Her books are sold all over the world.

She writes Mystery, Thriller, Paranormal, Romance, Suspense, Horror, Supernatural thrillers, and Fantasy.

Willow's books are fast-paced, nail-biting page-turners with twists you won't see coming. That's why her fans call her The Queen of Plot Twists.

Several of her books have reached the Kindle top 10 of ALL books in the US, UK, and Canada. She has sold more than three million books all over the world.

Willow lives on Florida's Space Coast with her husband and two daughters. When she is not writing or reading, you will find her surfing and watch the dolphins play in the waves of the Atlantic Ocean.

Tired of too many emails? Text the word: "willowrose" to 31996 to sign up to Willow's VIP Text List to get a text alert with news about New Releases, Giveaways, Bargains and Free books from Willow.

Where the wild
roses grow
EXCERPT

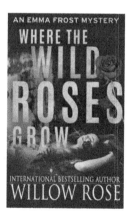

For a special sneak peak of Willow Rose's Bestselling Mystery Novel *Where the wild roses grow* turn to the next page.

Prologue
JULY 2015

She had almost given up on ever meeting that special someone. At the age of thirty-six, Bridget Callaghan had embraced the fact that she might end up alone for the rest of her life, just like her late Aunt Alannah, who had died in her home when Bridget was no more than ten years old. Bridget still remembered the horror she had felt when she was told that her aunt had been dead for weeks when she was found, and that her cats had eaten off half of her face just to stay alive, now that the hand feeding them had ceased to move. Bridget hated thinking about how lonesome her aunt must have been to the very end of her life, and she didn't like the fact that she might end up just like her. So, back then, when she had been no more than ten, on the brink of her life beginning, she had decided to never let such a horrific fate overcome her.

But life seldom turns out the way we wished for it to as children. And so it happened that Bridget now found herself alone in her small house in Enniskerry with no one but her cats to keep her company. There were days when she was terrified of her future, where she would wake up alone in her bed sweating from a nightmare, only to look into the eyes of her cats while she wondered how long they would wait after she died to start gnawing on her flesh.

But now, things seemed to have changed. Finally, after years of praying, she had met a man, a nice and decent man. Michael was his name. Bridget knew she wasn't as attractive as she had been in her younger years, but she wasn't ugly either. As a matter of fact, people still told her she was quite beautiful. That's why many in the small town wondered why she had never married and had children like all the other girls of the town. Bridget wondered that herself.

Some believed she was simply too beautiful for a man to handle. They simply feared her because she was so out of their league.

She had dated her share of men throughout the years, but only a few had stuck around long enough for her to get to know them properly, and the only one she had ever managed to actually dream of a future with, had turned out to have a wife and children in Dublin.

Bridget smiled at her reflection in the mirror and brushed her long blonde hair, thinking of this man that she had met. What she liked the most about him was the fact that he wasn't from Enniskerry. He had come to town just a few weeks ago, he said, and as soon as he had laid his eyes on her at the florist where she worked, he knew she was the one for him. That's what he told her while buying one bouquet of red roses after the other and telling her that they were all for her and he wasn't going to stop buying roses from her store until she agreed to go out on a date with him. Bridget had refused at first, but the man came back the next day and bought red roses from her store till there were no more. The very next day, he had returned and started all over until she had finally told him to stop it. She argued that he was going to go broke on buying red roses, and she couldn't let that happen.

"So, you'll agree to go out with me?" he asked with a handsome smile.

Bridget felt a tickling sensation inside and she knew then that she liked him. Never had a man pursued her like this before. And she had to admit, she really liked it. She liked the way he looked at her, she liked the way he spoke her name…how he tasted it like it was special.

"Could he be the one?" she asked her own reflection as she put on make-up. If that was the case, then it was certainly worth the wait.

Now Bridget wasn't stupid. She knew he was from out of town and just moved here; she knew almost nothing about him, and for all she knew, he could have an entire family somewhere, or he could be some pervert. In fact, that was why she had said no to him the first two days he had come to her store. But now she had decided to give him the benefit of the doubt. He deserved that much for his effort. And Bridget realized that this might be her last chance of finding someone to grow old with, someone who could make sure she wasn't left to die on her living room floor alone while the cats chewed on her nose. She felt hopeful that it wasn't too late for her. She never wanted children anyway, so that part didn't bother her much. It was the loneliness, the sadness of having no one in her life that made her miserable.

The doorbell rang and Bridget got up. She rushed to the door with all the anticipation of a first date, and then swung it open with a big smile.

"Hi."

The sight of the handsome man made her blush and she felt silly. He was wearing a nice gray suit and in his hand he was holding a single red rose.

"Hello there," he said, and handed her the rose. It still amazed her how he could have known that it was her favorite among flowers. It was very seldom that florists liked a flower as ordinary as the red rose. But it had always been her favorite. The fact that he knew that somehow told her he just might be the one. He just might.

He reached out his arm so she could grab it.

"Shall we?"

1

July 2015

"WHAT DO you mean we have to wait an hour? First you tell me we can't get the car we booked online, and now we have to wait for another?"

I stared, baffled, at the guy behind the counter. He looked like he had just graduated high school. I felt Morten's hand land heavily on my shoulder. "If that's the best they can do, then let us just wait," he said with a gentle voice.

I wasn't ready to give up the fight this soon. "No. I booked this car online," I said, and pointed at the receipt I had printed out before we left the house in Fanoe Island. "And now they want to give me this instead. It's half the size!"

Morten chuckled. "Now you're exaggerating. Besides, we shouldn't allow this to destroy our vacation, now should we?"

I growled. He was right. I just felt so cheated. I had paid for a much bigger and nicer car, and as soon as we reached the car rental in Dublin airport, they had told us we had to get another car. Not a word about compensation or even a little, "We're sorry for the inconvenience."

But Morten was right. We had finally managed to get away on a trip, just the two of us. It was sort of a make-up trip for a disastrous vacation we had taken six months earlier, where we had taken all of our children to Spain with us to visit an old friend of mine. The two teenagers had done nothing but argue about everything, and Victor had ended up throwing one fit after another, getting us thrown out of the hotel because he screamed all night, waking up the other guests. Jytte and Maya had been moping and not wanting to do anything, especially not with each other, and meanwhile, I had fought hard to keep Victor calm. Once we had set foot on our peaceful island again, Morten and I had promised each other that we were going to go on a trip soon, just the two of us.

So, here we were. In Dublin Airport trying to get a rental car, and already we had run into trouble. Maybe vacationing together simply wasn't our thing.

"We'll take it," I said to the teenager behind the counter. I felt determined to have a great time and enjoy my boyfriend. It was so rare we had time on our own and it was going to be great. No matter what.

I threw Morten a glare and he smiled triumphantly. He hated when I made a big deal about things.

"Let's sit over there while we wait," he said, and pointed at a row of red chairs leaned up against the window.

"Even the chairs are red-haired in this country," I groaned and dragged my suitcase after me.

It was no secret that Ireland wasn't my idea. It was Morten who wanted to go there. I wanted to go somewhere exotic with great food like Greece. We had discussed it for months until I finally had enough. I told Morten we could play Monopoly and the one who won would get to decide. I thought I could beat him, but…well, here we were in Ireland. Rainy, cold Ireland where sheep wandered the streets and potatoes were as exotic as it got. At least that was my presumption. I desperately wanted to be proven wrong.

We sat down. I grabbed my cellphone and turned it on, wondering if the kids were all right. My mom and dad had taken both them and the dogs in for the two weeks we'd be gone. School was out for the summer. They weren't exactly thrilled at the thought of us going on a vacation without them. Or the fact that they couldn't stay in their own house while we were gone. Maya was old enough to stay home alone, but after all she had been through and with her memory not having been fully restored yet, I felt very over-protective of her and I didn't like the thought of her being all alone in that big house. Victor didn't do well with change and had screamed when I told him he was going to live with his grandparents for two whole weeks. The past six months, his condition had gotten a lot worse, and he had become more and more introverted, even though he was getting help for it. I worried about him and his future. I didn't like the prospect of him spending his adult life in a home somewhere. I still believed he could manage to live a good life and be able to take care of himself. But my hopes were getting smaller, I had to admit. It was hard to watch. He was extremely intelligent, and I simply refused to believe he should be wasting away in some home just because he didn't quite fit into the way our society expected him to. I still thought he would make an excellent math professor or botanist one day. He loved trees and plants and he had a way with numbers that I had never seen before. Even his teacher in school had realized how well he did with math now and constantly gave him challenges that he aced completely. Stuff they taught at the universities. I clung to the hope that he was simply a misunderstood genius of some sort. But the fact that he wasn't even able to dress himself in the mornings if the clothes weren't put out properly or were in the wrong colors, told me living on his own one day was going to be hard. I had no idea how to help him. But regularity, routines, and schedules seemed to help. Now I had pulled him out of all that and placed him in a home he barely knew. I didn't feel good about it. My dad and Victor seemed to have a connection though, beyond what I ever had, and my father had told me to relax, that they were going to be fine, so that's what I tried to do.

"I think our car is ready," Morten said and got up. "The guy just waved at us to come."

I rose to my feet. "Finally," I grumbled.

Morten gave me one of those looks.

"Sorry," I said. "That was the last grumble you'll hear from me. I'll be good from now on. I promise."

2

March 1972

SHE WAS NAMED after the Irish woman who tried to shoot Mussolini. Not that she was in any way related to the real Violet Gibson, but her dad loved the story so much, almost as much as he loved his own little Violet, that he wanted her to have a name of significance. Violet was the only girl in a flock of five children, and as the youngest, she was also the most loved of all of them.

Growing up on a farm in a small town outside of Dublin, Violet would sit in her father's lap at night in front of the fireplace and listen to him tell the story of the fierce Irishwoman, Violet Gibson, one of four people who tried to assassinate fascist dictator Mussolini, and the only one who ever came close to succeeding, yet she had largely been written out of history. Her father would tell the same story he had heard from his own father…with the same enthusiasm and determination to not let this story of the brave Irishwoman be forgotten. Especially since they shared the same last name.

"See, my child," he would say with an almost deep whisper, letting her understand the importance of what he was about to tell her, "In the early years of his dictatorship, Mussolini was adored by Italians and admired by leaders across the world. People came to Italy just to hear him speak. In April 1926, at the ancient site of the Compidoglio in Rome, the petite, grey-haired Irish lady edged her way into the crowd that was waiting to greet him after his address to an international conference of the College of Surgeons, but she had not come to admire him. She was there to shoot him. Just as she pulled the trigger, he moved his head. The bullet hit his nose. At point blank range, she fired again, but—click—the gun jammed. She missed his bald head, but removed parts of his nose."

Violet's father pointed at his nose and made a sound like it was

274

ripped off. Violet giggled, then looked at him intensely. "But what happened to her? What happened after she shot off his nose?"

"She was taken away by the police. After some time in a prison in Italy, she ended up in St. Andrew's Hospital for Mental Diseases in Northampton. Spent the rest of her life there. Rumor has it she spent the rest of her life writing letters, asking to be released, but the letters were never mailed."

It was while listening to her dad's stories on calm nights like these that Violet understood that life was short and not always fair. A lesson she was glad she had understood early on in her life, especially when, two years later, her mother died at the age of only thirty-two. Once her mother was buried, she was left to be raised by her father and four brothers. Things changed at the farm. Her father didn't know much about raising a young girl, and he became strict and God was mentioned a lot when he spoke. Words like punishment and repentance were used daily in the house, while a nine year-old Violet tried to take the role of the mother in the kitchen.

In school, Violet got beaten up by the nuns a lot. She didn't always understand why, and that was probably why she kept getting herself in trouble. When she got back to the farm, she had to explain to her father why she had bruises on her cheeks, and when she did, he would slap her as well to make sure she didn't act badly in school again. Then he would ask her to leave him alone because he was tired from working all day on the farm. He had been tired like that ever since Violet's mother died, and his eyes had grown old. He never took her on his lap anymore and he never told the story of Violet Gibson again.

"Go away," was his reply if she asked. "You're too old for stories."

When she walked out of the living room, she could hear him sob, and she would think it was her fault…that she made him sad, that she could no longer make him happy like she used to.

In her room, Violet would throw herself on her bed and ask God why he had to take her mom away. But she would never receive an answer. All she could hear in her head were her dad's words:

"God didn't put us on this earth to make things easy for us. Life is a tough journey and dying is your prize for fulfilling it."

3

July 2015

"You look so beautiful," Michael whispered across the table.

Bridget Callaghan blushed and looked down. She couldn't believe him. He kept telling her how gorgeous she was, how her eyes sparkled when she spoke, how delicate her hands were. He smothered her in compliments. Not that she was complaining. On the contrary. She was quite enjoying this moment at the small pub. They had taken the car and driven into Dublin. It was her wish. She wanted to get away from Enniskerry and the staring faces. She, for one, knew how much they talked in her small hometown. She didn't want to ruin her first date with Michael wondering about others. In here, they were nobody. They could be anybody.

"So, why have you stayed in Enniskerry if you hate it so much?" Michael asked.

Bridget sipped her pint. She shrugged. "My friends are there. My family. I have the shop. I guess it's not all bad. It's all I have ever known."

"And your parents are still alive? Both of them?" he asked, tasting his shepherd's pie.

"Only my mom. I guess she is a part of the reason I stay. She needs my help. She's getting too old to take care of herself. She had me late in life. My dad, I never knew."

Michael smiled. "I see. Ever thought about looking him up?"

Bridget shook her head. "No. My mother never spoke of him. It would kill her if I started asking questions. I never really felt an urge to."

"You're not the least bit curious?" Michael asked.

Bridget shrugged. "I guess I never gave it much thought."

Michael tilted his head. "That's too bad. Everyone should know where they come from."

Bridget grabbed a forkful of her lamb stew and ate it. She didn't really like to talk about her family. Of course, she had wondered where she came from while growing up. But her mother had been very strict, and it was simply not something they discussed. Bridget never dared to ask. So, instead, she kept quiet. Like she had for most of her childhood.

"How's your shepherd's pie?" she asked, in an attempt to turn the conversation away from the subject of her lack of a father.

He smiled. Bridget liked his smile. "It's excellent. And your stew?"

She swallowed another bite, then nodded. "Quite good, actually."

"Marvelous," he exclaimed with a grin.

Jackpot, Bridget. You really nailed it with this one. He's perfect. Finally, you found someone. This one is a keeper. Play your cards right and you won't have to grow old all alone. No cats will get to eat your face.

Michael lifted his glass. "Cheers. To a wonderful date with great food and a lovely lady."

Once again, Bridget blushed at his kind words. It had been many years since anyone had called her beautiful. She knew she had always been one of the more attractive girls in the small town, but still. It wasn't something people told you. At least not where she came from. Her own mother had always thought of it as Bridget's curse…that her beauty was why she hadn't found a husband yet.

"You scare them away," she told her. "Men are terrified of beautiful women."

Over the years, Bridget had begun to think her mother was right. She had been known to scare a man or two away. Maybe it was because of her looks. Maybe it was something else.

Michael grabbed her hand in his. He looked at her pinky, then caressed it. The pinky was crooked and turning inward. The one thing that wasn't perfect about Bridget.

"I was born with it," Bridget said. "The doctor said it happens sometimes."

He laughed heartily.

"So, what do you want to do next?" Bridget asked when they exited the pub after finishing their dinner.

"Let's go back to Enniskerry," he said.

Bridget looked disappointed. Michael smiled, then leaned over and kissed her gently. He tasted of beer and shepherd's pie. She closed her eyes. Then she looked at him.

"Not to go home, silly," he said. "I want to take you to a special place. To my favorite place in the world."

4

July 2015

As I had expected, it was raining when we drove towards the hotel we had booked in a small town called Enniskerry, just outside of Dublin. The sun set just before we arrived, so it was both dark and rainy.

"It's over there," I said, and pointed out the window at a building with a sign saying Hotel Enniskerry.

Morten parked the car in front and we got out. I was soaking wet by the time we reached the entrance. A woman came out from the back.

"Yes?" she said with the cutest Irish accent.

That was the part I knew I was going to enjoy about vacationing here. I had told Morten I didn't want to stay in Dublin or any other big city. I wanted the countryside and all the Irish charm I could get. I wanted pints of Guinness and to eat in pubs with the locals.

"We booked a room," Morten said and showed her our reservations in print. The papers were soaked.

The lady smiled and nodded. She handed Morten a key. "Breakfast is at seven."

We took the key, walked up the stairs, and found our room after dragging our suitcases down a long hallway with old pictures of people I assumed to be dead. They seemed to be staring at us.

Morten fumbled with the key in the door.

"Hurry up," I said. "This place creeps me out a little."

Morten laughed. "You're kidding me, right? The big well-known mystery-author, Emma Frost, is frightened by a few old paintings in a dark hallway? You can write details about people getting brutally slaughtered, but you can't have a few old people look at you from a painting. You do realize they're probably dead many years ago, right?"

"That's the freaky part," I said. "Laugh all you want, just get us into the room. I have to pee."

Morten opened the door and I burst inside. The room was small, but very charming. In a tasteless kind of way. Flowered wall-paper all over and plastic flowers in vases, along with old porcelain figurines that I was terrified of accidentally knocking over.

I rushed to the bathroom and finished my business. The toilet was small, the sink made for midgets, and I don't think I could determine the color of the carpet in the bedroom, but still it had all the charm I was looking for. I had specifically asked to not stay in some big hotel chain somewhere. I wanted to be out among the locals, and so I had come here.

"So, what do you say?" Morten asked. He was the one who had booked the place, whereas I had taken care of the car.

I smiled. "It's not bad."

"You can do better than that," he said and threw himself on the bed. The springs creaked loudly.

"Guess we could do it on the floor, then," Morten said, and put his foot on the carpet. Was it green? I was inclined to say it was. But it had a little brown to it as well. And, in some places, it looked almost blue.

The floor underneath creaked too. I smiled and threw my suit-case on a small desk and opened it.

"The bath it is then," Morten said, and came up behind me. He grabbed me around the waist and tried to lift me, but I was too heavy. He kissed my neck and ears.

"You know we have to do it every day now that we're on vaca-tion, right?" he asked. "I mean, it's our only chance."

I let him hold me tight. I really enjoyed making love to Morten, but lately I had been feeling really insecure about my body. I had gained a lot of weight and it made me feel awkward when I was with him, since he was very skinny. He kept reassuring me that it didn't matter to him, but I wasn't so sure. In my everyday life, I could joke about my weight and feel good, but when it came to being naked, it was harder for me. I hadn't quite gotten used to being this big and kept telling myself I was going to lose it soon. I just really liked eating.

His hands were on my breasts and I closed my eyes.

"Are you up for a little action?" he asked.

"Mmm…maybe a little later," I said. "I am starving."

He made a disappointed groan and let go of me. I closed my eyes and bowed my head. I hated to disappoint him.

"Sure," he said, still with the disappointment of rejection in his voice. "Where do you want to go? I saw a list over here somewhere of places to eat in this town."

Order your copy today!

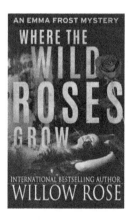

Made in the USA
Las Vegas, NV
21 January 2022

42056872R00173